D1240927

In loving memory of Russell Victor Pollero
March 9, 1947–June 4, 2014
His laughter was contagious and he was the
life of the party (unless I was telling my emu
story). He is sorely missed.

EXPOSED

CHAPTER ONE

Darby's eyes darted around the table, checking and recheck-
ing the two place settings. The placemats were exactly an inch
from the beveled edge of the glass table top. Wine glasses and
water goblets were precisely placed. Utensils, hand-polished
and sparkling, were laid out with precision. She lit the three
candles, symmetrically arranged in descending order and then
crouched down to make sure the flames flickered at exactly the
correct height.

The oven timer chimed. Darby tucked her blond ponytail
into the collar of her shirt, stuck a potholder on one hand and
eased open the oven door. The smell of fresh yeast rolls escaped
on a rush of hot air. Lifting the pan out of the oven, she placed
it on a trivet next to the cook top on the center island.

The kitchen, the entire house in fact, was immaculate to the
point of being austere. Like most homes in the exclusive en-
clave of Sewell's Point on Florida's Treasure Coast, the house
had a large, open floor plan with picturesque views of the in-

tracoastal. Hutchinson Island, a thin strip of barrier island, separated Sewell's Point from the Atlantic Ocean. It served a more important purpose, buffering the estate homes from the ravages of a direct hit from the hurricanes that roared in from time to time.

Of the five bedrooms, two had been converted into home offices. The master suite was spacious and the decorator had selected a Havana-style décor for the room. It was all muted greens, distressed wood, glass and iron. The only personal item was an eight-by-ten print of the formal engagement portrait that had appeared in the paper nearly fourteen months earlier.

Leaving the rolls to cool, Darby walked through the combination living room-dining room, down the long, narrow hallway. She stopped to absently pluck a slightly wilted petal from one of three dozen roses that had been delivered the day before. She swallowed a wave of nausea as the sweet, heavy perfume of the flowers surrounded her. Normally she enjoyed the scent of fresh flowers, but ever since becoming pregnant she'd found the odor revolting.

Turning the knob, she opened the door adjacent to the master suite and smiled. A soft, pastel mural with fairies and dragonflies had been painted earlier that day and this was the first chance she'd had to admire the artwork. It was perfect. Eventually, she'd have the remaining white walls painted some shade of pink. Or maybe green. She needed to make up her mind. The baby was due next month. Not much time left to procrastinate.

Speaking of time, she glanced down at her watch as she closed the door to the as-yet unfurnished room and went back to the kitchen. A rather uncooperative schnauzer had thrown her schedule off, so she had to keep moving in order to get dinner on the table at nine P.M. sharp. The keep-moving part was proving to be difficult since her belly had expanded. Carrying around the extra weight and girth, coupled with the long hours she worked as a vet, Darby was finding it a challenge to juggle everything that had to get done.

Taking the fresh asparagus from the refrigerator, she gently broke off the woody ends. Spreading the pencil-thin tips in a single layer in a dish, she chopped garlic, added that and some salt and pepper, and then tossed the vegetables with olive oil before placing them in the oven to roast. It wasn't until she lifted the lid on the double boiler that she realized she'd forgotten to turn the heat down on the burner. A good quarter of an inch of hollandaise sauce was scorched and crusted onto the bottom of the pot. "Beyond saving," she muttered.

Her heart rate increased as she furiously worked to wash and dry the pan, and then hang it back on the gourmet rack suspended from the ceiling. Darby used a half dozen paper towels to dry and polish the basin of the sink. At eight fifty-six, she dressed the salad and placed it on the kitchen table. Pulling a bottle of Alsatian *Sélection des Grains Nobles* from the chiller, she filled the Barona wine cooler with ice, then set it on the table next to the salad bowl.

At one minute before the hour, she heard the mechanical hum of the electric garage door opening. Darby plated the poached salmon and arranged lemon slices in a semi-circle around the platter. Taking the potatoes from the rarely used microwave, she placed them on a small serving dish, then reached for the breadbasket on her fourth trip from the table. She tossed rolls in as she went to retrieve the asparagus.

The minute she heard the door slam, she felt that sick knot of dread lodged in her throat. She turned and did one more visual scan of the table. Perfect. Just the way he wanted it.

Plastering a smile on her face as she pulled the elastic tie from her hair before giving it a fingertip fluff, she turned, folded her hands over the bulge of her stomach in an almost protective gesture, then waited for him to come through the garage entrance.

Sean Grisom was tall, muscular, handsome and smart. Light brown hair framed his darkly tanned skin. His shoulders were broad without being overly muscled. Thanks to good genes, he had a trim frame built for the designer clothing he favored. As usual, he didn't have a hair out of place.

That was one of the things that Darby had noticed about him at their initial meeting. He'd walked into her clinic, carrying a stray dog he'd found injured on the side of the road, and even under those circumstances he hadn't had so much as a speck of blood or dirt on him. When he'd asked for her help his voice had been deep and smooth, but it was his eyes that had melted her on the spot. When Sean Grisom looked at you, he was totally engaged—as if there wasn't another person on the planet. He was generous, too, promising to pay for whatever treatment the dog needed if she would just help him before the poor mutt died from his injuries.

To an animal lover like Darby, hearing the concern in his deep, sensual voice was payment enough. Of course she treated the dog. Some jerk had shot the poor thing with a BB gun. The surgery had been fairly simple and when she was finished, she was surprised to see that Sean had stayed, waiting patiently on news of a dog that wasn't even his. The next thing she knew, they were having dinner. Six weeks later, they were married.

"You worked late again," Sean said.

His voice was still deep but instead of smooth, it was laced with thinly veiled censure. Faux concern etched between his brows. A little over a year into the marriage and Darby knew him well enough to know that everything about this man was calculated and played precisely for whomever his audience happened to be at that moment in time.

Maintaining eye contact, she shrugged. "I had a problem patient but I was only there a little late." Ten minutes talking to a frightened little girl about her old dog's death. A few minutes well spent, as far as Darby was concerned. Except Sean wouldn't see it that way. Nobody should be more important to her than her husband.

"We've talked about this," Sean kissed her cheek as he placed his hand on her belly. "You're pregnant, Darby. It's time you stopped working. That's my child you're stressing."

"Pregnant, not disabled," she teased, hoping to ease the tension as she moved away from him to get the asparagus before they lost their crunch. "Would you open the wine, please?"

Sean went to the table and uncorked the bottle with practiced finesse. "Have some with me."

"I shouldn't," she said, adding the vegetable dish to the table.

"One glass a week," Sean countered, reciting the passage he'd read in one of her pregnancy primers.

She shook her head. "I had a glass at the restaurant two days ago, remember? Besides, I'm tired and wine would put me right to sleep."

"You're tired because you stand on your feet all day taking care of pampered pets when you should be here, at home."

What could she say? They'd had this argument many times since she'd found out she was pregnant. It always ended the same way—badly. While she was happy about the baby, the pregnancy had been unexpected. She'd been religious in taking her birth control pills but apparently she was part of the point-zero-one percent exception that proved the rule. Giving up her veterinary practice would mean giving up the only piece of herself she had left.

"I'll get a second wind," she promised as she sat in her usual chair and unfolded her napkin. She needed to steer him away from the whole working conversation. A knot was forming in her stomach and she felt the beginning of fear. For her safety and the safety of her baby, she had to calm Sean down before this took a serious left turn. So with a calm belying her true fear, she asked, "How are things at the restaurant tonight?"

Sean's eyes narrowed. "Is that some sort of polite way of pointing out that your practice is thriving while my business is stagnant?"

"Of course not," she said as her heart rate began to quicken. She took his plate to serve him so it would be ready when he sat down to join her. "I was just making conversation." Conversation she hoped would keep him from exploding.

"A new restaurant takes time to build a clientele."

"I understand that." Darby placed a portion of fish on his plate.

"It's going to take time."

She added vegetables and a potato. She tried to sound positive. "It'll be a success."

He glared at her. "Don't patronize me, Darby. I've got serious cash flow problems. Unlike you, I can't serve my guests kibbles and bits."

She drew in a breath and said mildly, "I'd be happy to write another check." Her trust fund was just sitting there. She didn't begrudge him the seed money for the restaurant. Paying him was a far better option than suffering the wrath of Sean.

"I need more than your monthly draw. Almost all of my vendors have upped their prices; some doubled, *tripled* the prices they were charging a few weeks ago." He began to pace. "If this guy I'm meeting in New York in the morning doesn't come through, I don't think I'll be able to keep the doors open for more than a month or so."

"You don't have to go to New York with your hat in your hand, Sean. I can ask my father to increase my allotment."

"Right," he spat, standing perfectly still as his fingers went white where he gripped the back of his chair. "Run to Daddy and tell him I can't support you."

"It's *my* money, Sean," she said as she reached out to pat his arm with her hand. "He's just the trustee and anyway, my father understands a new business requires cash. He knows there are times when you have to spend it to make it. And it is only money. He'll understand. He's a very—"

It took a second for Darby's brain to put it all together. Her cheek was on fire. She was on the ground, the chair teetering on top of her. The back of her head hurt where she'd hit the tile floor. As if in slow motion, she looked up in time to see Sean lifting the edge of the table.

Scrambling to her knees, she skidded along the floor as

plates and food rained down on top of her. Shards of glass pelted her skin like a thousand tiny pebbles as the tabletop crashed down, shattering all around her. Darby was vaguely aware of screaming as she curled into a fetal position when Sean yanked the chair off her and flung it through the air. It landed with a thud against the back of the family room sofa.

Then he was standing over her, his feet planted on either side of her body. He began thrashing her with something—the placemat, maybe. All she knew was that each successive snap of fabric bit her through her clothing.

"You stupid, *stupid* bitch!" Sean yelled.

"Sean!" she called, wrapping her arms around her belly as the beating continued. "I'm sorry. Stop!"

She pleaded with him, whimpering over and over. There was no response in his vacant eyes as they narrowed while he continued to thrash at her torso.

Then, as suddenly as it began, it was over. Just like always. Only this time was somehow different. It was the first time he'd attacked her while she was pregnant. She lay there, terrified, wondering if this was just the calm before the storm, or if he still intended to dole out more punishment.

Sean stepped away, tossed the napkin in the pile of food and debris, and then straightened his tie and smoothed his hair.

Darby remained cowering in the corner, following his every move like the trapped animal she was. When he reached for her, she flinched. Annoyance and disbelief were clearly painted on his features.

"Take my hand."

Hesitating for only a second, she reluctantly took the hand

he offered. Gently, he helped her to her feet and made sure she didn't lose her footing or cut herself on the glass and food strewn all over the alcove. Sean circled her in his arms and forced her cheek to rest against his chest. She felt his heartbeat. It was even and rhythmic. If she didn't know better, she'd have thought she'd imagined the whole ugly scene.

The feel of his hand stroking her hair as he kissed the top of her head made her skin crawl but she didn't dare pull away. Not when she was this vulnerable. Not when one well-placed punch could harm or kill her unborn baby.

Darby wondered how she'd gotten to this point in her life. She woke up in the morning afraid and fear followed her to bed every night. The only time she felt safe anymore was when she was at work. It was her haven. And yet here she stood, in the arms of her abusive husband, wondering for the umpteenth time how she could get out of this hell of a marriage.

"I forgive you," Sean said.

"W-what?" Darby was startled. What did she have to be sorry for?

Bracketing her shoulders in his hands, he set her back a foot or so and flashed her a brilliant smile. "It's okay," he said, using his fingertip to brush a strand of hair from her forehead. "I know you didn't do it on purpose."

"D-do what?"

"Burn the hollandaise." His finger hooked beneath her chin and he pushed her face up so their eyes met. "I smelled it the minute I walked into the kitchen. You should know better than to try to hide things from me, Darby. That's not how a marriage works. Now, come help me finish packing. I have to stop by the restaurant to pick up Roxanne on my way to the airport."

Darby was fairly sure he was taking Roxanne along for more than just assistance. She was also well beyond caring. As far as Darby was concerned, Roxanne was welcome to him.

"I think taking my assistant along will impress this guy. Send the right message, you know? After all, the key to this kind of deal is making the other guy think you're doing him a favor by letting him get in on the ground floor."

* * *

An hour later, sobbing, Darby dialed the phone, hiccupping as she struggled to speak. "M-Mom?"

"Darby, honey, what's wrong? Is it the baby?" her mother asked. "Will! Pick up the extension. Something's wrong with Darby and the baby."

Then her dad was on the line. "Did you call your doctor?"

"Not…the…baby." She hugged her belly protectively. "It's Sean."

"Something happened to Sean? Is he hurt?"

"No, Mom. He…he *hit* me."

"That son of a bitch," her dad said. "Where is he now?"

She could almost imagine her father's gritted teeth and see his blue eyes narrowed with fury. "Gone. Business trip."

"I'm coming right over," her dad insisted.

"No," Darby said, swiping at her tears with the back of her hand. "Sean won't be back until tomorrow. I'm going to get organized and pack. Then, if it's okay with you two, I'll come over first thing in the morning."

"If it's okay?" her mother parroted. "Don't be silly. You never have to ask to come home, honey. I'll come over to help you."

"Thanks, Mom, but I just need some time to sort through some stuff." *And clean up.*

"Yeah? What if the bastard comes back?" her father demanded. "What then? Has he done this before? Is that why you've been avoiding us the past few months? You need to have him arrested. Now. Tonight."

Darby pressed two fingers to her temple. The peppering of questions was precisely why she wanted some time by herself. "No, he's never hit me before." She lied. They didn't need to know about the slaps or back-handed blow-ups. "Don't worry. He won't come back. He's already on his way to the airport."

"How can you *know* that?"

"He's got an early meeting with a potential investor in New York." *And Roxanne in his bed.* "He won't bail on that kind of opportunity. The restaurant needs an infusion of cash."

"I've seen the bank statements, Darby," her father said with unfiltered disdain. "You've been infusing a lot of cash into that place. What's he been doing with all of it? Forget it. I don't really give a damn. Screw Sean. Wait until I get my hands on that piece of crap. He won't need any money where he's going."

"Calm down," her mother inserted. "The last thing Darby and that baby need right now is you going off picking a fight with a man more than half your age. Honey, what can we do?"

"You're doing it. I'll come by first thing in the morning. Before work, if that's okay?"

"Would you stop asking?" her mother admonished. "This is your home."

"Thanks."

"Are you sure you're okay, Darby? What about the baby? Maybe we should take you to the ER just to make sure."

"I'm okay. *We're* okay."

"Not if he hit you."

"He just slapped me," she fibbed, not wanting to give them a rehash of the actual events. That could come later, once she was safely ensconced in their home.

"Just?" her father scoffed. "*Just* slapped you?"

She massaged the back of her neck. "Let it go for now, Daddy," she said. "I don't really want to talk about it and the baby is fine."

She heard her father let out a long breath. "Well, I can't think about anything but that creep of a husband you've got. What kind of man hits his wife? His *pregnant* wife?"

"It's over now." Darby breathed in deeply. Feeling discomfort in her chest, she realized she'd cried hard enough to make her ribcage sore.

"It's far from over," her father countered. "I want to know exactly what that bastard did to you."

"I'm totally exhausted right now but I promise to tell you everything in the morning. Promise. I should be there before seven."

"Darby?" her mother asked, her voice so soft and gentle that Darby felt warm tears well in her eyes. "We love you, honey."

"I know. And I'm going to need all that love, mom. I can't, *won't* live this way. And I certainly won't raise my child with Sean and his violent temper. Tonight made that perfectly clear to me. My marriage is over."

* * *

Out of sheer exhaustion, Darby managed a few hours of fitful sleep before the alarm blared her awake at 5:45. Her back ached from sweeping more than two dozen dustpans full of glass-contaminated food and china from the floor, then depositing it in the trash can in the garage. Somewhere in the recesses of her mind, she realized it was a stupid thing to do. But the realization couldn't overcome the automatic reaction to eradicate all evidence of the fight. She didn't do it for Sean. No, on the off chance that her parents or an old friend dropped by, she didn't want to explain why the walls were splattered with salmon.

Covering for Sean had become a habit. A very bad one. As she tossed off the comforter she'd never really liked, she vowed it was the last time she'd make excuses for him. When she entered the adjacent bath and looked at herself in the mirror, she discovered she was smiling for the first time in, well, *forever*.

Rubbing her eyes, then her cheeks, she asked herself, "How did you turn into *this* person?" Holding her hair in a makeshift ponytail, she brushed her teeth and then splashed a handful of water in her mouth. After washing her face, she tossed her nightshirt into the hamper and got the pair of scrubs she'd set out the night before.

After applying just a hint of make-up, she closed her cosmetic case and added that to the suitcase before zipping it shut. It didn't make much sense to pack all her clothes. Most of them didn't fit right now, so she'd worry about that later. When she applied for the restraining order she could get the judge, or magistrate, or whatever you called them, to give her some time alone at the house to get the rest of her stuff. But for now, for today, she was content to take just what she needed for a week. By then, Sean would be back, he'd be served with the restraining order and she'd be on her way to being divorced.

The word was enough to send a shiver down her spine. No, she didn't—couldn't—stay married to Sean. But she'd never failed at anything before. Never.

Darby was smart enough to know that when it came to abuse, past behavior was the best predictor of future behavior. Given that Sean was getting worse by the day, counseling wasn't a realistic solution. No, she had to get out now. Before he killed her and the baby, a threat he'd made on more than one occasion.

After loading two suitcases into the back of her Grand Cherokee, she backed her car out of the driveway. Automatically she reached for the clicker attached to the passenger seat visor and pressed the button. The door descended about two feet before coming to a grinding halt. Then it bounced as the motor continued to whirl.

Sighing heavily, Darby got out of the car to see what was causing the malfunction. It took a minute, but she finally spotted a length of telephone wire looped around one of the slats. "Just what I need," she grumbled as she stood on tiptoe, trying to slap the wire out of the way. Darby gave up after three tries.

Like the house, the three-car garage was as neat as a pin. For once, Sean's insistence on order in all things worked to her advantage. The step stool was tucked between the shelving and the hot water heater. Even knowing that Sean wouldn't have an opportunity to react to any scuffmarks, Darby lifted the awkwardly shaped stool and maneuvered it over to the garage door. Once she had some height, it was simple to dislodge the cord. As designed, a safety feature of the door sent it backward, crawling up and along the ceiling. The phone cord disappeared into the void between the ceiling and the door. Oh well, she thought as she walked back to her idling car. Sean would take care of it. He didn't let things like strangely dangling cords—especially ones that impeded the garage door from working properly—go unattended.

The sun was just bleeding over the horizon as she drove the fifteen short miles to Palm City, the area where her family had owned a home since the 1890s. While the location hadn't changed, the homes certainly had. Her however-many-greats grandparents had built a modest, single-story wood frame dwelling smack in the middle of the original Hayes orange grove.

As the modest grove grew and expanded, so did the size and expanse of the home. She smiled with equal measures of respect and pride as she passed the remains of that first homestead. The only reason part of it was still standing was because of the adjacent cemetery. As common practice until the mid-1970s, all Hayeses had been entombed on that small strip of land. Part of the deal when the groves were sold off to a developer was that the family cemetery would be fenced and appropriately maintained. He'd kept his word.

Darby's stomach felt like a sack of unacquainted cats. She had always been so meticulous about her life. Driven, some would say. After her stint in the Army, she'd gone to college, then to vet school, and by age twenty-eight she had her own business with an impressive client base. How could all those aspects of her life be so right and her marriage be so wrong? Yes, intellectually she knew that leaving Sean was the safe and only option, but some small crumb in her brain kept harping on the failure aspect of throwing in the towel after less than two years of marriage. It wasn't supposed to be like this, but she couldn't risk the baby's safety, especially now that Sean was getting more violent with every encounter.

Traffic was light as she crossed the bridge over the St. Lucie River. The fresh scent of the ocean air dissipated under the weight of diesel fumes wafting up from the marinas below. Once upon a time in the not so distant past, all of the land on Monterey from Willoughby Road west had belonged to the Hayes family. Little by little, as snowbirds migrated from the north and population swelled up from the south, the groves had been sold off, leveled and replaced by gated communities, indistinguishable stucco homes, strip malls, and golf courses.

Martin County was in transition. More building, more families, less agriculture.

Darby suspected her father held on to one modest grove near Indiantown for sentimental reasons. He'd grown up working the groves. It was more than an exercise in nepotism. William Hayes loved the business. The scent of orange blossoms in bloom; the occasional flurry of activity to fend off an unexpected frost; the rugged machinery weaving through the rows, slicing off the ripe fruit to send it off to market.

Though they ever said it, Darby suspected her parents had thrown themselves into the business because they were married for nearly twenty years before Darby came along. Grace Hayes had been over forty when she had Darby. William had been fifty-one at the time.

As she approached the small, paved driveway leading to her parents' home, she saw several fire trucks parked at angles, blocking traffic in both directions. Automatically, Darby looked at the sky above the tree line, expecting to see a plume of dark smoke. Nothing. The sky was clear and blue save for a few puffy white clouds rolling in off the ocean.

A cold shiver crept up her spine. It appeared as if the emergency vehicles were in front of her parents' house.

Panicked, she placed the car in park. Darby unhooked her seatbelt and wriggled out of the car. The minute her feet hit the pavement, she did her best to run at the same pace as her rapid heartbeat.

As she neared the fire trucks, she caught sight of a previously obscured ambulance, parked on the west side, its doors open. A man sat on the fender, sucking oxygen through a clear plastic mask affixed to his face.

Holding her stomach to lessen the effects of her vigorous movements, Darby jogged over to the ambulance. She'd moved beyond palpable fear to utter panic.

"You a doc?" the EMT asked, his fingers pressed to the pulse point of the police officer's wrist.

"Vet," she answered. "What happened?" She turned her head, getting on tiptoes in a futile attempt to see her childhood home through the thick shrubbery vining through the six-foot iron fence.

"Carbon monoxide," the EMT explained. "Harry, here, got a few whiffs. The oxygen is just precautionary."

Darby's mind was spinning. Ignoring everything but the dread gripping her chest, she pivoted on the balls of her feet and started toward the house. She got all of maybe ten feet when a tall, lanky patrolman held up his hand.

"Sorry, ma'am. This is—"

"My parents' house," she finished, watching him blanch slightly. "What's happened?"

Crooking his thumb behind him, he said, "I've got to radio the sergeant. Just a minute."

The patrolman turned sideways and whispered muffled words into the microphone clipped to the shoulder of his beige uniform shirt.

"He'll be right here," the patrolman said. "Why don't you come over here. Wait in the shade," he suggested, pointing her toward a small area under a canopy of palm fronds.

Just as she took her first step, four men dressed in street clothes filed past her, pushing two gurneys. The fact that they were in no particular hurry, and that white body bags were neatly folded atop each gurney, confirmed her worst fears. Her vision started to spin and she got that rollercoaster feeling—like her stomach was dropping out. This couldn't be happening. Darby clutched her stomach and felt warm tears slide down her cheeks.

Darby felt her knees buckle, then everything went fuzzy.

As if viewing the scene from underwater, Darby felt the patrolman lift her up and carry her to the ambulance. Gently, she was placed on a stretcher and the EMT who'd been working on the officer turned his attention to her. Though her head was spinning, she brushed his hands away.

"I'm fine."

"You're at risk for shock," the EMT insisted. "Your BP is too low. We've got to get you to the hospital."

"But my parents. Are they…are they…?"

"I'll ask one of the officers to follow us to the ER." He gently lifted her arm and secured a blood pressure cuff, then attached leads to her chest to monitor her heart. The sirens came on at the same time as he reached beneath her to secure a fetal monitor around her abdomen.

"I'm Pete," he said as he fiddled with myriad machines in the ambulance.

"Darby," she said, barely feeling the continuous stream of tears sliding down her cheeks. No one was telling her anything, but she knew. She just knew that her beloved parents were gone.

The EMT offered a weak smile as he donned a stethoscope and listened first to her heart, and then pressed the single-head stethoscope at various places on her bulging abdomen. "What's your OB's name?"

"Meredith Price. Why? Is there a problem?"

He shook his head and patted her hand. "Not that I can see, except for those," he said, pointing to the small red welts on her side. "Look a little like hives. Do you have any allergies? Eat anything new or different?"

Out of sheer habit, she lied, shaking her head. She wasn't ready to admit they were just the latest in a long list of bruises and welts left by her husband's beatings. She wondered if she'd ever have the nerve to tell the whole truth about Sean. It was hard to imagine, since she'd also have to admit that she'd chosen him. For that she felt a twinge of responsibility.

"Said you were a vet, right?" he asked rhetorically. "Any chance something at work might have caused an allergic reaction?"

"Not sure." The truth lingered on the tip of her tongue. The taste was bitter but it was far overshadowed by concern for the fate of her family. "My parents?" she pressed.

The ambulance came to an abrupt halt outside the emergency room of Martin Memorial North. After being rolled into an exam area, Darby waited more than three frustrating hours badgering anyone and everyone about her parents. After what felt like an eternity, a representative from the Martin County Sherriff's office poked his head through the flimsy curtain.

"Mrs. Grisom?"

"Darby Hayes Grisom," she both corrected and replied as she leveraged herself up on the bed with her elbows. "What happened to my parents?"

"First, I'm Sergeant Joe Ciminelli. Secondly, is there anyone here with you?"

"No, my husband is on his way home from a business trip. His flight landed a little more than an hour ago."

The sergeant's brow furrowed. He ran his palm over his bald head, then hooked his hand at the back of his neck. His pale brown eyes were somber and fixed on a point just above her head.

"Is there anyone who could come to be with you?"

Darby's whole body was stiff, braced for whatever news he seemed so reluctant to deliver. "No. Now, please tell me what happened to my parents."

"I'm afraid there was an accident."

Accident? What kind of accident kills two people? "Excuse me?"

Sergeant Ciminelli moistened his forefinger, then flipped through the small notebook he'd pulled from his breast pocket. "I'm very sorry to have to tell you this, Mrs. Grisom, but your parents passed away in their home sometime during the night."

"How?"

"All indications are that the on-off switch on their car was left in the 'on' position. Carbon monoxide leaked into the home."

"Impossible," Darby said, emphatically shaking her head.

"Ma'am," the sergeant began, his tone sympathetic, "I know this is a terrible shock, but tests conducted inside of the home confirmed a high concentration of carbon monoxide. Unfortunately, it's a very deadly gas. Odorless, colorless. I know this probably isn't much of a consolation, but in most cases, the victims fall asleep, then succumb to the fumes."

Darby raised her hands, waving away his words. "I mean it's impossible that my father would have left his car running. He checked things like that. He was very cautious. Nothing was ever neglected. Were you in the house?"

The officer shrugged his muscular shoulders.

"Did you see a single thing in need of attention? He washed the range hood every single day, for god's sake. This wasn't an accident. He was a detailed person. Practically anal about safety. He would not have left his car running in the garage."

He reached for the small box of tissues and handed her one. Darby looked down at it as if he'd handed her a foreign object.

She only vaguely realized she was crying. Tears of sorrow, yes, but salted with disbelief and frustration. "There has to be some sort of mistake. Something you missed."

"Your parents' neighbor was walking her dog and heard the engine running. She used her spare key to enter the house and, well, then she called police. She said your parents were lying comfortably in their bed."

"Something is wrong," Darby insisted.

"I'm very sorry, Mrs. Grisom. There was no sign of a break-in. And now the medical examiner has confirmed the cause of death with blood samples taken from the dec—from your parents."

Darby replayed the last twenty-four hours. Her parents' death was just too coincidental. She'd reached out to them for the first time in her marriage and they'd been dead before morning. Somehow Sean must have known she would contact them. But how could he be in New York and Florida at the same time? Darby didn't know, but she was certain he was behind this. There was no way her father would have been so careless with his new push button-start car. It just didn't make any sense. Darby's sorrow took on an edge of fury when the sword of certainty stabbed through her. "My husband killed them. He knew the garage access code. He must have taken a later flight or something."

"Excuse me?"

"It had to be Sean." She dropped her head, closing her eyes as hot tears fell freely. Her whole body shuddered as sobs wracked her body. Darby embraced her belly, holding on to the baby for dear life. Scrambled, jumbled thoughts raced through her head in a fragmented marathon. Memories: her mother's face; the feel of her father holding her hand as they walked along the beach; the smell of her mother's perfume; the joy in their eyes when she'd told them they were going to be grandparents. Other memories, too, like the first time she'd dropped by the restaurant, unseen and unheard as she watched her husband stroke his fingertips along Roxanne's throat. And the bad, ugly ones: Sean losing his temper time and time again. The cold, emotionless look in his eyes before he exploded in anger. Things being flung against the walls. Finding her beloved German shepherd dead in the parking lot of her clinic—suspecting him, yet deluding herself into believing Sean had had nothing to do with the dog's death. The coincidence had been just too great: the night before she'd found the dog, Sean had *suggested* she get rid of it. According to him, too much of her time was spent walking and caring for the dog. They'd argued to a stand-off. The dog had been dead less than a day later.

The similarity now was too great. As much as she didn't want it to be true, it made sense. Brushing at her tears with the backs of her hands, Darby couldn't look at the officer as she quietly said, "My husband killed them."

"It was an unfortunate accident, Mrs. Grisom. Besides, I thought you said your husband was out of town."

"He was. But he did this. I know it." Fueled by grief, conviction, and a sense of security due to her surroundings, she began to open up to the officer. "Sean is a very possessive man. We had a fight last night and he—"

"Apologized."

Darby's head whipped up and her heart stopped as she saw

Sean walk into the exam room. Dropping his garment bag in the corner, he came over and gathered her stiff body in his arms.

"Sweetheart, I'm so sorry." He dusted her head and face with kisses. "I should have been here for you. I'm so sorry this happened when I was away."

Planting her hands on his chest, Darby shoved him away. The last thing she wanted was to feel his hands on her. She would never have had the nerve to do such a thing if it wasn't for the officer standing right there. She didn't care what her parents' deaths looked like; she knew Sean was behind it. She looked up at him and saw the raw anger in his eyes and a lot of her bravado faded away. Now she was back to being scared witless. The exchange seemed to intrigue the officer, but Darby didn't care. For all his polish, Sean was a murderer. She saw that truth with absolute clarity. Now her only priority was to save herself and her baby from the lunatic she'd married in haste.

"Get him out of here!"

"Darby—"

"Mrs. Grisom," Sergeant Ciminelli began, "I realize you're upset."

"He killed my family," she said in a deadly calm tone.

Sean backed away from the bed. As he did, he reached into the pocket of his suit coat and produced two rumpled boarding passes. "I've been in New York since yesterday evening." He patted his other pockets, then pulled a folded slip of paper from one and a business card from another. "This is my hotel receipt and the name of the gentleman I met for breakfast."

"See what I mean?" Darby asked. "Who but a guilty man would carry his alibis around in his pockets?"

"Let's step into the hallway," Sean suggested, placing his arm around the shoulder of the officer, guiding him out of the room.

Darby slammed her head against the pillow and again hot tears welled in her eyes. Grabbing the call button, she pressed it over and over until a petite and clearly irritated nurse entered the room. In the split second the curtain was drawn back, Darby saw Sean and the sergeant sharing a handshake.

"Yes?" the nurse asked as she gave cursory glances to the machines tethering Darby to the bed.

"I need a phone."

"We don't allow telephones in the rooms. Is there someone I can call for you?"

"Yes. I need the police."

The nurse blinked, then peered back over her shoulder as she pushed apart the curtain. "Officer?"

"Not him," Darby cried. Too late.

Sean and the officer returned. It didn't take a rocket scientist to see that the sergeant was totally charmed by Sean. The sergeant took up a position at the end of her bed next to the nurse while Sean moved to the head and draped his arm around her shoulders. "I was just explaining your condition to the policeman." His fingers dug into the flesh at her shoulder.

Ciminelli smiled understandingly. "I've got three kids myself. My wife went a little hormonal with each one. She had all sorts of weird thoughts and cravings. Got so I was afraid to walk in the door after my shift. Never knew what was going to set her off."

"Darby's normally very rational," Sean said, brushing a kiss to her temple. "Don't you have something to say to the officer, sweetheart?"

Darby pressed her lips tight.

Sean squeezed her shoulder harder. "Darby, the officer checked. He spoke directly with Roxanne."

"Roxanne would lie for you," she whispered under her breath.

Sean sighed heavily. "Sweetheart, I thought you might still be…confused, so I made sure the officer called the airline to verify that I was on the flight. The hotel verified that I checked in and even told the officer what I ordered from room service and when it was delivered. The investor I was meeting as well as the restaurant staff verified that I attended the meeting. So, don't you think it's time for you to apologize to the officer for making extra work for him?"

Darby had no idea how he had managed it, but he had. Now she looked like the crazy one. And worse yet, she was at Sean's mercy, which was a terrifying thought. What would happen once they were alone? She shivered just thinking about the potential punishment for calling him a murderer in public. She had that trapped animal feeling again and she couldn't stop crying. No one believed her but she didn't know how he'd pulled it off; she just knew he had. Just as she knew the officer wasn't going to believe a word she said. Darby felt defeated. She gave up. "I'm sorry."

"Don't give it a thought, Mrs. Grisom. I know it was just the grief and the hormones talking. I gave your husband everything you'll need to make the, um, final arrangements for your parents."

"Thank you."

The nurse followed Ciminelli out of the room. Darby braced herself, fully expecting to suffer the wrath of Sean. Instead, he was just looking at her as he arranged the hair framing her face.

"I'm sorry, sweetheart. I always liked your parents," he whispered against her ear.

"Ummmm."

Then calmly and quietly he added, "If you hadn't called them, I never would have been forced to kill them."

CHAPTER TWO

Darby cradled the large urn against her swollen belly as she walked the short distance from the chapel to the car. She didn't speak, she didn't cry, but most importantly, she didn't flinch when her husband, the man who'd murdered her parents, tightened his grip on her shoulder.

She knew better. Any infraction, real or perceived, could have the potential to bring about dire consequences. Sean opened the door to the champagne-colored Jaguar and held her elbow as he guided her into the car. Anyone witnessing the scene would have immediately thought him the most kind, considerate husband on the planet. A genuinely sweet man attending to his grieving, pregnant wife getting through the sudden, shocking, *accidental* death of her parents.

"I'm so sorry," she whispered to the cold, enameled urn.

Sean leaned in, locking his choleric green eyes with hers. "So am I." He crooked his forefinger beneath her chin, forcing her head up. "You left me no choice, sweetheart. There are always dire consequences when one exercises poor judgment. If you hadn't involved them, I wouldn't have been forced to take such drastic action."

"I know; you've already explained that." Since the scene in the hospital, Sean had admitted that their house had been wired for both video and sound. It was only then that Darby put two and two together and realized that the loose wire she'd found in the garage was part of the surveillance. But all traces were gone now; nothing was left that would allow her to prove to the police that Sean had listened in on her call to her parents after his attack. The creep factor, knowing he had been watching and listening to her every move, was gigantic. No wonder he'd seemed to know every time she had coffee with a friend or received a phone call when he was out of the house. She felt as if she'd married her stalker. And she didn't know what he'd do next; she just knew she had to find a way to leave him and keep the baby safe.

"I'm sorry," she said, her sentiment for the urn and not for her psychotic husband.

Her response seemed to placate him. Moving closer, he pressed a kiss against her lips that made bile rise in her throat. The scent of his cologne mingled with the stench of her revulsion. Darby clutched the urn tighter and went through the mechanical motions of kissing him back.

After helping her with the seatbelt, he closed her door, went around to the driver's side and slid gracefully inside the car. Sean coaxed the engine to a soft purr, and then shifted into drive. Darby let go of the urn with one hand to tug against the snugness of the seatbelt. The brilliant morning sun and clear south Florida sky seemed cruel and mocking given the turbulent emotions she had no choice but to tamp down. Reaching up, she took her sunglasses off the clip on the visor and slipped them on her face.

Instinctively, she stiffened. Maybe she should have asked him if it was okay to shield her eyes from the sun. Darby never knew what might set him off. But she did know what he was capable of. It had been four days since the last vestiges of his mask had slipped. Four days since he'd killed her mother and father. Four days since she'd tried, in vain, to convince the police that he was a murderous monster.

Not that she could prove it. No, Sean was far too smart to leave tracks. Darby pressed her back against the seat.

The sergeant had made it perfectly clear he thought she was crazy or hormonal or both. Maybe if she spoke to someone else, someone higher up on the law enforcement food chain. Maybe then she could convince someone that Sean wasn't what he seemed.

If he found out, she had no doubt he'd beat her again, or more likely, kill her. She was only safe because of the baby. Sean was fixated on the baby. And not in a fatherly way. No, Sean just knew that the baby would be a strong way to control Darby, with the added benefit of having her own trust fund from the Hayes Foundation. Darby knew Sean would use the baby like a club to beat her into submission. The only reason he wanted the baby alive and well was so he could take over as her trustee. Too bad for him; Darby was already named trustee, and she wasn't about to abdicate that role to Sean.

Sean was treating the baby as if she was going to be an extension of his warped world. Darby wasn't going to allow that to happen. She needed a contingency plan, and she needed it fast.

"I'm sorry, sweetheart, but I have to go to the restaurant. Roxanne can't handle it alone."

"I'll be fine," Darby replied, secretly grateful that she wouldn't have to suffer his company. Even if it was only for a few hours, anything that kept the two of them apart was a bonus. Darby was very near the point of a complete meltdown. The situation robbed her of sleep and with no outlet for her emotions and no real friends with whom she could confide, each day felt like an eternity. She didn't have any idea how long she could handle living with, talking to, or sharing a bed with the man who had taken so much from her.

Absently, she rubbed her belly. In a month she'd have the baby. Instead of looking forward to finally meeting her daughter, she was terrified. Sean had killed her parents without hesitation. How easy would it be for him to kill a helpless infant?

"Darby?"

The sound of Sean tersely barking her name brought her back to the present. "Sorry, I must have gotten lost in my thoughts."

Sean placed his hand on her leg. "I asked what you had planned for the rest of the day."

"I've got to arrange for someone to pack up my parents' things and put them in storage."

"Good. The house needs to be sold. The sooner the better. The last thing I want is you hanging on to it, treating it as some sort of a shrine. We have to move on with our lives. I've been thinking."

He began making small circles on her inner thigh with the tip of his thumb. Darby hugged the urn tightly, desperately battling the strong urge to shove his offensive hand off her leg. *I'll bet you have.* "About?"

"The sale should bring half a million or more easy. I checked with your family attorney. Those proceeds aren't part of the trust, so we can use that money to spruce up the restaurant. I'd like to expand. By adding a deck, I can take advantage of the water views. Maybe even construct some sort of gazebo to rent for weddings or charity events."

"Mmmmm."

"With you closing your practice, we can focus all our efforts on making the restaurant a success."

Darby was taken aback. "When did we decide I was closing my practice?" *No way*, she thought. Her clinic was the only thing she had left. Sean had killed her parents and alienated her from all her friends. If she lost her job as well, there would be nothing left of her own. She couldn't handle the thought of losing the last vestiges of her old life.

His fingers stilled, then pinched into her skin. "Would you prefer our daughter was raised by a stranger? You had a charmed childhood. You have no idea how that feels. I barely saw my mother when I was growing up. She was either out working or exhausted from working. I'd rather not have this baby than subject her to the kind of childhood I was forced to endure."

Not have this child. The comment chilled her to the core. "I was thinking I could just work in the mornings. Before you go to the restaurant."

"So now you're telling me you can't be bothered raising our child? That you'd rather give rabies vaccinations?"

Hearing the dangerous calm in his tone, Darby immediately backtracked. The calm scared her because it usually led to something worse. She was too terrified to argue, so she decided simply to deflect. "You're right, of course. With all that's happened, I wasn't thinking clearly."

"Good," he said.

His grip loosened, as did Darby's tensed muscles.

"What about the rest of the day?"

"I have a doctor's appointment. I can reschedule if—"

"No." His hand slipped up to rest on her stomach. "We can't risk anything happening to the baby, right?"

"Right."

Darby didn't take an easy breath until Sean had dropped her at the house and she'd watched him drive off. Not that she felt all that comfortable at home. *Home*—only in the most general definition of the word.

Just to demonstrate his total immersion in her life, Sean had played a tape of the phone conversation with her parents. He didn't say how long he'd been tapping the phone, but his doing so explained a lot—like the incident a few months back when he'd known she'd disobeyed him and met her mother for lunch. And how he knew her every coming and going.

It wasn't just tapping the phones. Darby now knew that hidden cameras covered every inch of the house, a fact uncovered when the nursery muralist called to apologize for getting paint on one of the lenses. Assuming that the camera was a pre-installed nanny cam, the artist had just wanted to follow-up to make sure the camera was still in working order.

Alerted, Darby went room to room under the pretext of dusting and found no fewer than two dozen cameras hidden in various places, none larger than a pencil eraser. It was a terrifying trip around the house—uncovering cameras in every room, sometimes more than one—not knowing how long he'd been taping her. She felt totally violated and completely mortified. There was even a camera in the bathroom. It was terrifying to see just how far he'd gone to keep tracks on her. She shivered at the memory.

No, this house wasn't a home. It wasn't even a house. It was a prison and Sean was her warden.

Though she had no appetite, Darby knew she had to eat something. Opening the fridge, she starred at the contents for a long time before settling on a yogurt. Hoisting herself up on to one of the barstools at the center island counter, she managed to choke down the food while trying not to look in the direction of the electronic eye mounted in the smoke detector. There was no way of knowing if Sean was watching her live or taping the footage or both. Regardless, she didn't want to let on that she knew about his surveillance equipment. When she was finished, she rinsed and dried the yogurt container, then took it to the recycle bin in the garage. She thoroughly washed and dried the utensils before she put them in the Fisher-Paykel dishwasher. Then finally, she wiped and polished the stainless steel sink.

Somberly, she took the urn into her office and placed it on a shelf in the closet. Kicking off her modest heels, she turned on her laptop to check her online calendar. She was fairly sure her OB appointment was at one o'clock, but she wanted to confirm. Opening the program, a ding sounded to let her know she had new messages in her inbox.

Sean often emailed her the minute he got to the restaurant with instructions—clothing to be taken to the dry cleaners; comments on trivial things like the living room drapes having fewer than four crisp folds; his preference for the dinner menu. Given the current situation, Darby went immediately to her inbox. Scrolling down through several advertisements, she saw an email from Sean marked with a red exclamation point. Every communication from her husband was marked high importance, so she clicked the mouse button and brought up the reading pane.

The body of the message was simple—*open immediately*. She heard Sean's commanding voice in her head as she read the two words. Without hesitation, she clicked the paperclip icon and waited for the document to upload.

A cursory scan of the opening line strangled the breath from her body. The room started to spin and she thought she'd get physically ill.

Sudden Infant Death Syndrome (SIDS) accounts for more than 2,000 deaths a year in babies from 2 to 4 months of age. Often called the 'silent killer,' many researchers agree prevention efforts like placing the baby on its back when sleeping or napping have been marginally successful. . .Sometimes it is impossible to tell the difference between SIDS and suffocation.

Slamming the laptop closed, Darby brushed perspiration off her forehead with trembling fingers. "Oh God!" she whispered as she retrieved her shoes. Off balance and hobbling down the hallway, she managed to get her shoes on before she reached the kitchen where she retrieved her purse and keys. Darby gulped air into her lungs, forcing it past the lump of fear clogging her throat. Her chest was tight and her heart pounded in her ears.

She tore out of the garage, sideswiping the empty trashcan in the process. In the rearview mirror, she watched it spin like a top before coming to rest in the middle of the street. As she drove, Darby wept uncontrollably. She needed help. She needed a plan. And she needed it now. But with her parents gone, who could she trust?

* * *

Darby stood out among the women assembled in the pastel yellow and green waiting room of Dr. Price. But this had nothing to do with her puffy red eyes and tear-stained cheeks. She was clad in her sober black dress and simple strand of pearls, and her hair was twisted into a neat bun. The other women wore bright, happy colors that matched their pregnancy glows. Seeing them only served to darken Darby's mood. What she wouldn't give to be one of those women.

A cheery brunette nurse called her back into the exam area. Her bright smile dimmed. Apparently she wasn't as oblivious to Darby's appearance as the other patients seemed to be.

She rubbed a reassuring hand down Darby's back as she led

her to the scale. "Dr. Price told me about your parents. We're very sorry for your loss, Mrs. Grisom."

"Thank you," Darby replied through the fog of her private despair.

"Hummm."

"What? Is there a problem?"

"You didn't gain an ounce. In fact, your weight is down a little. I know this is a difficult time for you, but you really need to take care of yourself and that baby." After making a notation on her chart, the nurse escorted Darby into an exam room and gave her a paper gown.

As she was placing her clothing on the hook next to the exam table, a small poster caught her eye. "You're not alone. Everyone gets the blues," she read. Almost immediately, her brain kicked into high gear. Was this a possible way out? It can't hurt to give it a trial run.

By the time the doctor arrived, Darby was ready to test drive her idea.

After offering her condolences, Dr. Price had her lie back on the table. "Losing your parents this close to your due date is tough, Darby. Thankfully, you've got that gorgeous husband of yours to help you through it."

"I suppose."

"Not all husbands are so hands on," the doctor commented.

"He is that. Is there maybe a counselor you could recommend?"

"I know someone who specializes in grief counseling. I've referred patients to her before."

"I don't want Sean to know."

The doctor's head came up as she yanked off the latex gloves with a sharp snap. "He probably knows you're grieving, Darby. It's perfectly normal."

Darby shook her head as the doctor gave her a hand sitting up. "It's not just the grief. I've been feeling…well…before my parents…Before that, I was having thoughts. Inappropriate thoughts."

The doctor's eyes narrowed as she scooted closer on the wheeled stool. "Like what?"

"You know we didn't plan this pregnancy."

Dr. Price nodded. "Surprises can be good."

Summoning all her nerve, Darby took a deep breath and said, "I'm not sure I'm ready to be a mother."

Offering a small smile, the doctor said, "Eight months too late for that decision. Besides," she added, patting Darby's foot. "Most of my first-timers get the jitters when they get close to term."

"This is more than jitters."

"How so?"

"I have these thoughts. Kind of like daydreams, only worse."

"Like?"

"Like the baby would be better off without me as her mother."

"Darby, do these thoughts include hurting yourself in some way?"

No, I've got Sean for that. "Not hurting myself, no."

Taking the prescription pad out of her purse, Dr. Price scribbled for a few seconds, then handed the paper to Darby. On it was a name and a phone number. Darby recognized the area code and her heart sank. "I can't go all the way to Ft. Lauderdale. I don't want Sean to know what I've been thinking. He'd be devastated if he knew about this. You won't say anything, will you?"

"I can't," Dr. Price promised. "Privilege. But I see your point. When I spoke to Sean a little while ago, he mentioned that he thought you might be having some difficulties."

Darby felt her eyes grow wide. "You spoke to Sean?"

"He called and asked for any information I had on SIDS. He explained that you'd been acting—his description—irrationally for a little while now and he thought it was as a result of reading about SIDS on some online site. By the way, didn't I tell you to stay away from e-zines and other unreliable stuff on pregnancy and parenting? If you want to read a book, read Dr. Spock. An oldie but a goodie."

Darby wondered if there was any part of her world Sean hadn't violated. Probably not. "Isn't there anyone close by I could talk to?"

Maybe it was the desperation in her eyes, or outright kindness on the part of the doctor. The reason was irrelevant. Dr. Price reached for the phone and within five minutes, she'd gotten the therapist to agree to make an exception and meet Darby at the OB's office. The first session was scheduled for three the next afternoon.

If she was going to pull this off, Darby had to do some research. Fast.

After leaving the doctor's office, Darby was waiting to cross to the parking lot when she noticed the sign on the building across the street.

"Law offices of Jack Kavanaugh." She'd never heard of him but that worked to her advantage. As did the fact that all she had to do was cross the street. Given the fact that he was video and audio taping her, Sean was probably checking the odometer on her car as well.

When the light changed and the little silhouette of a person illuminated, she carefully made her way across the brick crosswalk, stepping carefully as she traversed the uneven stone. The strong scent of garlic from the pizza shop around the corner battled for supremacy with the sweet aroma of chocolate from Kilwin's, historic downtown Stuart's landmark candy shop. The blend was nauseating, made worse by the oppressive heat from the full sun above and the heat reflected off the street. Being dressed in all black didn't help.

The building sported a fresh coat of terra cotta paint on its stucco exterior. A large plate glass window just to the left had his name freshly stenciled in gold lettering, followed by the phone number. The six-paned door was primed but not yet painted. Tucked into the inside of the lower right-hand corner of one of the windowpanes was a small, flat plastic clock. "Just great," Darby grumbled after she tried the door, only to find it locked. "Liar," she said to the clock, which incorrectly said Jack Kavanaugh, Esquire would be back at one-thirty. It was already a few minutes past two.

She had taken a half step back from the door when it flew open. Her first impression of the man wasn't positive. He was tall and muscular, with jet-black hair and light brown eyes. His hair was disheveled, falling down on his forehead even after he'd raked his fingers through it in a futile attempt to make himself more presentable. It would take more than finger combing his hair for that to happen. He was wearing khaki slacks that had never seen an iron. He'd paired the rumpled slacks with a short-sleeved olive shirt, ditto on the lack of pressing, and a haphazardly knotted tie in a god-awful paisley pattern. The ensemble was completed by a pair of flip-flops that had some miles on them, judging by the frayed stitching.

Generally speaking, he looked a lot more like a lifeguard than a lawyer—at least none of the lawyers she'd ever met. Then again, all the ones she knew were from the upper echelon of the local legal community. They had large, impressive offices professionally decorated. Large, impressive staffs to tend to every need. Doors with proper coats of paint.

* * *

"Sorry," he said as he put his half-eaten chili dog on the table next to the door and extended his hand.

The blonde didn't respond. He looked at his outstretched hand and realized some of the chili had dripped onto his palm. "Sorry," he mumbled again as he stepped aside and waved her inside.

She was very pretty, very, very pregnant and based on the Prada bag and shoes, very, very, *very* rich. He felt his shoulders tense. Pretty was good. Pregnant was good. Rich spelled trouble.

Leading the way, he ushered her past what would have been his secretary's desk—if he'd had a secretary, which he didn't—into the cramped ten-by-twelve office. He transferred a stack of files from one chair to another and offered her a seat. "I'm Jack Kavanaugh," he said as he moved behind his desk and sat down.

"Darby Gris-Gray," she said.

Lie number one. "Mrs. Gray," he greeted. "What can I do for you?"

"What do you know about family trusts?"

Leaning back, he studied her for a minute. The dark circles could be a side effect of being pregnant. By the time she'd gotten to son number six, his mother had had circles under her eyes as black as a football player's anti-glare grease. The woman's makeup was subdued but smudged, most likely from crying, judging by the redness of her eyes. That too could be chalked up to the pregnant factor. Tears came with the territory. Under normal circumstances, he'd bet her eyes were her best feature. Even now he could see hints of gray-green that had him picturing her in a different way.

That was a first. Jack had never been one of those guys who got turned on by the whole miracle-of-birth-making-a-woman-glow crap. Nope. Pregnant women looked uncomfortable, drained and waddled instead of walked.

"Mr. Kavanaugh?" she prompted.

The scintilla of turned on evaporated when he heard the snobbish, dismissive tone in her voice. Apparently this one had her fair share of arrogance. He should have shown her the door. The last thing he wanted to deal with was some prima donna. Then again, if he wanted to help Michael, he needed all the money he could get.

Michael, his oldest brother, was incarcerated for killing their father. He was the reason Jack had gone to law school: he wanted to get Mike out of jail ASAP. Mike wasn't some maniacal killer; he'd just been protecting their long-suffering mother from a beating. Unfortunately, ASAP wasn't moving as fast as he'd like it to, so he needed clients like Mrs. Whatever Her Name is.

"Family trusts?" she asked again, more irritated.

"Right, family trusts. Well, I know poor people don't have them."

She pursed her pouty lips together as she began to stand. "I'm sorry, I seem to be wasting your time. I was looking for a *real* attorney."

"Yale real enough for you?" he asked, leaning on his elbows to enjoy the curtain of shock as it rolled down her face. "Setting up a new one or making changes to an existing one?"

She hovered, half in, half out of her chair, then sat back down. "An existing one."

"Beneficiaries?"

"That's what I want to change."

He looked at her tiny, pointless designer purse. She'd be hard pressed to put anything more than a lipstick in that. Oh well, the idle rich often went for form over function. He'd spent enough time in their company to know that was a fact. Being a scholarship student did have its advantages.

Jack didn't want to like her. Most of his clients were pro bono or paid the minimal amount. His true specialty was criminal law, but criminal cases were expensive to defend so he needed the subsidy of clients like the pretty blonde across from him.

But Jack was a tad weary of pretty blondes. His law school sweetheart had been a blonde and as soon as she'd found out he wanted to do pro bono instead of taking his Yale degree on the fast track to a well-paid partnership, she'd bailed. Thanks to that experience, he'd become a tad weary of women in general. He had kind of made a deal with himself to avoid relationships until he'd garnered Mike's freedom. Right now he was tied up in the appellate process.

Still, he asked the question just to gauge her reaction. In truth, it wasn't as if he had anything more pressing to do. He had only opened his practice a month earlier. Clients weren't exactly lined up around the block. "Who is the executor?"

The polite smile she'd obviously been struggling to keep in place slipped. She recovered quickly, though. This wasn't the first time Darby Whatever Her Name Really Was had been forced to camouflage her emotions.

"The executor passed away."

"Is there a substitute trustee named?"

"Yes, but that's one of the things I want changed."

"The other being?"

"The beneficiary."

"If it's a family trust, then I'm assuming the new beneficiary is a blood relative?"

She nodded and rubbed her belly. "I want to turn over the whole trust to a friend."

Lie number two. "Because?"

She blinked. "Why does that matter? I'm the only beneficiary of the trust still living. All the money is mine. I'm just trying to know the legality of transferring it to another person."

He nodded in the direction of the gazillion-carat diamond on her left ring finger. "Do you have a prenup?"

"No. Why?"

Rich and dumb, every man's fantasy. Well, not every man. Jack preferred brains over bucks. Not that he'd eliminate a woman as date potential just because she earned a decent living. But that was the difference. People who earned their money were completely different from the ones who had it placed in their lap on the day they are born; people like the woman sitting across from him, all prim and proper.

"Well, for starters, your husband could claim any interest earned during your marriage is a matrimonial asset. That is what this is all about, right? Hiding money from your husband in contemplation of a divorce?"

"N-no."

Lie number three. Sorta.

Clearly flustered, she dashed out of his office as if the devil himself was chasing her.

Going to the door, Jack watched as she crossed the street and got into a tan SUV. He made a mental note of the license plate number, then grabbed the now cold chilidog and took a bite.

The fact that she'd stumbled when he'd brought up divorce intrigued him. He knew she was lying, but sensed there was something more to that lie. If he was a betting man, which he was, he'd bet she was about to give birth to a baby that wasn't going to look a whole lot like her husband. "Friend," he scoffed, now back in his office as he reached for his phone. "Lover is probably more like it."

He pressed the numbers from memory.

On the second ring, his brother said, "Declan Kavanaugh."

"Jack Kavanaugh," he replied, mocking the clipped cadence of his older brother's speech.

"What do you want?" he asked with half-hearted irritation.

"Why do you automatically assume I want something?"

"Don't you?"

"Well, yes. But that's beside the point."

"Paying job, or gratis?"

"It's not a job; it's more like a favor. You know," Jack leaned back in his chair and rubbed the back of his neck with his free hand. "The kind of thing one brother does for another."

"No, a favor is when I do work for you and you don't pay me."

"C'mon, Declan. All I need is one license plate run. It'll take you five seconds, max. Just run the numbers through your fancy database thingy and give me a name and address."

"It's a subscription service," Declan grumbled. "I pay for it. A concept you don't seem to grasp."

Even though he was on the receiving end of a lecture, Jack could hear his brother's stubby fingers clicking away on the keyboard.

"The car's registered to Grisom, Sean Francis and Grisom, Darby Hayes. One-three-seven Blue Marlin Way, Sewell's Point." Declan let out a long, low whistle. "Nice part of town. You can't tell me this is some pro bono thing. I won't buy it. Sewell's Point? No way."

"She isn't a client." That much was true.

"Potential client?" Declan asked.

"Nope. Thanks for the info. I owe you a beer."

"Forget one beer. At this rate, you owe me a whole damned brewery."

"I'll get right on that," Jack said before placing the phone back on its cradle.

* * *

"I can hardly hear you, Darby."

Darby cupped her hand over the mouthpiece, trying to muffle the noise of the breeze and the traffic on Federal Highway. The sky had turned a threatening shade of gray as thunderclouds prepared for the afternoon downpour.

"Sorry, I'm at a pay phone."

"A pay phone?" Lyssa Chandler repeated. "They still have pay phones? Is something wrong? Did you break down? Is it the baby?"

"No. Lyssa, this is personal. Just between us."

"If it's about my bill, I—"

"No. I need a favor. Can you meet me at the deli next to Stratton Realty?"

"Sure, when?"

Darby checked her watch. "Ten minutes?"

"Um, sure. So long as you don't care that I've been working and not primping. I'm covered in paint and not really looking my best."

"Whatever. Just do me a favor?"

"Anything," Lyssa replied. "After everything you've done for me and Mr. Wiggles, I'd walk through fire for you. You know that, right?"

"I hope you mean that," Darby said. "See you in ten."

Nine and a half minutes later, Lyssa's Toyota zoomed into the lot. The neon yellow car suited the big, colorful personality of its owner.

Lyssa was forty-two, single and a brilliant illustrator. Darby had been seeing Lyssa and her cat, Mr. Wiggles, almost daily for the past three years. The cat suffered from feline leukemia, requiring close monitoring and daily injections. By rights, the cat shouldn't have made it past the first few months, but somehow he kept hanging in there.

Lyssa was the consummate artist. She wore outrageous, neon-bright clothing and her hair was always gelled into some spiky, gravity-defying shape. She had at least a dozen earrings in her left ear and a heart the size of Montana. The only thing she lacked was family. Lyssa's parents had died in a car accident when she was a child. Her grandparents, neither of whom lived long enough to see her graduate from college, had raised her. No siblings, no aunts, no uncles, no cousins. She'd married young, but that had only lasted a few months.

Darby was such a wreck over what she was about to propose that she was actually shaking. It was a hastily crafted plan, but it was the best thing she could come up with. The sacrifice was so huge she wasn't sure she could do it. Well, she'd cross that bridge when she came to it.

Lyssa greeted Darby with a tight hug. "I'm sorry about your folks. I have a casserole in the car. I wasn't sure if you'd want me to drop by your house." Lyssa paused long enough to push her black-rimmed, rectangular glasses up on the bridge of her nose. "I didn't—"

"I don't have a lot of time," Darby interrupted, pulling Lyssa into the deli and steering to the far back, away from any other patrons. "I need a huge favor."

"What do you consider huge?"

"I'm going to kill someone and I need your help."

CHAPTER THREE

Jesus Christ, Darby!" Lyssa said in a forceful whisper.

"Hear me out," Darby pleaded. "But I don't have a lot of time." Darby shared what Sean had done to date and the fact that she couldn't prove any of it. Sean was a lot of things, but stupid wasn't one of them. When she finished, she added, "But he doesn't know about you, Lyssa."

Lyssa ordered a small coffee and once the waitress left she asked, "How does that help?"

"Even if he finds out, which he won't, he'll never connect you to this."

"But your baby," Lyssa said, each syllable tinged with anguish.

"My baby is better off with you than with Sean. I can't protect myself, let alone her." Tears welled in her eyes.

"But you'll go to jail," Lyssa reasoned.

Darby nodded. "But I'll go knowing that my baby is safe and loved with you."

Lyssa shook her head. "I don't know, Darby. Can't you just get a restraining order and a divorce?"

Darby took the email from Sean out of her bag. "He's already threatening to hurt her," she said as she handed over the SIDS article. "Subtle, but I get the point. If I make any move he doesn't like, I'm positive he'll kill the baby. And I have thought about divorce. Sean can charm the white off rice; he'd get visitation and if that happens I'll never see my daughter again. And I know him. Eventually the baby will inspire his ire and she'll be helpless against his temper. Please, Lyssa. You aren't *taking* her, you're *saving* her." Darby checked her watch, then leaned closer to Lyssa. "I don't have much time and you're my only hope. Just promise me you'll think about it. Sleep on it and give me your answer tomorrow when you bring Mr. Wiggles into the office."

Lyssa let out a long, slow breath, then relented. "Okay."

Darby battled tears, checked her watch, and stood up. She held Lyssa's gaze. "Not to get overly dramatic, but my daughter's life depends on you."

* * *

Darby checked her rear mirror every few seconds as she drove to her doctor's office. Sean had seemed to accept her lie that she was taking some Lamaze classes with her OB/GYN. Probably because he had no interest in the actual birthing process. Or, she thought with a shiver dancing along her spine, he hadn't swallowed her explanation and was following her from a safe distance, waiting to pounce. God, she was getting paranoid in addition to being afraid of her own shadow.

Darby was still at a crossroads about money. The family trust was worth middle seven figures, and she wanted to protect that for her daughter. But if her daughter was declared dead and Darby was arrested and convicted for the crime, the trust would go to her closest living relative—Sean. No matter how she racked her brain, she couldn't think of a way around that inevitability.

By sheer, dumb luck, she ended up parking in front of the law offices of Jack Kavanaugh. Needless to say, their meeting the prior day hadn't accomplished much. He hadn't made a particularly good first impression, but then again, neither had she. Darby wasn't usually rude to people, but she had been curt to Mr. Kavanaugh. Perhaps she should apologize.

Perhaps she was making an excuse to see him again. She wondered where that thought came from. Her life was a cluster and she was curious about an attractive man? There it was again—*attractive*. When had she decided he was attractive?

The minute he'd opened the door.

Okay, so the chili dog was a bit of a turn off, but he was definitely handsome and had great eyes. Almost the color of café au lait. And they were expressive. So much so that she was fairly certain that he'd seen right through her pitiful lies.

Darby wriggled herself from behind the wheel and went across the street to her doctor's office. Again, the waiting room was full of glowing women rubbing their distended bellies. God, how she envied them. This should have been one of the happiest times in her life but it was nothing but pure hell.

The receptionist showed her into the conference room. It was a long, narrow room with a highly polished oblong table surrounded by ten leather chairs. There was a woman standing by a counter against the wall, checking the contents of the refrigerator there. In a matter of seconds she grabbed a container of cream, then turned to smile. Darby placed her around thirty-five, with sandy blond hair and blue eyes. She was wearing a simple Lilly Pulitzer shift dress and white sandals. Then she said, "Good morning, I'm Dr. Pointer."

"Darby," she replied as she moved in to grasp the offered hand. "Thank you for meeting me here. I hope it wasn't too much of an inconvenience."

Dr. Pointer shook her head. "Not a problem. I like road trips. Sometimes being cooped up in an office all day can make you nuts."

"That's why I like my job. Every day is different."

The doctor gestured toward a seat. "You're a vet, right?"

Darby nodded. "Everything but exotics." She felt herself relax a bit. "I hate snakes."

"Me too." The doctor pulled out a yellow legal pad and a pen. Then she dug into her bag and produced a microrecorder. "Do you mind?" she asked.

"No, doctor."

"Call me Fran," she corrected. "So I hear you're having some troubles."

Darby's hold on her purse tightened so much that her knuckles went white. And smelling the coffee but not being able to have any only seemed to make her more tense. Quickly, Darby went through all the information she'd studied on the computer. She needed to pull this off if her plan was going to work.

"I'm not sure I'm ready to have this baby."

Fran offered a compassionate smile. "I think it's a little late for that. What *exactly* is it that has you so worried?"

"I just don't feel like I'm ready. I'll be totally responsible for this little girl and I think she deserves better."

Fran began to take notes. "No help from your husband?"

"Oh, he's very excited. Ever since the sonogram he's been very into the idea that he's passing on his genes. Like she's an extension of him."

"That sounds kinda normal, Darby. A baby has a way of solidifying a marriage."

Or destroying it. "I know; I'm not making any sense."

"You're conflicted," Fran said. "Are you sure this isn't a reaction to losing your parents last week?"

Darby felt that jab through her heart. "Yes." *That was my dirtbag husband.*

"Were they excited about the baby?"

Darby nodded. "My mother has—had been buying baby things for months. I wanted her to be in the delivery room when Mia is born." *And she would have loved seeing her granddaughter born.*

"And that caused a problem?"

Darby shrugged. "My husband wanted it to be just the two of us." *And if my husband doesn't get what he wants...*

"And do you always do what your husband tells you to do?"

"He's the more rational of the two of us. I tend to be more emotional." *And I don't want another beating.*

"You know," Fran began as she scooted her chair closer and patted Darby on the knee. "A certain amount of anxiety is perfectly normal. And in your case, just losing your parents...well, that amps it up to a new level."

This was not working. Darby had to ramp up the issues just to get this doctor's attention. As much as it disgusted her not to out Sean for the creep that he was, she knew in her heart that getting Mia to safety had to be her top priority. "I think about hurting myself," she said on a rush of breath.

Fran's face went blank. "Tell me why and how."

"I think I'll be a lousy mother and Mia deserves better. I have these daytime fantasies of killing myself."

"And Mia?"

"That's the only thing stopping me. I don't want to hurt her."

"Have you told your husband about these feelings?"

Darby vehemently shook her head. "Sean would be furious if he knew."

Fran's head tilted to one side. "Furious?"

"He even sends me articles about SIDS and other infant mortality things so I'll be vigilant."

"Sounds like more of a taunt than vigilance," Fran opined. "Whose idea was this pregnancy?"

"It was an accident," Darby admitted. "Birth control failure. Sean and I had never planned on having children."

"Why?"

"Why?"

"Yes. Why did you and your husband decide not to have children?"

"Sean always liked being a couple. He thought having a baby would take time away from our relationship."

"But he's come around now?"

"We both have," Darby said. "Sean likes knowing his immortality is assured. When I saw her face on the 3-D imaging scan, I fell in love."

"So what's happened since then that makes you think you won't be a great mom?"

"There's just so much responsibility. What if I get it wrong?"

Fran chuckled. "Trust me, we all get it wrong every once in a while. Babies are pretty resilient, Darby. You'll be amazed how fast you fall into a routine. And if you think you love her now, wait until you actually hold her in your arms."

Darby felt a single, hot tear slide down her cheek. "But what if I don't? I read up on bonding. What if Mia and I don't bond? That thought makes me feel so sad all the time." The truth was she had already bonded with her baby, and knowing she had to give her up was tearing her apart inside.

"You just lost your parents. I think that might be the reason for the sadness."

"I had it before they...passed."

"Sad enough to hurt yourself?"

"I don't know," Darby answered. "I just know that in two weeks I'll have a baby who is totally dependent on me and I'm not sure I can protect her."

Fran sat back and studied Darby quietly. When she couldn't stand the silence any longer Darby asked, "What?"

"'Protect her' is an interesting choice of words. Protect her from who or what?"

Darby's heart skipped. "Me, I guess. She'll be so helpless."

"Do you think your husband will be hands-on?"

"My husband is always hands-on," Darby said, hoping the irony didn't drip off each syllable.

"What about friends? How is your personal support system?"

"I've kinda lost touch with people since I got married. You know how it is. Once you get married you tend to shy away from your single friends."

"Who do you socialize with?"

Darby dropped her gaze. "My staff, I guess. But I'm giving up my practice once the baby is born."

"Why?"

"My husband came from a single-parent household. He feels very strongly that I should stay home with the baby. Maybe when she goes to school I can start over again."

"Can't you compromise? This could be one of the reasons you're so sad. You have a wonderful reputation, and didn't I read that your husband owns a restaurant?"

"Yes, Tilefish Grille on A-1-A. It's been open about six months."

"Maybe you could work in the mornings before he works in the evenings."

"I don't think that would work."

"So, you lose your parents, you lose your career, and now you're gaining the responsibility of a newborn. Darby, you have every reason, several of them to be exact, to be down in the dumps. I'm not comfortable prescribing medicine this late in your pregnancy but I have a feeling that once you hold your daughter, this sadness will go away. But until then, I'd like us to meet once a week. Okay?"

Darby nodded, then gathered up her things and left the office. She was just approaching the driver's side of her car when Jack Kavanaugh came around the corner. He had files tucked under both arms and a briefcase in one hand. Then there was the deli bag he had dangling from his mouth.

Sighing deeply, Darby went over to him and took the files from under his right arm so he could fish out his keys to the front door of his office. She followed him in with his files.

"Thanks," he said after he dropped everything on a chair and retrieved the files from her hands. In the process, his fingertips brushed the back of her hand, and she felt a long dormant tingle in her stomach. She jerked back as if he'd bitten her. "Happy to help." She wondered where *that* sensation had come from. It was disconcerting, to say the least. Finding him attractive and responding to his touch—no matter how brief—scared her. It reminded her of how quickly she had fallen for Sean, and that wasn't something she wanted to repeat.

He was smiling at her and that simple expression made her feel weak in the knees. Then she remembered it had been more than a month since she'd last seen her knees. How could he be offering that sexy half-smile to a woman with a belly the size of two basketballs? Darby felt her cheeks burn with embarrassment. "Have a nice day," she said, turning to go.

"I'd like to repay your kindness," he said.

His voice was deep and sensual. Darby tried to figure out how and why she could be feeling so drawn to another man when her world was basically crashing down around her.

"No need," she said.

"How about I do that trust work for you?"

He was so tall she had to bend her neck to meet his gaze. His eyes were rimmed in inky lashes. "That's okay. I'll find someone else."

"If we're just talking a change of beneficiaries, it'll only take me a few minutes."

Darby drew her bottom lip between her teeth then let it slip back into position. "I just want to make sure my daughter is taken care of."

"Not your husband?" he asked as he nodded toward the five-carat ring on her pregnancy-swollen finger. "No. I want an independent trustee."

"Do you have the document with you?"

She shook her head. "I can fax it to you when I get back to my office."

He reached and took a business card off the table and handed it to her. "Just send the trust and the name of the new trustee and I'll have it done in a day."

"My husband can't know about this," she warned. "And I want to continue to be trustee if and until my situation changes."

"Like a divorce?"

"Something like that."

"Done."

"Thank you."

Darby shook his hand and again the grasp lasted just a fraction of a second longer than it should. Her hormones were definitely out of whack. Like any man could find her attractive with her huge belly and puffy ankles.

Darby next went to the bank and spent an hour with the manager, filling out forms. The saddest part of her duty was handing over her parents' death certificates. Sean always opened the mail, and he'd been very excited that the documentation had arrived so quickly. He was practically giddy and very quickly told her what she needed to do. Go to the bank, have them change the trust over to her name, and bring home a cashier's check.

As much as it irked her to give him a single dime, she knew she had to play this right for the next two weeks, or until whenever baby Mia came into the world. Her heart ached knowing she wouldn't be able to raise her beloved baby. And yes, she had money at her disposal, but money couldn't stop a determined man like Sean. No, this was the only way to make certain the baby was safe. All she could hold on to was the hope that at some point down the road, some miracle might happen and they would be reunited. For now she had to focus on keeping the baby safe and making sure she crossed all the Ts and dotted the Is because her plan had to come off perfectly if it had any hope of working.

The banker gave her two checks and a folder. Darby thanked him and went out to her car. Using the razor blade she'd brought from home, she slit the lining of her bag and slipped one of the checks inside. Then, with thread and needle also from home, she carefully stitched the slit closed. She smiled at the perfect row of stitches. Being a vet did have its advantages. She tossed the thread, needle, and blade in the trash can outside the bank, then got back into her car and headed to her office.

Darby was too preoccupied to notice her surroundings as she drove south on Route 1 to Jupiter. Her office was in a strip mall at the intersection with Indiantown Road. She checked her watch and realized she was ten minutes late. Fear tensed her whole body. She couldn't afford to be late to meet Sean for dinner.

The minute she walked in the door, a chorus of barking began, although not all of the animals were into it. There was Helda's old hound dog lying on a dog bed in the waiting area who didn't even bother to lift his ears. Helda, her receptionist, greeted her as she came around to the back of the reception area. Darby was putting on her lab coat when Helga said, "Light afternoon, but we do have an emergency on the way."

Darby had a private emergency going. She loved everything about her clinic: the people she worked with and the pets she'd gotten to know over the years. They were like a family, and Darby was the one giving up everything while Sean just kept on leeching his way through life. It wasn't fair and that made her angry as hell. She was going to have to give up everything for a man she loathed.

Darby sighed and nodded and began rounding up the three veterinary assistants who were the backbone of her successful practice. It was killing her to know that in a matter of days they'd be out of work, but she needed and hoped she could find a replacement fast who could take over her practice. She moved that to the top of her to do list.

Surely there was someone out there who'd want to work a half mile from a beautiful sandy beach. She put up a quick ad on craigslist and an almost immediate response made her smile.

"Bring in the first client," she said as she came out of her office and took a quick look at her messages. Nothing earth-shattering. Three messages were from patients with new puppies and four were from Sean. Fearing repercussions, she dialed Sean.

"Where have you been?" he snapped.

"Hello?" Apparently she wasn't being followed. "I went to the bank like you told me to do. It took some time," she explained as she fingered through her file drawer and pulled out a copy of the Trust. Too bad Sean couldn't see what she was doing as they spoke. If he even got a whisper of what she was planning, he'd probably beat her senseless. Darby knew she was taking a risk, but Mia was worth it. She had to keep telling herself that. Knowing her baby would be safe and loved was the only way she could function, especially after Sean's ominous email about SIDS and suffocation. She couldn't risk a divorce with visitation. Sean was just evil enough and angry enough to kill the baby just to make Darby hurt. Well, she wasn't going to give him that chance. "And now I have to see patients, okay?"

"I'll see you for dinner at eight."

"Okay."

"Darby?"

"Yes?"

"Say it."

"Say what?"

"Tell me you love me."

She closed her eyes and grimaced. "I love you."

"You don't sound convincing," he taunted.

"I love you," she said again, trying to make it sound better.

"Good. After dinner you can show me how much."

"Sean," she sighed. "I feel like an over-inflated beach ball."

"I'm sure you do but I've been patient. I've given you a week to mourn, now it's time things got back to normal."

She lowered her voice. "I wouldn't have needed a week if you hadn't killed them."

"Don't blame that on me, sweetheart. You're the one who went running to Mommy and Daddy."

This subject made a knot form in her stomach. Besides, she needed him to think all was normal if her plan was going to work after Mia was born. "I'm sorry. I really do have patients and I don't want to be late."

"Good. From now on, I don't want to hear you mention your parents. What's done is done. Agreed?"

She raked her fingers through her hair. "Yes."

CHAPTER FOUR

In between a well check on a German shepherd and cat with respiratory difficulties, Darby started a cover letter to go with the fax to Mr. Kavanaugh. In language somewhat resembling legalese, she wrote that if she was unable or unwilling to carry out her duties as Trustee then…she found herself stuck. She definitely couldn't make the new trustee Sean. Especially now.

Darby looked back on her time with Sean and an ugly puzzle took shape. She thought about the way her dog Samson had mysteriously died from ethylene glycol poisoning. When she'd found him in the garage, he was dead next to a pool of the neon green liquid, yet there had been no bottle of anti-freeze in sight. Then there was the slow but methodical way Sean had managed to alienate nearly all her friends and family. Hell, it wouldn't be a shock to discover that he might have married her for her money.

She realized she couldn't name Lyssa as the trustee because Sean was sure to hunt her down, and then he'd find that the baby was alive and well. And Sean would be more likely to take baby Mia away someplace where Darby could never find her again. Her heart was breaking bit by bit as she contemplated her bleak options.

She would miss all the firsts—first word, first steps, first day of school, all those Christmases. Tears began to trickle down her cheeks. She needed to think. And fast.

But right now she needed to give some immunizations to a Maltese.

She dried her tears as best as she could and went to the exam room. The poor little dog was curled at the back of her carrier, shivering. Her owner wasn't much braver. "How's"—she paused to read the chart—"Molly doing?"

Mrs. Littleson smiled. "Fine until I put her in the crate. She knows a trip in the carrier usually ends up in a shot or two."

"Let's see if we can't get her to come out." Darby reached into her pocket and laid a small trail of liver treats from the inside of the carrier onto the cold metal table. Tentatively, the tiny animal sniffed and ate her way out of the cage. As soon as she did, Darby put the crate on the floor and Molly reacted by practically leaping into her owner's arms. "Do you want to hold her while I give the injections or would you rather one of my vet assistants do it?"

"Vet assistant," the woman answered instantly. "I've had five kids and I can't even count the number of times one of them broke something or needed stitches. I can handle that, but when it comes to my sweet baby Molly, I just can't stand the thought of her being hurt."

"I understand," Darby said. She stepped out the back door

into a long corridor that was used mostly for storage. This route was also a way for Darby and her staff to move the animals from area to area without stressing them too much. "Peggy?"

The cute redhead turned and she offered a smile. "Need me?"

"Just for a few minutes."

Peggy brushed off the front of her scrubs and twisted her long, curly hair into a bun. Peggy had been with Darby for a little over five years and she was just two months away from graduating with a degree in Veterinary Science. The plan had been for Peggy to join the practice after school, and suddenly Darby got an idea. But it would have to wait until Molly was finished with her appointment.

"Can you come to my office after we finish with Molly?"

Peggy seemed perplexed but answered, "Sure."

A few minutes later, there was a knock at Darby's door. "Come in," she called.

Peggy stuck her head in and asked, "Is now a good time?"

Darby nodded. The office was simply furnished and very neat. There was a wedding picture on the credenza behind Darby's desk and framed diplomas hung on the walls. The walls were painted beige with pale blue trim, giving the room a beachy feel. The only other photograph in the room was a framed shot of Darby and Sam on Hutchinson Island.

Peggy appeared nervous, so over the muffled sounds of barking dogs, she tentatively took a seat, teetering on the edge as if she might need to make a fast getaway.

"C'mon," Darby chastised as she rubbed her belly. The baby was unusually active today. "You're acting like I'm going to fire you. I'm not. I have a proposal for you I'm hoping you'll like."

Peggy seemed to visibly relax. "Are you okay?" she countered. "Your eyes are all red and you look exhausted."

Darby waved her hand dismissively. "You try to sleep with someone kicking you in the kidneys all night."

Peggy's bright smile returned. "Guess that is a bit of a bitch. Why don't you go home for the afternoon? There's nothing on the schedule I can't handle."

"Which is why I want to talk to you." Darby sat back in her seat, trying to get comfortable in the chair. "I got an email a few minutes ago from a guy I went to vet school with. He heard I was thinking of closing my practice because of the baby and he's interested."

Peggy was positively beaming. "Really?"

Darby nodded. "Yep, but there's a catch."

Peggy deflated a bit. "He gets to hire his own staff?"

"No, nothing like that. He lives in Rhode Island and wants to make a change."

"That's great!"

"But he only wants to stay for a few months. Three, to be exact. At first I dismissed the idea, but I figured Carl could fill the void until you get your license, then you can take over."

"What about you?"

I'll be in jail. "I'm not sure I'll be coming back after the baby. And I'd appreciate it if you wouldn't share that for now."

"Darby, I appreciate it, but I can't afford to buy your business. Hell, I'll be about seventy when I pay off my student loans."

Darby smiled for the first time in a while. "I'm not talking about selling you the business. I want to give it to you, no strings."

Peggy scratched her head. "I know this is kinda personal, but how will Sean feel about this? I mean, not to speak out of turn, but he doesn't act like the kind of guy who would approve of you just handing over a practice you spent years building."

"You let me worry about Sean." *And God knows I do.*

Peggy shifted nervously. "I think you should wait until after the baby comes and you've talked to Sean to make this decision. Let your friend Carl come down and then we can revisit this after he has experienced a Florida summer. Darby, you can work a limited schedule. You can even bring baby Mia to work with you. You have six women here who would gladly watch over her while you saw patients."

That was my plan until my husband killed my parents. "Sean really wants me to stay home with her."

"You're my boss, but you're also my friend, so as your friend…screw what Sean wants. He doesn't even go to work until noon. You could just work mornings. You have options."

If only Peggy knew. "I think a clean break is the best course of action." Now was good time to enhance her plan. "Besides, I don't know anything about babies. I'm scared to death I'll be a horrible mother."

"What are you talking about? You're compassionate and smart. You'll figure out the whole baby thing in no time."

"Or, I'll screw up royally."

Peggy's brow pinched. "You won't screw it up. Darby, I've never seen you scoff at a challenge. I don't have any experience with this, but I'm sure you'll be a great mom."

"We'll see."

Peggy stood up. "Well, for now I'm just going to operate under the assumption that you're coming back." She started for the door. "By the way," she asked with a wicked grin. "Any chance Carl is gorgeous and single?"

"Yes on both counts."

Peggy let out a long sigh. "Thank you, Jesus."

Once she was gone, Darby hoped she had planted the seed subtly. Wiggling her computer back to life by the mouse, she stared at the screen, unsure what to do. Peggy would make a wonderful trustee except that she knew about Lyssa and would notice her absence. She couldn't risk turning over the trust to anyone who could make the connection. What she needed was a total stranger whom she could trust. But that was easier said than done. Too bad there wasn't a "Trustworthy Strangers" section in the Yellow Pages. Her phone buzzed and the receptionist informed her that Lyssa and Mr. Wiggles were waiting for her in Exam One.

When she went to the exam room, Lyssa looked terrible. "I haven't gotten any sleep all night," she began on a rush of air. "Darby, I'm not sure I can go along with your plan."

The words felt like a sucker punch. Panic made her breath catch in her throat. She was working so hard at making this work, and Lyssa was the key. "Please don't say that, Lyssa. You really are my only hope," Darby practically begged.

"I went online last night, and judges tend to favor custody to the mother when an infant is concerned. You can get a divorce." She stroked the cat in her arms as she spoke.

"Lyssa, he killed my parents because of me. What do you

think he'll do to a defenseless baby if I do something else to inspire his temper?"

"So take the baby and run."

Darby let out a slow, painful breath. "You don't know Sean. He'd find me and I'm starting to think that he only wants this baby because she comes with her own trust fund. He knows hurting her—hell, even killing her—would be his best revenge if I stepped out of line. If I get a divorce, he'll get visitation. I'll be forced to send my helpless baby to a psychopath. I can't risk that. He made my parents' deaths look like an accident. He'll do the same thing to the baby. And then he'd probably find some way to blame me. I've thought about every possible scenario and the *only* way to keep the baby safe is to keep her away from Sean."

"You'll go to jail."

Darby nodded. "I know."

"Maybe for the rest of your life."

"I know that, too. Just take her someplace you've never been. Someplace where no one would think to find you. Okay?"

Lyssa hesitated.

"Please?" Darby pressed. "I need to know Mia will be safe no matter what."

"When are you thinking of doing this?"

"I'm not sure. But when it happens, you'll have to be ready to go quickly." Darby reached out and grabbed Lyssa's hand. "Please?"

"I can't believe I'm doing this."

"Thank you."

* * *

Darby dressed carefully for her dinner with Sean. He could get quite angry if he didn't care for her clothing choices. Unfortunately, at present, her choices were limited. She settled on a snug little black dress and a pair of heels that had her back screaming even before she finished securing the strand of pearls around her throat. She fought back tears; the pearls had been a gift from her mother on her wedding day.

Her thoughts drifted back to that time. She hadn't thought it was possible to be that happy. She had a man who adored her and she'd loved him by the end of their first date. She rubbed her belly. "How did everything go so wrong?"

She'd probably have a long time to contemplate that question when she was in jail. For now, she just needed to get through the night.

Tilefish Grille was an upscale restaurant a block west of the beach. It was done in black and gold with hints of red. Which made it unique in Martin County. Florida is a pretty casual place, but Sean had insisted that an upscale restaurant was just what the small county needed.

She entered through the double doors and was greeted by the low sound of classical music pumped into the dining room. There were twenty-seven tables and a private room on the opposite side of the building. The hostess was nowhere to be found, so as she weaved through the tables, she acknowledged the patrons, passed the coffee station, and pushed into the kitchen.

The smells were heavenly. Which they should've been, given

that the chef was making six figures—the only way Sean could lure him away from Palm Beach.

She knew immediately that something was wrong. No one made eye contact with her. She avoided the bustle of the kitchen and walked through the salad station toward the door marked PRIVATE.

As soon as she opened the door, she knew why the staff had been so uncomfortable. Roxanne, the restaurant's hostess and Sean's assistant, was curled up in his lap with her hand down his pants. At least the auburn-haired bimbo had the decency to look mortified. Sean's expression was impossible to read.

Darby's back stiffened as she stepped back, closed the door and retraced her steps. When she got to the dining area, she went over to Gary, the bartender. She reached into her purse and said, "Sean is in the middle of something. Please give him this when he's available." She handed over the fifty-thousand-dollar check.

"Will do," he said as Roxanne came out of the kitchen with Sean hot on her heels.

Anger and humiliation surged through her as Darby pivoted and went toward the front door. Sean blocked her way.

"We have to talk," he said softly.

"About what? The weather? My favorite color? The hand job you were getting from your assistant?"

"You were early."

He said it as if it was a rational excuse. "Sorry I interrupted," she said blandly. She didn't much care that he was fooling around with Roxanne, but she had to admit that having it happen in front of the entire staff was pretty humiliating.

Sean grabbed her upper arm and squeezed tightly. "I want you to come back to my office."

"I want to go home, Sean." She jerked free. "Every employee in this place knew what you were doing. They couldn't even look at me."

He grabbed her a second time. "I'm not asking," he said in that tone that chilled her to the bone. "Let's go."

Darby plastered a well-practiced smile on her face as Sean's large hand held her like a vise. The only time her resolve faltered was when she passed Roxanne, who was reapplying her lipstick. Contrary to what Sean thought, he couldn't read her mind. If he could, he'd know that she hated him. For the past, the present, and the future.

She wanted to scream at the woman. Not out of jealousy; she wanted Roxanne to take her cheating, murdering husband. God knew she was finished with him. All she had to do was think about her parents and she was ready to crumble into little bits and pieces. The only thing holding her together was her plan to keep Mia safe.

The instant he closed the office door, his hand was around her throat, squeezing. She was plastered, her back crushed, against the wall. Instinctively, she dropped her purse and started clawing at his hand. It had no effect.

Sean was glaring down at her with what looked like total hatred in his eyes. Just as Darby was ready to pass out, he let go. She slid down the wall, crumpling on the floor. After coughing and sputtering a bit she gulped in oxygen. Sean said, "Get up."

In a less-than-graceful fashion, Darby rose, rubbing her neck. Her bare neck. She looked down and saw that the floor was littered with her pearls. The strand must have broken during the encounter. She opened her purse and began the task of picking the pearls up off the floor. Not an easy accomplishment with your belly in the way. Sean sat behind his desk while she spent the better part of five minutes hunting around.

By the time she had what she hoped was all of them, she was seething and terrified all at once. "What do you want?" she asked as she inched toward the door.

"Did you bring the money?"

"Gary has it. I gave it to him as I was on my way out." Sean was silent for a moment. "Is that all?" She rubbed her tender throat.

"People will notice if you don't stay for dinner."

Darby shook her head. "Your whole staff knows you were in here with Roxanne. That's about as much humiliation as I care to take for one evening."

"If you were keeping up your end in the bedroom, I wouldn't have to look elsewhere."

Furious that he had broken her pearls, totally humiliated, and angrier than she had ever been in her life, Darby said, "I stopped caring what you do when you killed my parents." With an abundance of caution, Darby reached behind her and turned the knob just in case he came around the desk and grabbed her again. "In fact, why don't you spend the night with Roxanne tonight? Finish what you started." Darby had the door open and was back in the kitchen, hoping there was safety in public. It worked. She glanced behind her and Sean was standing in the doorway seething, but stationary.

Darby got into her car and locked the doors before she started the engine.

* * *

Sean took her seriously and didn't come home. Darby's back was aching, probably from wearing heels the night before, so she was slow to get out of bed.

She couldn't wait until baby Mia arrived and she could go back to drinking coffee. Orange juice just didn't cut it. She got dressed and realized she had a problem. She had deep purple bruises around her throat where Sean had choked her the night before. Going to her closet, she switched out her scrubs for a lighter pair, then grabbed a lightweight turtleneck. She felt like an idiot. It was going to be in the mid-eighties. She went back into her closet and selected another pair of scrubs and a scarf. This look was only slightly better than the turtleneck, but it hid the bruises. It did not, however, hide the bruises on her arm from Sean dragging her through the restaurant. So she went into the bathroom and carefully applied some makeup. It wasn't perfect, but it was good enough and she could always put on the sweater she left at the office for days when she got chilly. Though those days had been few and far between since she'd been pregnant. If only the spasms in her back would go away.

It was just about sunrise and she wanted to be out of the house before Sean returned. The baby was very active, which made her back hurt more. It was going to be a long day.

But a good one. She had a seven o'clock appointment with the psychologist and a nine o'clock appointment with her OB/GYN. She could use the break in between to grab breakfast at the Sammy J's in Cove Plaza. It was a small place tucked into a corner behind a doughnut shop with great food. Darby had bacon on the brain as she drove away from the house.

Traffic was nonexistent, so she was in front of the doctor's office in no time. For some reason she glanced across the street at the darkened office of Jack Kavanaugh. A plan began to take shape: perhaps the trustworthy stranger was just a few feet away.

She had extra time, so she turned her car around and made the quick round-trip in less than twenty minutes. She was looking through her tote bag, out in front of the doctor's office again, when a knock on her car door window jolted her back to the present. It was Dr. Pointer. Darby left her tote in the car, taking just her purse inside. Hearing the pearls roll around in it was an unhappy reminder of the night before.

They went to the conference room and try as she might, Darby couldn't get comfortable. She was shifting around in her seat like a toddler.

Without preamble Fran asked, "How have you been feeling?"

Darby shrugged. "About the same. Well, almost the same."

"Meaning?"

Darby glanced away, unable to maintain eye contact. Lying didn't come naturally to her. "I've had some dreams."

"About?"

"Hurting myself." She paused. "Hurting the baby. I just don't know how I'm going to cope with a newborn. I don't have any practice with babies. When other girls my age were babysitting, I was at the barn." She lifted her head. "One year in high school my parents let me raise a pig for the county fair." She smiled at the memory. "Most people don't realize that pigs are smarter than dogs. By the time the fair rolled around, my pig could sit, stay, lay down and offer his hoof. We won first place." Her expression changed again. "Then I learned that Patty—that was my pig's name—was off to slaughter. I put up such a fuss that my father ended up buying the pig for me. We were inseparable until she died when I started Vet school."

Fran's eyes followed her every gesture. It was unnerving.

"Darby, how can you think you'll be a bad mother with your history?"

"Because it doesn't include handling a newborn."

Fran leaned back and her head tilted sideways. "Want to tell me about the scarf?"

Darby reflexively touched the soft fabric. "Scrubs are pretty androgynous, so I like to spruce them up now and then."

"And the bruises on your arm?"

"I went one-on-one with a pit mix yesterday. I get bruises all the time. You can ask my staff."

Fran moved her seat closer. "Are you safe at home?"

Darby pretended to be shocked by the implication. "My husband loves me," she insisted. "He's totally devoted."

"What about the baby?"

"What about her?" Darby replied.

"How does your husband feel about the baby?"

Darby shrugged. "So maybe he wasn't thrilled at first, but once he saw the sonogram his whole demeanor changed. He's really excited." She proclaimed by rote.

"There are places I can recommend for you. Places where you and your baby will be safe."

Darby gave a dismissive wave of her hand but she couldn't maintain eye contact. "Even if Sean didn't want the baby, which I'm telling you is false, he knows the baby inherits from the family trust and he wouldn't be able to resist that kind of money."

"So you fight about money?"

"No more than other couples." *That sounds lame, even to me.*

"That doesn't make sense, Darby. Your family is prominent and very wealthy. You were an only child. You mentioned in passing that your husband owns a struggling restaurant while you have a thriving practice. It wouldn't make sense for him not to feel a tad emasculated and possibly take his frustrations out on you."

"How many times do I have to tell you Sean isn't like that?" *Wrong! Sean is* exactly *like that.*

"If you say so." The doctor reached into her bag and took out a business card that she slid across the table toward Darby. "Margaret Hindel is a friend of mine and she runs a safe house for abused women."

"I'm not—"

"I know. I just want you to have a resource in case you ever need it."

God, if only it was that simple. Darby rubbed her aching back as she glanced up at the clock. "Same time on Thursday?" she asked.

The doctor nodded. She reached out her hand and closed it over Darby's, then said, "If you need me, any time, just call."

"Thank you," Darby replied as she slid her hand away.

She greeted the staff at the doctor's office on her way out.

She wasn't particularly hungry, but she knew the baby needed some fuel. Glancing across the street, she noticed the lights were on in the Law Offices of Jack Kavanaugh.

Stopping at her car, she pulled out the tote and walked over.

She was totally unprepared for what she saw. Jack was definitely an attractive man, but unlike the other times she had seen him, today he was sporting a gunmetal gray, custom shirt with a lavender tie, and his dark hair looked recently cut and styled.

And he smelled good.

And Darby was being a fool. *Haven't I learned my lesson about lust at first sight? God knows I'm paying for it. Dearly.*

"Do you have a few minutes?" she asked.

"I don't have to be in court until ten."

Well, that explained the suit and tie. He ushered her inside his cluttered office. Darby thought he was in dire need of a secretary and a trip to the Container Store.

"I assume this is about your family trust?" he asked.

She nodded as she pulled the document out of her tote and handed it to him. "It's pretty straightforward. Upon my parents' death, I became trustee." She was talking while he thumbed through the pages. "Obviously there has to be an adjustment for my daughter. Should anything happen to me, she'll need a trustee to handle the money and investments until she reaches the age of twenty-five. As you can see, the trust will pay for her living expenses, her education, and her needs as she grows up, but the bulk of the money stays in the trust until she's an adult."

Jack placed the papers on his desk. "The way this is set up, you became the trustee the moment your parents died. I'm not sure what you want from me."

"If something happens to me, I want to name a successor trustee for Mia."

He pointed at her belly. "Mia?"

Darby nodded and smiled, then she absently rubbed her belly as she spoke. "I need someone trustworthy and knowledgeable."

His expression showed that he suddenly understood what she was getting at. "You do know I handle mostly criminal cases, right?"

"Then you'd be perfect because it would be a crime for my husband to get his hands on the money. We both know that if I was out of the picture, Sean would be the logical substitute trustee."

" 'We both know'?" he prompted.

What the hell, he wasn't going to judge and if he did, she had nothing to lose. Darby untied the scarf around her neck and rolled up her sleeve, baring the litany of bruises.

Jack's expression changed and his brows pinched. "Your husband beats you?"

"So now you know why I can't let him have control of what is rightfully Mia's."

"Why are you so sure you aren't going to be around? Is it so bad that you think he'll kill you?"

She shook her head. "So long as I keep giving him money for his failing restaurant, I'm safe."

"You don't look too safe," he countered.

"I can handle Sean."

"Looks like you're doing a stellar job, from where I'm sitting."

"I don't need lectures, Mr. Kavanaugh."

"Jack," he corrected. "You need a divorce and an Order of Protection."

"Which he will ignore, and the only thing that will come of it is he'll be even angrier. And I'm his favorite target when he's angry."

"I have a brother who's a PI. We could set up surveillance and—"

"I already know what I'm going to do. Now I just need to take care of the Trust."

Jack took out a legal pad. "Who do you want to designate as the new trustee?"

"You."

He looked up and she met his gaze. Seeing his light chocolate eyes made her stomach flip flop. God, she was such a loser. *What kind of woman lusts after a man when she's almost nine months pregnant and about to pull off a brilliant plan that will put her away for a long, long time?* "You," she repeated. "I need someone I can trust who won't be intimidated by Sean. He is sure to go batshit when he finds out about this. But there are two people who will contact you. Please, and this is very important. Please do not let anyone know about these two women."

She handed him her business card with Peggy's and Lyssa's names written on the back. "Give them whatever they need but make sure you keep anything they tell you secret. And don't let Sean find out about them."

"Anything else?"

"Yes. I can't tell you when; you'll just have to trust me on that one. And the—Oh!"

"What?" Jack said as he ran around the desk to where Darby was doubled over.

"Back ache. Nothing major, just another one of the joys of pregnancy." Slowly the cramp stopped and she looked at the clock. "I have to go to the doctor's office now."

"Nice idea," Jack said. "You don't look very good."

"Thank you."

"I didn't mean it that way. Should I help you over?"

"Sorry. But don't walk me; I'd like to keep our relationship quiet for now." She reached into her purse, ripped the lining and gave him the second cashier's check, for five thousand dollars. "What do I owe you?"

"Fifteen hundred."

"Here," she said as she handed it to him. "You can just keep the remainder in escrow. I couldn't risk writing you a check in case Sean goes over my records."

Darby was in agony by the time she waddled across the street. She went to the receptionist, who immediately looked concerned. Then Darby realized she'd left her scarf at the law office. She covered the purplish bruises with her hand. Again in the course of fifteen minutes, her back cramped and she doubled over.

She heard the receptionist call for the nurse. Together, the two of them got her back into an exam room. Darby couldn't get comfortable. The sharp pain was now starting near her spine, then wrapping around her abdomen.

Her OB/GYN's partner came in; Dr. Moser had an odd smile on her face. She snapped on a pair of exam gloves as Darby removed her scrub bottoms and sat with a paper blanket draped over her on the edge of the exam table.

"Is an internal exam good for the baby this close to delivery?" Darby asked.

The doctor laughed. "Did you not read a single baby book? A due date is a guess at best. When did the back pain start?"

"Last night."

"And you didn't think to call?"

"And tell you what?" she asked as she scooted down and placed her feet in the stirrups. "That I had a back ache from wearing heels last night?"

"No, but you could have told me that you were in a stressful situation with your husband and I could have admitted you for observation."

"I didn't know that," Darby said on a sigh.

Then her body seized and the doctor calmly said, "Breath like this…hee, hee, haw, haw. Shallow, little breaths will help with the pain."

Darby did as she was told, but the pain didn't seem to want to go away. It wasn't until the cramp stopped that she realized the doctor had already removed her gloves and called out for one of the nurses.

"Darby, what you have, and have been having since yesterday, is back labor. You're already seven centimeters dilated, so I'm thinking you're going to have this baby in a matter of hours."

Darby blinked. "But she isn't due for another month."

"Yeah, well, interesting thing about babies: they have their own sense of timing. The nurse will help you get dressed, I'm going to call for an ambulance to take you over to the hospital."

"I can drive. It's not that far away."

"You can't drive. What you can do is call whoever you want in the delivery room with you."

Darby immediately thought of her mother and tears slipped down her cheeks. She didn't want Sean there, but she knew the potential danger of not telling him. Reluctantly she dialed his cell. It went to voice mail.

"I'm in labor. I'm having the baby at Martin Memorial North."

Maybe she'd get lucky and he wouldn't check his messages.

The ambulance was there in a matter of minutes and her exit via stretcher didn't go unnoticed by the shopkeepers and the people on the street. But the last face she saw before they closed the ambulance door was Jack Kavanaugh's, and he gave her an encouraging smile.

CHAPTER FIVE

Six weeks had passed since Sean had burst into the delivery room wearing a crisp shirt and the hint of Roxanne's perfume. Things were getting worse, but Darby so adored her baby girl that she was having second thoughts about her plan. She was so enchanted with her daughter that she couldn't imagine handing her over to Lyssa. She kept having fantasies about Sean being hit by a train, or falling victim to some other unforeseen disaster, and she often woke in a cold sweat. He was coming home at night less and less, so Darby was almost hopeful that he was going to leave her for Roxanne. Anything that got him out of the house would make her plan unnecessary.

Until this morning, this is, when Sean had backhanded her for not fixing a bottle fast enough. It was the first time he'd struck her since the first pediatrician's visit, when the doctor had voiced concern about Mia's lack of weight gain. He suggested they put the baby on formula. So after the visit they'd stopped and bought several varieties of formula, then went home. Sean had made her put the baby in her cradle while she made a bottle, but before she'd had the chance to even open the container, he'd shoved her into the wall. Darby slid down, off balance.

"You can't even feed our daughter," he growled at her before he kneed her in the ribs.

Mia was crying but Darby was afraid to stand until Sean stormed off. As soon as he was out of the house, Darby comforted her daughter. She had worked hard at keeping up a pretext of indifference when it came to the baby. She did it around everyone. It was only when they were alone that she was able to cuddle and coo with Mia. And that was only because she had scoured the house, and found and destroyed all of Sean's micro-cameras. She had paid a price for destroying Sean's cameras, but it had been worth it. She treasured every second she had alone with her daughter. She assumed the phone was still tapped, but so far he hadn't said a word about the missing cameras. But what could he do? Call the police and ask for their help?

She fed Mia, then put her down for her morning nap. She went into her bedroom and lifted her T-shirt and saw the beginnings of a decent-sized bruise where Sean had kneed her. What if Mia had been in her arms? As much as she didn't want this, she had to do what was safe for the baby.

All of her appointments with Dr. Pointer since the birth had been low-key, and Darby had made a special effort to seem as disinterested in the baby as possible. She'd taken Mia to her clinic and behaved the same way while the staff passed the baby around. It gave her a chance to say hello to Carl and to give

Peggy Jack Kavanaugh's business card. "If you need anything, cash or anything, call him."

"Who's he?"

"Don't ask and please don't tell anyone about him. Okay?"

Peggy agreed. Then Darby went to the bank to make another withdrawal so Sean could keep his restaurant afloat for another month. Finally she ended up at her doctor's office.

"She's precious," Dr. Moser said.

Darby shrugged and offered a weak smile. What she really wanted to say was that Mia was a wonderful baby who was sleeping through the night and only cried if she needed food or a diaper change. That Darby was hoping for a miracle, and Sean would get struck by lightning or something equally lethal.

It was killing her to continually pretend that she wasn't all that interested in her precious baby. She was having fantasies at night, too: being quite the marksman, she would lie in her bed and shoot him right between the eyes. But then her conscience would get the better of her. How would she ever be able to explain to Mia that she'd killed her father? More than that, Darby worried that she'd be no better than Sean if she acted on her fantasies.

No, this was the best option. She'd made certain that her gynecologist and her therapist thought she was suffering from postpartum depression, and hopefully their eventual testimony would mitigate any punishment she might get from the court. Still, the thought of missing so many of Mia's firsts…

She knew Lyssa, and knew her friend would send her updates, but that wouldn't be the same as experiencing them.

Darby's exam was unremarkable, other than that she was

cleared to resume sexual activity. Like that was going to happen. It wasn't until she went to sit up and her paper gown slipped that the latest bruise showed. Dr. Moser's brows arched.

"What happened?"

"I fell over the ottoman. Luckily I wasn't holding the baby at the time."

The doctor didn't seem to be convinced. "Darby, are you in trouble?"

She shook her head. "Just clumsy," she said as she fought back tears.

"Stay here," the doctor said as she left the room. She was back in less than a minute with a business card. "This is the name and address of a shelter. It's got 24-hour security."

Darby sniffed. "I'm fine, really."

"This kind of thing doesn't usually end well."

"I can protect myself," she insisted. "I was ROTC in college and did two tours in the Middle East. I was at the top of my class at the range. I'm a crack shot."

"Do you really want to kill your husband?"

She scoffed. "No. The courts don't look kindly on women who shoot their husbands. Can we change the subject?" Mia started to get fussy.

"Are you still seeing Fran?"

Darby nodded. "She's a good shrink. I like her."

"Use her as a resource, Darby."

* * *

She hadn't seen Jack Kavanaugh since the day of Mia's birth and now she was crossing the street to his office. He was even more handsome than she remembered. Not preppy handsome, but rugged handsome—like Matthew McConaughey if he went back to shaving, and if he had black hair and chocolate-colored eyes. Chinos and a rumpled dress shirt with the sleeves rolled up to his elbows seemed to compliment his laid-back style. Darby's stomach clenched when his eyes met and held hers. "Well?" he prompted.

"Well what?"

"Are you going to introduce me to your baby?"

Darby had all but forgotten that the handle of the baby carrier was in the crook of her arm. "Sorry, yes. This is Mia Grace." She went to place the carrier on top of his desk but winced when her injured side complained. "My mother's name was Grace, so I went with it."

"I?"

"Yes."

"Your husband didn't care?"

"It just wasn't important to him, so he left it up to me." *Which earned me a slap on the back of the head in my hospital room.*

Darby undid the maze of clips and clasps that kept the baby safely in the carrier. She was about to get her when Jack went right in and lifted her out of the carrier. "She smiles," he said, clearly enchanted.

"You must have children," she said with an unexpected twang of disappointment.

"Nope. But I've got a big family and I'm the second oldest, so I've had more than my fair share of baby duty. Now I have some nieces and nephews, so I keep my skills sharp."

She watched in awe as he made silly raspberries and funny faces to a delighted Mia. It made Darby's heavy heart that much heavier. Sean's only interest in Mia was her Trust, and he'd been haunting Darby for weeks to have it updated. He would on occasion comment on how pretty she was, but only in the context of Mia having his good looks. He wanted not just to include Mia by name to the Trust, but to add him as a trustee so Darby wouldn't have to go to the bank every time he needed cash. Right; like he gave a flying fig about whether Darby would be inconvenienced.

"What's wrong with your side?" Jack asked without taking his attention off the baby.

"Tripped and fell. Nothing major."

Jack cradled the baby in one arm. "Do people actually buy that bullshit from you?"

"It's not—"

"Let me guess. Your husband was cleaning his fist and it accidentally went off."

Darby ignored the comment and reached into her tote. "Here's the changes I want made to the Trust. All signed and notarized, but I'd appreciate it if you wouldn't make this public. Okay? I need your word that no matter what, you'll keep this information confidential."

He handed the baby to Darby and she pressed little kisses against her nearly bald head while Jack went into his desk drawer. He held the paper straight while she signed.

"So what's the plan?" Jack asked.

"I never said I had a plan," Darby replied.

"Do I look stupid to you?"

"No. Are we done now?"

"Something tells me we aren't."

* * *

Darby got back home around three, relieved when she didn't see Sean's car in the garage. She fed Mia, then put her down for a nap and called the restaurant. Sean was there and he came on the line, so she calmly asked, "Will you be home for dinner?"

"Yes. Eight o'clock. Did the doctor clear you for sex?"

"Yes," she answered, knowing full well it wouldn't happen. "Any preference for dinner?"

"Snapper. I brought some home last night. It's in the refrigerator. A salad and a baked potato."

"Okay."

"I'll see you then."

"Good-bye."

Darby didn't have much time. Which was both good and bad. Getting everything ready kept her mind off what she was about to do. She couldn't go there and keep her sanity at the same time. Just the mere concept of handing over Mia had her hands shaking and her stomach in knots. No matter how hard she concentrated, her mind was whirling with potential alternatives, but none of them worked through to the desired end. If she left Sean would retaliate, and he'd retaliate by hurting the baby. Darby couldn't risk that. She had set up the postpartum depression issue and hopefully that would be enough to get her a life sentence with the possibility of parole.

Using one of the disposable cell phones she'd picked up at a convenience store, she called Lyssa and told her where to meet her, then she was all about setting the scene. It was the last thing she wanted to do.

As much as it pained her, she took a thin needle and pricked Mia's tiny foot. She fussed a bit, then went back to sleep. Darby pressed the pillow from the rocking chair against the droplets of blood, then left it at the end of the crib.

Then she went into the garage and pulled down the stairs to the attic. Inside was a cache of baby clothes, bottles and formula she'd been stockpiling since coming home from the hospital. The two suitcases fit in the back of her SUV. She went back into the attic and got a conversion stroller so Lyssa would have a car seat and a stroller.

The whole time, Darby was crying. No, sobbing. The idea of giving up her baby was harder than she had imagined. She kept telling herself it was important to keep the baby safe. Sean was getting nastier by the day and he came home less and less frequently. Darby didn't give a damn if he was with Roxanne, but she knew he wouldn't leave her until he got his hands on her money.

She'd had more than two months of planning and Jack Kavanaugh on her side. She stopped for a minute, wondering why she was thinking about her lawyer. No, not thinking about him, more like feeling fascinated by him. Like she didn't have enough going on in her life—a life that would soon put her behind bars, possibly forever.

But there was something about her attorney that made her weak in the knees. It was totally inappropriate, save for the fact that he seemed like such a nice guy. For a nanosecond, Darby even considered calling him and asking for his advice. Then she remembered that he was an officer of the court and would have to turn her in for "killing" her daughter. Still, she felt as if he might understand her plight. Just as she felt a return in affection. No, she continued her internal discussion, she couldn't get Jack involved. The fewer the people who knew the truth, the better.

The car was packed; all she had to do was drive to the assigned meeting place at Jonathan Dickinson State Park. The location was perfect. They exchanged everything in plain sight since it was a tourist destination. Two women handing off suitcases didn't draw attention.

But when it came time to hand Mia over to Lyssa, Darby began to cry. She kissed her baby's forehead, smelled her skin, rubbed the soft fuzz growing on her head. All she had to do was let go. It literally felt like she was ripping her heart out of her chest.

"You don't have to do this," Lyssa insisted. "I'll help you."

"No one can help me," Darby said through her tears. "When I told the police that Sean had killed my parents, they laughed at me and called me hormonal. You know Sean; he's so charming on the outside, no one believes he's a total prick on the inside. I'd rather die in prison knowing my daughter is safe than live with the fear that he'll hurt her."

Darby handed over the untraceable cell phone and then the baby, and said, "Just go. Please?"

"Darby, I—"

"Go!"

Darby sobbed as she left the park, looking back in her rearview mirror to watch Lyssa putting Mia in the back of her Toyota.

"Stop," she said aloud as she wiped her tears and fought to regain control. If her plan was going to work, she needed to be as calm as possible.

She made one stop at a small grocery store, balling up a chicken inside one of Mia's blankets, so it looked kind of like she was carrying a newborn. Then she got in her car, drove around the block several times, then, careful to make sure the store's video surveillance caught her on tape, she went behind the building to the canal and tossed the blanket-encased chicken, hearing it splash into the murky water. She stood there for a few minutes, then watched as the inevitable happened. Several alligators arrived, ripping and tearing at the blanket until they dislodged the chicken and began spinning to claim their prey. Darby had seen enough.

She got home with plenty of time to set up the house. She took all of Mia's things and placed them in her room, including bottles and anything that reminded her of her beautiful daughter. Once everything was in place, she picked up the receiver and dialed 911.

"I need to report a murder," she said.

"Ma'am?" The dispatcher questioned her as if she'd heard wrong. "Did you say a murder?"

"Yes. I just killed my baby."

Lights and sirens started arriving within minutes. The first to arrive was a Martin County patrol car. A very muscular officer got out of the car and Darby stood at the door and watched him approach, praying she could pull this off.

"I'm Deputy Benson." He took a small notebook out of his breast pocket. "You called in a murder?" he asked, rather casually, she thought.

"Yes."

"And the victim is?"

"My daughter. I killed my baby."

His head whipped up and he regarded her in a totally different light. For her part, Darby was struggling to keep her tone and expression as blank as possible.

"Can I come in and look around?" the officer said, then he reached for the radio clipped to his shoulder and called for backup and forensics.

"Yes. But she isn't here."

"Where is she?"

"I smothered her, then threw her in the canal off A-1-A."

"Ma'am," the officer began, "for my personal safety, I'm going to have to handcuff you."

Darby turned around and grimaced when she felt the cold metal close against her skin. Leading her by the elbow, he steered her to the sofa and gave her a gentle tug so she'd sit down.

"Don't move," he cautioned.

She was trying her best not to move but that was difficult, given the fact that her heart was pounding. What if the police didn't buy her story? What then? Darby grimaced. She hadn't thought about that contingency until just now.

More sirens sounded and in a matter of minutes a half dozen deputies had swarmed on her house. Darby kept her eyes fixed on the clock. It was ten minutes before eight. Sean would be here momentarily. And with all the officers present, for once she didn't have to be afraid of her husband's cruel retribution. That knowledge cloaked her in a sense of calm, bordering on feeling meditative. For the first time in months she didn't have that sinking sense of foreboding in the pit of her stomach. For the first time she knew he couldn't hurt her or Mia. She fought back the tears that threatened when she thought of her little girl. A female deputy came and stood over her. "Are there any weapons in the house?" she asked.

Darby nodded. "There's a nine millimeter in the master closet in a lock box and an M80 rifle in the closet of my office. First door on the right. Ammunition for both guns are in the garage on the top shelf behind the paint cans."

The deputy stepped away and was soon replaced by a plain-clothes detective. Darby's hands were beginning to tingle from the handcuffs.

Suddenly there was a loud commotion out front. Darby recognized Sean's voice. He was none too pleased to learn the police would not let him in the house. Darby relaxed a little. Even though her heart was in tatters, she felt safe for the first time in a very long time.

"Mrs. Grisom, I need to read you your rights."

"No, you don't," she said. "I killed my daughter."

"Where is she?" he asked.

"In the canal."

"You threw your newborn in a canal?"

Darby blinked. "She was already gone," Darby explained. "I smothered her with the pillow in her crib."

"Can you tell me why?"

She hung her head. "I'm a bad mother. So I sent her to God."

The officer looked like he wasn't buying her story.

"I can take you to where I threw her body into the canal," she offered.

"Mrs. Grisom, I need you to understand your rights before we go further." He read the list she had heard on television shows her whole life. "Do you understand these rights?"

"Yes."

"And do you wish to talk to me?"

"Yes. I am talking to you. I killed my baby." She spoke in a monotone, not wanting to betray any of the paralyzing emotions coursing through her body.

Yet a third officer was left to stand guard over her while the detective went down the hallway. When he returned, his expression was stone cold. He was followed by an officer carrying her gun in its lock box in an evidence bag.

The detective returned. "Your husband is outside," he said. "I need to go speak to him. Deputy Renna will take you down to the homicide office and I'll meet you there."

"Okay."

Darby kept her head down as she was marched out of her house in cuffs. Her neighbors were out in force. Sean and the detective were at the side of the house, and when Darby glanced in his direction, she was stunned to see—well, *not see*—the anger she'd expected. If she didn't know better, she'd think he was relieved to hear his child was dead. How was that possible?

Darby was placed in the back of a squad car and driven to

the local police station. The place smelled like stale coffee and cherry air freshener. There was a worn linoleum floor and gray walls genuinely in need of some paint. The deputy who had her by the elbow unlocked the door to a tiny room and then put Darby in a chair. Only then did she unlock the handcuffs. Darby rubbed her sore wrists but her freedom didn't last long. She was told to extend her left arm, which she did, and then a cuff was reattached to that wrist and the other end was attached to an iron loop bolted to the table.

The laminate table top had several etchings. Most were foul and vulgar; the rest were, she assumed, initials. As she sat there her adrenaline started to crash, so she put her head down on her arm and willed herself to stay strong.

They left her in that room for two hours and seven minutes, until yet another pair of detectives entered carrying notebooks and coffee. "Want some?" the shorter of the two asked.

"Please," she responded.

"Cream and sugar?"

"Black," Darby said.

The detective stepped out and was back in just under a minute. While he was gone the other detective remained mute. It was disconcerting.

He passed her the coffee and said, "I'm Detective Lange and this is Assistant State's Attorney Matt Johnson."

He opened a leather portfolio and took out a slip of paper, which he slid across the table to Darby. "These are your rights," he began.

"I already told you I don't care about my rights."

"Then I need you to initial each box and sign it."

Darby sighed and did as asked and slid the paper back to him.

"Walk me through what happened today," the state's attorney asked.

Before she could answer, there was a knock at the door. The detective got up and stepped out for a minute, speaking in whispered tones to another man Darby could only see in silhouette.

He came back to the table but didn't sit down. "This interview is over," he announced. Then looking to the state's attorney he said, "Her lawyer is here and he invoked for her."

"What lawyer?" Darby asked.

"David Greer," he answered and Darby noticed something pass between the two men.

"What?"

"Greer is the best defense attorney in Martin County."

"I don't know David Greer and I didn't hire an attorney."

"Your husband did."

CHAPTER SIX

David Greer looked like a stereotypical successful attorney: silk suit and tie, posh leather briefcase, and a Presidential Rolex attached to his left wrist. Darby was definitely not glad to see him, even if he was a complete stranger, because Sean was with him.

Darby braced herself, waiting for Sean to attack. Instead, he came around the table, hugged her awkwardly since her wrist was cuffed to the table, then he kissed her cheek and brushed away her tears. She wasn't sure why she was crying; she was just so confused by his response.

"They're going to transfer you to the jail," Mr. Greer said. "So we don't have much time. Tell me what happened."

Darby launched into the events of the day, keeping her gaze on the handcuffs and her voice as calm as possible. "Sean can tell you; I wasn't a good mother. Mia deserved better, so I sent her to God."

"Have you always had these religious feelings?"

"No," Sean answered for her. "As far as I know the last time she was in church was on our wedding day."

"I couldn't even feed her correctly," Darby continued. "She cried a lot and no matter what I did, I couldn't comfort her."

"When did these feelings start?" Greer asked.

"When I was pregnant."

"What?" Sean demanded. "Why didn't you say something to me?" She could see his temper beginning a slow boil.

She glanced up at him. "I think you know why. What does it matter? I did it and now I have to pay the price."

"Did you talk to anyone?"

Darby nodded. "I saw a therapist for the last two months I was pregnant. And I told my OB/GYN. I think I knew before she was born that I was going to fail as a parent."

Sean knelt by her, holding her free hand. "You should have come to me," he said in a tone she recognized as insincere. To the untrained ear, it was that smooth, comforting tone that had first attracted her to him. Only now she knew better. That tone was his gateway into a hellish life with a brutal man.

"I'll need names and a retainer," Greer said. "They'll take you before the judge tomorrow morning and I'm going to try to get you out on bond."

"Really?" Darby asked, terrified.

"Don't get your hopes up, Darby. Beautiful, wealthy professional kills baby and tosses her body in a canal is a press wet dream. I don't think a judge is going to grant bail in your case. But we might have another option."

"Which is?"

"Let me talk to your doctors. We might be able to work on a diminished capacity defense."

"I knew what I was doing," Darby insisted.

Greer placed both his palms down on the table and leaned toward Darby. "And you have to stop saying that to anyone and everyone. Do not discuss your case with anyone. Okay?"

She nodded.

"My checkbook is at the house but if you can bring it to me, I'll be able to pay you."

Then Sean said, "We should probably do a Power of Attorney so that I can pay your legal bills or whatever comes up while you're…indisposed."

"I can't think about that now," Darby said. *And hell will freeze over if he thinks I'd ever give him Power of Attorney.*

Sean gave her a hug and as he did, he whispered into her ear, "You'll pay for this."

* * *

Darby was taken down a dark hallway to a row of cubicles. A metal stool was in front of each cubicle. The deputy had her stop at one, then said "Sit."

Darby did as she was told and found herself staring at a bored-looking woman in uniform at a computer terminal. The handcuffs were removed.

"Full name?"

"Darby Hayes Grisom."

"Address?"

Darby answered every question while absently rubbing her

wrists. The questions seemed endless and pointless. What did her financial information have to do with anything?

"Do you have an attorney?"

"Yes." She gave the woman Mr. Greer's information.

Next she was taken to the shower room, where she was strip-searched by a female deputy, then provided with a pair of orange scrubs, white panties and a white sports bra. She was crying as she stepped into the shower as commanded and got out when the deputy called her name.

Before she got dressed, the deputy had catalogued her belongings—dress, shoes, undergarments, ring, a cell phone, bracelet, etc. As soon as she was dressed, she was handed a bedroll and pack of personal items and told to follow the deputy. She was taken to a large dorm with double tiers and an open center with chairs and tables bolted to the floor.

"Take bed three," she was instructed.

Darby went to bed three and tried not to notice the attention she was garnering from the other inmates. Several yelled, "baby killer" in unison and then an alarm sounded.

The inmates immediately got on their beds and Darby did as well. Several deputies came in the unit, one directly to her. "Get your bedroll and your things."

Darby did as told and the chants and jeers continued and grew louder as she was escorted out of the dorm. "We'll put you in a segregation cell," the deputy said. "Obviously your reputation has preceded you."

Apparently there was a pecking order in prison, and Darby realized she was low woman on the totem pole. She was already worried but having more than a hundred women yelling

and spitting in her direction turned that worry into abject
fear.

Darby was put into a small cell with a small glass window. It
smelled moldy and musty and there was some black gunk stain-
ing the air vent on the ceiling. But it was better than being in
that hellhole with those other women.

Darby cried softly. It was one thing to know she had made
the right decision, but an entirely different thing to have to live
with it. She didn't have a watch, but she guessed she'd dozed off
from sheer exhaustion sometime near dawn. She was awakened
moments later when a trustee arrived with her breakfast tray.

The least offensive of the offerings was the instant coffee
with powdered no-dairy coffee lightener. She preferred black
coffee but figured this cup would need a little help. The remainder of the tray consisted of a scrambled egg, juice, two strips
of turkey bacon and two slices of white toast. There were no
condiments, not even salt and pepper.

Given that she was terrified of what the day would bring,
Darby settled for the rancid coffee and sipped the juice. She
learned an important lesson, too. The same person came
around to collect the tray before she'd even finished the juice.
Apparently one didn't linger over meals in jail.

Darby looked in the plastic baggie she'd been given and
found a toothbrush and toothpaste. She went over to the sink,
which was bolted to the wall next to the commode, and held
her hair back with one hand while she brushed her teeth. The
baggie also contained a small, cheap black comb that took her
several minutes to pull through her tangled hair. Technically
speaking there was a mirror above the sink, but previous resi-

dents had scratched off the reflective surface. The last items in the baggie were a rough, worn washcloth and a small bar of no-name soap which she moistened and used to wash her face. It left her skin feeling tight and dry. Apparently there was also no moisturizing in jail, either.

Just as she was finishing up, the guard appeared and told her to stand up and walk backward to the door. She slipped her hand through the narrow slot and felt cuffs being snapped in place. "Where am I going?" she asked.

"Court," the guard replied.

It wasn't exactly a direct route to court. First she was put in a holding cell, then she was escorted in through a side door, to a hallway where she joined another half dozen shackled women. They formed a single line, then boarded a dark green bus for the short trip to the courthouse.

They went in a back door and each woman was placed in a single cell. Darby's nerves were frayed to near breaking by the time her name was called and a deputy led her into the court-room. Compared to what she'd seen on TV and in the movies, it was small and darkly paneled, with an impressive bench for the judge. That seat was vacant when she went and stood, knees week, next to her attorney.

Darby was nervous and rattled by the press in the gallery. As she walked into the courtroom, it seemed like a thousand cam-eras were pointed her way, including television cameras from the three local channels. She shuffled to the long table with the de-fense placard on it, nearly tripping several times. It wasn't easy to walk with her ankles and wrists shackled. She was wearing a bright orange jumpsuit and her hair was tucked behind her ears.

The judge entered. Everyone rose and then sat down once the judge was seated, and her case was called. "State of Florida versus Darby Hayes Grisom."

"Your honor," Mr. Greer began immediately as he rose and buttoned his jacket. "Mrs. Grisom is a suicide risk and as such, defense moves to have her transferred to an appropriate mental health facility for observation. In addition, the defense believes Mrs. Grisom is and/or was suffering from a mental illness at the time of the crime and asks the court for a competency hearing prior to the defendant offering a plea."

As she looked around the gallery, she was stunned to see Jack Kavanaugh among the vultures. He was in the back row and his eyes followed her like tractor beams, but she couldn't read his expression. Had Sean already discovered the changes she'd planned for the trust? No, she decided. Sean wanted revenge and part of that revenge would be finding a way to get to her money. If he knew she had already changed the document, he never would have gotten her a lawyer and be playing the bereft yet understanding husband.

Darby watched him on the news the previous night, through the thin sliver of window in her cell overlooking the common area. Sean had insisted that she was not guilty, but rather suffering from postpartum psychosis. Here was a twist she hadn't expected, a deviation from her plan. Darby had hoped that setting the stage by seeking help for depression she might, just might, get a lighter prison sentence, allowing her to reunite with Mia. She never dreamed her actions would become a plausible defense. Nor had she thought Sean would be leading the charge.

Now she was terrified of getting out of prison. After his whispered threat, she knew he'd kill her if given the chance.

A deputy was stationed behind her; Sean was in the front row. It seemed like the judge was taking an inordinate amount of time deciding what to do with her. Then he removed his glasses and looked at her and said, "Mrs. Grisom, based on the affidavits provided to the court as well as a sworn statement from your husband, I believe a competency hearing is in order. Therefore, I am ordering that you be transferred to Green Haven for observation and assessment by the state's psychologist."

"Excuse me, your honor?" Greer said.

Clearly the judge didn't like to be interrupted. "Yes?"

"The defense respectfully requests that our own psychologist be able to monitor that evaluation as well as any evaluations the defense may require."

"Fine," the judge said, then he looked at the state's attorney. "Do you wish to add anything at this time?"

"No, Your Honor."

"We'll set this matter for preliminary hearing after such time as the mental health professionals have had an opportunity to examine the defendant."

Darby startled when he slammed his gavel on the desk. "What does that mean?" she asked Greer.

"You'll be transferred to a secure mental health facility."

"I don't have to go back to jail?"

Greer put papers in his briefcase and said, "Yes." He turned to the deputy behind them and asked, "Hey, Fred? Can she get a hug from her husband?"

He shrugged. "A quick one."

Sean came around through the swinging doors and wrapped his arms around her. He grabbed her and since she was off balance because of the shackles, she practically fell into his embrace. Darby quickly regained her balance and put as much distance between her and her husband as was humanly possible. Yes, she might have been the one who sent Mia away, but he was the reason she'd been left without a choice. At that instant, Darby tensed automatically, and realized Jack Kavanagh had witnessed the awkward moment.

"That's enough," the deputy said, taking Darby's arm.

"I'll come see you tomorrow," Sean said in a whisper.

"Please don't," Darby countered softly. "After what I did I can't even look you in the eyes."

He offered a menacing smile. "I know. Why do you think I'm doing it?"

Darby was led back to the holding cell adjacent to the courtroom. It was in a series of small cells, each with a sink, commode, and table with attached seats. Everything was bolted down, stainless steel, and smelled of sweat. Darby sat on one of the benches, rubbing her arms where they'd been cuffed for the hearing. She was only there for a few minutes when the guard came and told her that her attorney was here.

"Mr. Greer?" she asked, confused.

"Guy named Kavanaugh."

"Tell him to go away."

The guard disappeared, then returned and said, "He said to tell you either you could talk to him or he could talk to your husband."

Darby sighed. "Okay."

In minutes, Jack was let into her cell then locked in. Darby was still having trouble getting used to the sound of the metal bolt as it slid into the locking mechanism.

Unlike Greer, Jack carried a backpack, not a briefcase; and he was dressed in his normal casual style. Not that she was in any position to discuss style; she was wearing an ill-fitting tangerine jumpsuit.

"You are full of surprises, Mrs. Grisom," he said as he took the seat across from her.

"I killed my own baby."

Jack shook his head. "No you didn't."

"Please keep your voice down," she insisted.

"Then explain to me what's going on because right now I'm getting the sense that you've involved me in some sort of conspiracy."

"Which is why I didn't want to see you. But since you're here, do you have the Trust papers?"

"Yes."

"Let me sign them."

"Not until I know what's going on."

"I killed my daughter and now I'm going to jail. I want you to use the family trust for Lyssa Chandler. Send her whatever she needs whenever she needs it. And Peggy from my office might call, too. Give her what she needs as well. I don't have any other relatives so this is what I want done with the money."

"You have your husband."

She pulled her lower lip through her teeth. "The only thing

I want from my husband is a divorce. Can you do that? While I'm in here?"

"Sure. But you have to come clean with me. I'm your attorney, remember. I can't repeat anything you tell me in confidence."

Darby raked her fingers through her hair.

"You can trust me," he prodded.

"Right. Why should I?"

"When I saw the news last night I knew something smelled fishy. I saw you with that baby. No way did you kill her."

"They found her blood on the pillow I used to suffocate her before I threw her in the canal."

"Bullshit."

"Sean doesn't think so."

"Your husband is a dick. Why didn't you tell someone?"

"I did," she said as she felt tears sting her eyes. "I told my parents. The next day they were dead."

"And no one looked at Sean?"

"I don't know how he did it, but he had his whole alibi in his jacket pocket. The police thought I was being hormonal and dismissed me. All I could think of was how long it would be before Mia did something that made him angry. I couldn't let that happen."

"Well, you certainly came up with a creative and complicated way to keep that from happening. I'm sure I'm not the only one who saw the bruises. Why not get a divorce and a restraining order?"

"Because we both know Sean would have gotten some sort of visitation. I couldn't risk that. Now I can divorce him."

"Actually, you can't. Not without revealing that Mia is alive. Otherwise it's considered a fraud upon the court."

"Well, shit." Darby's mind was racing a mile a minute. "What if he divorces me?"

Jack shook his head. "Same problem."

"Then how do I get him out of my life?" she asked.

"I read in the newspaper that you were ROTC and a sharpshooter. Why'd they have you training search-and-rescue dogs?"

"Every member of my family has done military service," she explained. "And I am a good shot. But in those days women weren't placed in combat roles. Are you saying I should have killed *him*?"

"Better plan than this mess you've gotten yourself into."

"Except then I'd have to explain to my daughter that I killed her father."

"And that's better than explaining to her why Daddy beats on Mommy?"

"Okay, so I'm back to how do I get myself out of this *and* keep Mia safe."

"You don't happen to have any witnesses to any of his battery, do you?"

Darby smiled for the first time in forever. "I don't, but he does."

"I don't follow."

"Sean had the whole house wired with cameras. He's been taping everything that goes on."

"Where are the tapes?"

She shrugged. "I have no idea. But based on a few things he's said, he could watch them at work on his computer."

"How did you manage to make it look like you killed the baby with cameras everywhere?"

"I destroyed them one by one."

"Were they hardwired?"

"No, they had little antennas. About the size of a dime, maybe smaller."

"Probably has the video stored off site. Have you seen a bill or an invoice for anything like that?"

"No, but he would have that sort of thing sent to the restaurant. So what's the plan?" she asked.

"First we go to the cops and tell them the truth and then—"

"No!" Darby shook her head vehemently. "I won't reveal Mia's whereabouts until you can guarantee that she'll be safe from him. Mia is my number one concern." Darby wiped away a stray tear. "I want to trust you, Mr. Kavanaugh, but I'm running a little low on trust these days."

"I'm not your husband, Darby. And please call me Jack. I think any man who hits a woman should be hung by his testicles."

That coaxed a smile out of Darby. "Yes, you are the antithesis of Sean. Is there any way I can get out of this mess without putting Mia in danger?"

"Would you settle for supervised visitation?"

"Supervised by who?"

"The court appoints people. They're trained and vigilant and if Sean so much as whispers anything inappropriate to the baby, they revoke his visitation."

"How long would this supervision last?"

"Until your husband proves he's no longer a threat."

She shook her head. "Sean can really turn on the charm."

"I don't know. First, let's get you out of here," Jack said.

"I'm safer here," Darby insisted. "Go see Peggy at my clinic. She has copies of all my keys, including keys to the restaurant. Go see if you can find the tapes or anything else that will make a judge understand why I did what I did."

"Doesn't the restaurant belong to Sean?"

She shook her head. "Technically, it belongs to me. The deed is in my name alone."

"And the house?"

"Mine, too."

"The cars?"

"All mine."

"No wonder he wanted to have children with you."

"Thank you for pointing that out."

He reached out and patted her hand. It was quick, but then again so was the little skip in her heartbeat. "I'm sorry. But once they transfer you to Green Haven, you'll be on a seventy-two-hour hold. Even if you produced Mia for the court, getting you out of there will be nearly impossible."

"I can stand anything for three days."

"Let's hope so. And Darby"—he stood—"be honest with the therapists. Talk about Sean, but try to avoid discussing Mia because we can't have you lying to the state's shrink."

"Okay."

"How can I get in touch with Lyssa?"

"You can't," Darby said. "She'll call you."

"When?"

"When she gets settled."

"When will that be?"

"I honestly don't know. I didn't want to know in case my plan didn't work."

"From now on do me a favor?"

"Yes?" She met his eyes.

He gathered up the executed trust papers. "No more plans. You suck at them."

CHAPTER SEVEN

Green Haven appeared to be anything but a haven. It was a stark two-story building five minutes from the jail. Darby was once again in shackles as she was led into the building. Her shackles were removed and she was led through a metal detector, then the deputy who had driven her over signed a form and left Darby in the care of a pretty Latino woman. She wore scrubs and looked more like a nurse than a jailer and that was comforting...

Until for the second time in about twenty-four hours Darby was forced to undergo another strip search. For a rather modest woman, it was a humiliating part of the check-in process. The nurse handed her a pair of green scrubs, white granny panties, and a sports bra. Once she changed, Nurse Garcia had her select a pair of shower shoes from a wall of cubbies just outside the strip-down room.

She was led into a smaller room with a table and two chairs. Garcia took one and motioned Darby to the other. They spent an hour going over a list of questions. Darby didn't lie, but she did fudge a bit when asked about wanting to hurt others. She wanted to hurt Sean, but she figured she'd save that one for the shrink.

After the interview, Garcia got a handful of hospital bracelets, pulled a red one out of the batch, wrote on it with a sharpie, then had Darby hold out her left arm. "What does red mean?" Darby asked.

"The doctor will explain all that to you."

"Is that my next stop?" she asked.

The nurse smiled. "Maybe tomorrow. Dr. Radcliff has already been here today."

"So what do I do until then?"

"Attend sessions."

"Sessions on what?"

"Drug and alcohol abuse, parenting, marriage and family issues, art therapy, group therapy. We have a full program here."

"So I get to make macaroni necklaces until tomorrow?"

"No, you'll meet with our staff therapist, but Dr. Radcliff is the court-appointed doc you have to meet with."

"If he knew I was coming, why not wait?"

Garcia snorted. "Honey, he has a lucrative private practice. Only comes here when the court involves him in a case. He loves to testify."

"Great."

"C'mon, I'll show you to your room."

Darby followed the nurse, taking in her surroundings. There was a circular nurses' station in the middle of a large common area, and there were dormlike rooms down hallways spaced out like the spokes of a wagon wheel from the central station. The place smelled of pine cleaner.

Garcia opened one door. "This is your room." It was maybe seven by ten, with a cement rectangle topped by a two-inch pleather mattress pad in it. Darby started to step in but Garcia blocked her way. "You have to go to the main desk and get your assignments first."

"Assignments?"

"What you'll be doing between meals. This room is only for sleeping."

"There's no bathroom," Darby noted.

"You can press the button by the door, but it may take a while for anyone to get here. We have a small staff overnight. If you'd be more comfortable, you can have an adult diaper."

"So I'm locked in at night and locked out during the day?"

"Right. You missed lunch."

"That's okay."

"Good, because we don't have a cafeteria. Dinner is at six."

Darby went to the nurse's station and was given a piece of paper. Her first assignment was to attend a drug and alcohol program. "I don't have a problem," Darby told the nurse.

"Fine. But you still gotta go."

Darby looked at the rest of her "activities" and wondered why on earth she'd been sent to this place. Just about everything, save for her appointments with counselors or group therapies, was geared toward drug and alcohol aversion. It was going to be a long seventy-two hours. She didn't want counseling. She wanted Mia back. Darby gave herself a little

mental tongue-lashing. Here she was griping about her surroundings when she was really just trying to focus on anything other than Mia. About now would have been bath time.
Mia loved splashing the water and Darby could practically
close her eyes and smell the scent of baby shampoo. Darby's
heart constricted. Maybe Jack was right. Her plan was littered
with flaws.

* * *

Jack kept his phone with him at all times, hoping beyond hope
that Lyssa Chandler would call him sooner rather than later.
He pulled into the circular drive at Darby's house, got out and
went to the front door just as the sun was setting. Using the
keys he'd gotten from Peggy at Darby's vet clinic after making sure Sean was at the restaurant, he let himself inside her
spacious home. It was a far cry from the modest house he was
renovating in Palm City. It was also the cleanest place he'd
ever seen. Well, except for the baby's room. The crib had been
stripped and moved away from the wall.

    He'd decided it was better to take a look around when he
knew Sean would be at the restaurant. Hopefully he'd find
something that could support Darby's story, if he didn't hear
from Lyssa before Darby ended up locked up for good. As
her attorney, he was able to visit her, but at Green Haven,
they made doing so very difficult—mainly because they
didn't like anything that interrupted their strict schedule.
Jack had represented a schizophrenic man a few years back
and he'd learned then that getting into Green Haven outside

of visiting hours could be difficult.

He felt a rumble of fury go through him as he thought about Darby in that place. For a rich woman, she was very down to earth. The more he learned about her, the more intrigued he became. She was a very attractive, down-to-earth woman. He gave himself a mental bitch slap. Nothing good could come out of lusting after a client. Especially when that client was chin deep in crisis. Even once he had proof that Darby had faked the whole thing, she'd probably be arrested for filing a false report, and about six other felonies and misdemeanors. He had to make things right before things went any further.

Having grown up in a house where domestic violence was the norm, Jack wondered if his attraction to Darcy was somehow linked to his difficult childhood. As much as he tried to chalk it up to that, he couldn't get past the desire he felt for her. Even when she was wearing her jail garb. She'd managed to make that jumpsuit sexy and that took some doing. No, wanting Darcy had hit him like a brick. He couldn't recall the last time he'd felt such a strong pull of desire for a woman. It wasn't as if he lived like a saint. Far from it. He'd just never had this kind of reaction before.

In the hallway he stopped and picked up a framed wedding photograph. He'd never seen *that* smile on Darby's face. Once he thought about it, he realized that wasn't true. He'd seen that smile when she'd brought the baby to his office. She must have been crazy afraid to think up this nutty idea. Man, but Jack would enjoy about five minutes alone with Sean.

Swallowing his anger, he made his way through the house,

checking for additional cameras or some hint as to how Sean was broadcasting to his office at the restaurant. Going from room to room, he hoped to find something out of the ordinary that she had missed.

He went into a guest room that appeared to be the catch-all room. There was a bed, but it was buried under a stroller box and some smaller boxes, and then on top of that were neat piles of men's and women's clothing. He found more men's clothes hanging in the closet. Spreading the clothes apart, he noticed an attic access panel. He went and got one of the kitchen chairs, stood on it and pushed aside the wooden panel, then hoisted himself up. He was forced to crouch in the dimly lit space. This wasn't going to work. He needed a flashlight.

He found one in the garage and went back to the side attic. With the flashlight in his mouth, he again hoisted himself into the small space. Much better. He had a bright view of the insulation, ventilation and other expected pipes and items. Then he saw the black box plugged into an exposed outlet affixed to one joist.

He went over and examined it. It had three lights on one side: two were solid, the third was blinking. He was no expert in electronics but if he had to guess, he'd bet the blinking light meant there was something wrong with the feed. He unplugged the box, deciding he'd drop it by a friend of his who knew everything there was to know about electronics. He checked his watch. Sean's flailing restaurant closed in a half hour and he didn't want to be caught in the house. Sean didn't know about him yet and he wanted to keep it that way, at least for now. Hopefully Sean didn't have any other cameras Darcy hadn't found.

At least nothing damning until he had solid evidence of his violent nature to show the court. Hopefully it would be enough to keep a judge from coming down hard on Darby for wasting police and court time.

With the black box tucked under his arm, he left and headed to downtown Stuart. There was a three-block area on the waterfront popular for its shops and restaurants, and Jack parked his black Escalade nearby, then took the box and walked to the second-story apartment off Osceola Street.

Tony Altemonte—Big Tony to his friends—opened the door and welcomed Jack with a slap on the back. He was a giant of a man, six-six and close to four-hundred pounds. He was dressed in shorts and a button-down shirt, only the buttons weren't buttoned and his massive belly and hairy chest hung out for all to see. "Haven't seen you in forever."

"Been busy," Jack said.

"A man should never be too busy to play poker."

Jack smiled. "Okay, I just got tired of giving you all my money."

"Whatcha got there?" Big Tony asked, pointing at the black box.

"I was hoping you could tell me."

Big Tony took the box over to what should have been the kitchen but had been reconfigured into a series of computer screens, CPUs, keyboards and a bunch of other electronic components Jack couldn't name. Big Tony took a half-smoked cigar out of the ashtray and placed it in the corner of his mouth.

Thankfully, he didn't light it. Jack hated the smell, which was the real reason he'd pulled back from the weekly poker games. Big Tony and his friends were all cigar smokers and by the third hand, the air would be thick with choking smoke.

"Sit," he told Jack as he reached into a box next to his seat. He pulled out some cables and plugged them into the machine. "What we have here is a Bluetooth DVR—Digital Video Recorder."

"Does it have recordings on it?"

Tony took a look at a laptop he'd attached the other end of the cables to, punching a few keys on it and staring at the screen for a moment. "Full. About one-hundred-fifty hours."

"Can I see what's on it?"

"Not in my apartment," Big Tony said with a chuckle. "I'll put it on a portable hard drive. Just plug that into your TV."

"Thanks," Jack said.

"Thank me tomorrow," he said. "It'll take time to transfer the files."

"Early tomorrow?" Jack pressed.

"Not before ten," he said.

"Thanks again."

Jack let himself out and then drove over to the Tilefish Grille. The place was dark save for the red haze from the illuminated exit signs. There were no cars in the parking lot, so he drove around the back and parked away from the security cameras. Grabbing a baseball cap from the back seat and pulling it low, he kept his head down as he went to the back door.

He tried three keys before he found the one that fit the bolt. He opened the door and heard the unmistakable sound of an alarm beeping. He glanced around and found the keypad and entered the code Darby had given him: the date of their wedding anniversary. For some reason that annoyed Jack. And it wasn't just because she was married. It was because she was married to a man like Sean. *You have to be a special kind of asshole to hit a woman.*

He walked through the spotlessly clean kitchen. The scent of food still hung in the air and Jack's stomach growled. He hadn't eaten in a while. Spotting the door marked OFFICE he used the keys to open that door as well.

It wasn't a very big space, maybe ten by twelve, with pale blue paint on the walls and a tile floor that slanted slightly toward the drain in the center of the kitchen. Jack had worked at a few restaurants during his college years so he knew all about that drain. It was so the floor could be power washed. He'd been the grunt-level employee who'd done the washing.

There was a pegboard on one wall covered with labeled clipboards for various vendors, and one for scheduling. There was a U-shaped desk and an expensive executive chair. Beneath the desk was a safe. The top desk drawer was locked and Jack didn't have a key for it. The same was true of the file cabinet. He was about to give up when he bumped the desk and Sean's computer came out of hibernation mode.

Making himself comfortable, Jack began to click around the machine. He noticed a small envelope icon in the tray and clicked on it. Sean's email opened. It was very revealing. Literally. In a folder titled "exhibits" he found at least a hundred emails. Each email contained an embedded photo. Many were all of one woman, even though you couldn't see her face. The images ran the gamut from seductive poses to graphic porn. They dated back over a year. He could tell by the hips that the woman wasn't Darby. Well, that and the red hair. There was a second set of emails, again with nudes, again with a redhead. Based on the date stamps, these were newer; he also based that conclusion on a mole near this woman's right pelvic bone that hadn't been in the first group of emails. Obviously Sean had a thing for redheads.

Other than a penchant for dirty emails, Sean's emails were mostly about him holding back payments to various suppliers. Jack found a spreadsheet and it appeared the Tilefish Grille was deep in the hole. He also saw a pattern of large deposits. He'd bet the bank they were infusions of cash fresh from Darby's accounts.

Jack looked around the desktop and found a stack of pink message slips. All of them save one was from a vendor, but that one caught his attention. The callback number was familiar but he couldn't place it. So he did the the obvious. Jack took out his cell and dialed the number.

"Hello?"

"Who is this?" he asked pleasantly.

"Who is this?"

"My name is Jack Kavanaugh and I—"

"Oh, thank God," the woman gushed. "I'm Peggy Tillman. I work for Darby and I'm here at the clinic."

"Why?"

"The alarm went off and I'm the secondary contact on the account. The police are here now."

"I'll be right over."

After carefully locking up the restaurant, he drove to the clinic and found two deputies talking to a woman. Jack took one look at her and had a pretty good idea he'd seen her before. *All* of her. Peggy was the redhead with the mole. So if she was Darby's close friend, why was she sending sexy emails to Sean?

CHAPTER EIGHT

Peggy escorted the deputies inside. She silenced the alarm and then she and Jack stayed behind while the police cleared the building. If there had been an intruder, he was long gone.

The authorities asked Peggy to take a quick look around the clinic to see if anything was missing. She went to the cash box beneath the counter and showed them where the lock had been jimmied.

"How much cash is normally on hand?" one of the deputies asked.

"A hundred dollars or less. Most of our clients pay by check or credit card. There's a safe, too."

Jack tagged along to Darby's office and the safe under her desk was standing wide open. "That's odd," Peggy mused. "All Darby keeps in here are important papers. Deeds, bank statements, that kind of stuff, birth certificates. No cash."

"But it's always locked?"

Peggy nodded. "Always."

"No one else has the combination?"

Peggy blushed. "Maybe her husband. Unless…"

"Unless what?"

"We have a new vet on staff with Darby having the baby and all. Maybe she gave it to Carl for some reason."

Jack asked, "But wouldn't he know the alarm code?"

"Yes," Peggy said. "But I can call him and see if he came by this evening."

Jack met and held her gaze. "Then why don't you give your friend Sean a call and see what he was doing an hour or so ago?"

Peggy blanched and there was a definite tremor in her hand as she dialed Carl. He hadn't been to the clinic. Peggy made a production out of pretending to look Sean's number up on the contact list. She explained the reason for her call, then said a few "um-hums," and then she hung up. Smiling nervously at the deputies, she said, "Case solved. Sean needed to get Darby's checkbook out of the safe."

The deputies went on their way. Peggy and Jack lingered in the parking lot.

"Thank you for coming all the way out here," Peggy said as she started to go to her car.

Jack blocked her. "Does Darby know?"

Peggy's eyes closed and she let out a long breath. "No. And I'd like to keep it that way. My thing with Sean lasted about six weeks. It took me that long to realize he wasn't interested in anything other than keeping tabs on Darby. He wasn't interested in me; he's obsessed with her."

"She thinks you're one of her best friends."

"I am," Peggy insisted. "You just don't know Sean. When he

turns on the charm, he's practically impossible to resist."

"Was he ever violent with you?" Jack asked.

Peggy's pale skin blushed a dark crimson. "He can be pretty kinky in the bedroom."

"Define kinky."

"He's into dominance and punishment. The last time we were together like that he ignored the safe word and kept whipping me, only instead of calling out my name, he was screaming for Darby. That was enough for me to realize that he had a dangerous side he couldn't control."

"Did you ever think he was hurting Darby?"

She shook her head. "Girls talk sometimes and Darby was pretty clear on the fact that she wasn't into sex games. I think Sean is a sadist but if you won't take my word for it, try chatting with his newest plaything."

"Roxanne?"

She nodded. "I've only met her a couple of times but I think she's just as kinky as he is."

"Did Sean ever hit you? Slap you?"

"Only during role playing."

"But you said he blew off your safe word. Isn't that a huge no-no?"

"Yes."

"Do you think he's capable of hurting someone?"

She thought about it for a few seconds, "Maybe. If he got mad, I guess."

"Would you be willing to testify to that?"

"Testify? You mean admit in court that I cheated with my best friend's husband? Not a chance."

"Darby doesn't have much of a chance unless the people around her start circling the wagons. Darby will forgive you; you know that and so do I."

"How is it you know her so well?" Peggy asked.

"I have experience with guys like Sean. And all I care about right now is making sure Darby doesn't spend the rest of her life in jail."

"But she killed little Mia," Peggy said with compassion. "I know she had to be desperate or in the throes of some sort of psychotic break, but do you really think you can get her off with a slap on the wrist?" Peggy peered up at him. "Wait! You aren't even her attorney. I was in the courtroom. David Greer was her counsel."

"For the time being, yes. I'm afraid of what Sean might do if he knew Darby had contacted an attorney when she was still pregnant."

"She was going to leave Sean?"

"I can't comment," Jack said. "But she could really use your help, Peggy. My legal strategy depends on being able to prove that Darby was desperate and Sean was dangerous. Can you do that?"

"On one condition," she said.

"Name it."

"Will you tell her about me and Sean and tell her how sorry I am? I don't think I can face her and say those words."

"Consider it done."

* * *

Nights were long and lonely for Darby. Even though the hand-cuffs and shackles were gone, she felt more like a prisoner than she had at the county jail. Green Haven was a loud and scary place.

As required, she'd gone to the drug and alcohol aversion meeting and all that had come out of that was a stern lecture by the group leader that the first step to success was admitting you had a problem. Darby's failure to acknowledge a problem with alcohol was considered an act of defiance.

But her surroundings had thrown her for a loop. One young woman sat in a chair with a blanket pulled over her head and rocked for the entire fifty minutes. Another guy was tasered halfway through because he jumped out of his seat and began ranting and threatening the counselor. The one she couldn't fig-ure out was the seemingly normal woman in her sixties who had voluntarily signed herself in, yet she didn't seem to have any problem. Oh, and she was given a pass on the failure to admit drug and alcohol abuse.

The bathrooms were kept locked at all times and she had to go to the nurse's desk for a key. There were special phones on one wall and at certain times of the day you could make an out-going call to a local number. Darby had no way of checking on Mia. She longed to hear Mia coo. That could only happen if she had the disposable phone with her. Darby had purchased two throwaway phones so she could keep in touch with Lyssa but unfortunately, her phone had been in the pocket of the black dress she'd been wearing when she was arrested. She assumed the phone was in the jail's property room and made a mental note to ask Jack if he could retrieve it for her. She just needed a good excuse, though, because she just wasn't ready to admit that she had a possible way of locating her daughter. She knew he'd insist that she return the baby immediately in order to end her legal troubles. Doing so might help to do so, but it would also open up the possibility of Sean getting visitation rights. He'd already killed her parents; Darby had no doubts her sweet baby girl could suffer the same fate.

After breakfast, which was a bagel and cream cheese with real, freshly brewed coffee, Darby was scheduled to meet with first the psychologist and then with Dr. Radcliff. His was the opinion that mattered. As an added bonus, she was not required to participate in physical fitness, which this morning was a game of basketball.

Darby found room 110 and knocked gently on the door. A soft male voice ushered her inside.

"I'm Dr. Fisher," he introduced himself.

He looked like a Dr. Fisher. He was short, with a full beard and hair in need of a trim in the back. His clothing was rumpled, so she immediately looked on his left ring finger and found it bare. *All work and no ironing makes for a very wrinkled psychologist.*

He was glancing through a rather thick folder. Darby couldn't imagine what was in there, given that her life behind bars was only forty-eight hours long. She decided to sit quietly while he finished perusing the pages.

"You've been charged with a very serious crime," he finally said.

"I understand that."

"Did you understand what you were doing was wrong when you suffocated your daughter?"

"No," she said without lying. "What I did was try to save my daughter."

"You believed you were a threat?"

"I knew I couldn't protect her."

"I see here that you lost your parents two months ago," he began. "Did that play a part in your decision making?"

Darby's stomach clenched. Reliving the past six weeks was more than painful, it was cruel. "Only insomuch as I'd lost my support system."

"How do you feel about what you did now?"

"I feel like my heart has been ripped out of my body but I know what I did was for the best. I don't know any other way to explain it to you."

"What about your husband?"

"My husband is a very angry man."

"Because you killed his baby?"

"His anger predates what happened with the baby."

"Are you saying you were abused?"

Darby took in two deep breaths. "I've been choked, kicked, slapped, punched and kneed. I think that qualifies."

"But you never attempted to leave," he said, as if the situation was her fault. "Nor did you tell your OB/GYN, your therapist or anyone else."

"But they all knew," Darby countered, her voice slightly raised. "They would see the bruises and give me referrals and names of shelters and other useless options."

"Why do you think they were useless?"

"Because if I left him, he would have hunted me down and killed me. Those are his words."

"Yet he got you an attorney to fight the charges. A very expensive attorney."

Darby scoffed. "Money is no object to him because it's all my money."

"Did you argue about money?"

"Not really. I gave him what he needed. He just hated the fact that he had to ask."

"Did you tell your parents about the abuse?"

Darby's eyes filled with tears. "I called them after a particularly bad beating when I was eight months pregnant. The next morning, they were dead."

"And you blame your husband?"

"Absolutely. Especially when I discovered that he had tapped the phones and wired the whole house for video. I don't know how he did it and still managed an alibi. He admitted to me that he killed them. Then he told me it was my fault for involving them in our problems. So yes, my fear that I couldn't protect a helpless six-week old was and is very valid."

"Okay." He snapped the binder closed. "Wait here, the doctors will be in to see you shortly."

In the pit of Darby's stomach churned a combination of frustration and fury. "Why did I think this stupid plan would work?" she muttered just as the door opened.

The first person to enter the room was a tall, thin guy in his early sixties wearing a silk suit and tie, followed by a friendly face that almost immediately put Darby at ease. It was Fran Pointer, the therapist she'd seen through those last dark days of her pregnancy. The last man in was her attorney, Mr. Greer.

The room was a bit cramped but they managed to cram in

around the small conference table. Fran was to her left, Mr. Greer across from her, and the man who introduced himself as Dr. Radcliff was to her right. She could smell his cologne—Versace—and it was a nice change from the scent of the industrial cleaner that permeated Green Haven.

Dr. Radcliff took out a minirecorder and a pad, as did the other two. Darby was the only one without the ability to take notes, but then again, pens and pencils were off the list at the mental health facility—they were considered potential weapons.

"Mrs. Grisom," he began, making the introductions. "My job is to evaluate you and let the court know if I think you can appreciate the consequences of your actions and/or assist your counsel in your defense. Do you understand that?"

"Yes, she said, twisting the hem of her scrubs around one finger. "But this is all unnecessary."

One graying brow arched. "How so?"

"I've been lying since—"

"My client," Greer interrupted, "will answer your questions, but please, Mrs. Grisom, don't offer information unless specifically requested by the doctor."

"But there's been a terrible mistake," Darby insisted.

"I think I mentioned that to you, David," Fran said with conviction. "Darby was my patient for more than two months but it only took me two visits to see that she was being severely abused by her spouse. I'm not sure what will come out of her mouth next, but she'll do anything to keep her husband at bay."

"Even kill?" Greer asked.

"Sean is the killer," Darby muttered. "He killed my parents."

Dr. Radcliff thumbed through his notes. "The medical examiner determined that your parents died from accidental carbon monoxide poisoning."

"Sean had the means—he knew the garage code. The motive—he was furious that I had told them about the beatings—and the opportunity. He must have taken the late flight to New York, killed them, and then flown in for his breakfast meeting."

Greer practically scoffed. "That's a very convoluted story, Mrs. Grisom. And we're veering far off our stated purpose here. I need you to be more cooperative."

Tears burned at the backs of her eyes. Tears of frustration and tears of anger. She'd lost faith in her plan so she didn't know what to do. Jack had warned her not to go into too much detail before he did whatever he was doing and even though it made no sense at all, she trusted his advice.

"May I speak to Dr. Pointer privately for a moment?" she asked.

"That's not how this works, Mrs. Grisom. All I need from you is some basic information and then I'll file my report with the judge."

"As will I," Fran interjected as she reached out and patted Darby on the leg.

Darby just surrendered to the inevitable, folded her hands in her lap and answered questions in fairly single-syllable answers. She confirmed everything she'd told the police to date—never claiming it was true, just that it was what she'd said and done at the time.

"How long prior to the birth of the minor child did you start planning the crime?"

"Mia," Darby said softly.

"Excuse me?"

"You called her 'the minor child.' Her name is Mia."

"Was," the doctor corrected. "Is there some reason why you can't refer to her in the past tense?"

"It's too painful," Darby replied honestly.

"Okay. But when did you start having homicidal thoughts?"

"When I was about eight months pregnant."

"Can you think of what may have triggered those thoughts?"

Darby looked down at her lap. "Things at home weren't good and I feared for her safety."

"Did you reach out to anyone?"

"Dr. Pointer."

"Did you tell her things at home were tense?"

"I didn't have to," Darby answered. "She saw the bruises for herself."

"How did your husband feel about the mi—about Mia?"

"He was thrilled to be passing his genes along to another generation."

"And that made you angry?"

Darby turned and looked at her attorney. "How much longer do I have to do this? All we're doing is covering the same ground over and over and nothing has changed. Mia is still gone."

CHAPTER NINE

All Darby really wanted to do was crawl into a nice comfy bed and cry herself to sleep. But that wasn't a possibility. Green Haven's strict schedule meant that after being grilled by the court appointed lawyer, then chastised by her own lawyer for what he felt was evasive behavior on her part, she was emotionally spent. Only Fran seemed realize that there was more to this than Darby suddenly having a psychotic break, but Darby didn't tell her everything. Not until she spoke to Jack. And she hoped that was soon. She had learned a thing or two about mentally ill criminals. In order for her to walk out of Green Haven, she'd need a majority of three shrinks to find she was neither a danger to herself or others. She had Fran on her side and she'd meet tomorrow with the second staff psychologist, and if all went well she could change her plea and bail out.

But before that happened she needed to make sure it was safe to bring Mia back.

The next morning, Darby was in the middle of art

therapy—she was weaving a placemat out of construction paper strips. It was slow going because a staff member had to cut
the strips since she couldn't be trusted with scissors.

"Grisom?" a guard asked.

She nodded. "Your attorney is here."

"Do I have to see him?" she asked, not really relishing the
notion of a second lecture in as many days.

"Follow me."

CHAPTER TEN

Darby was led through a different part of the wagon-wheel maze, in the opposite direction from where she'd had her disastrous meeting with the psychiatrists and Mr. Greer. Her attorney was obviously back for a postmortem of how she'd done. Somehow that made the placemat seem infinitely more appealing.

She noticed the faint scent of his cologne before his silhouette was fully in view. "Jack?" Her heart skipped a beat and she felt immediately comforted by his presence.

He turned and greeted her with a warm smile. "How are you doing?"

Darby waited for the guard to leave and then honestly answered, "Lousy. I miss my little girl."

"Sit," he said, waving his hand in an arc near the chair. "Some weird stuff has been going on."

"Weird? Weirder than confessing to a murder that didn't happen? Or weirder than being locked away with some seriously troubled people?"

"I'm sorry. I know this must be tough," Jack said. "But first, let me get you caught up." He told her about the break-in at her office, and as gently as possible he told her about Sean and Peggy.

He watched her expression and braced himself for some sort of reaction. Nothing. Hearing that the woman she had mentored had had an affair with her husband didn't seem to faze her. Darby never ceased to surprise him. "Can you think of any reason why someone would break into your clinic?"

She shook her head. "We keep maybe a hundred dollars in petty cash."

"That's missing."

"There are drugs in a locked cabinet in Exam Room One. But I'm the only one with a key. Or I was. I turned the key over to Carl when he arrived to take over the practice. Was the door pried open?"

"No. What about the safe in your office?" He watched some of the color drain from her cheeks.

"Paperwork mostly. My financial records. I've been sneaking them out of the house a little at a time since the weeks before I had Mia. Our birth certificates, passports—that sort of thing. I was hedging my bets in case Sean decided to take the baby and run."

"Why would you think that?"

"He had me take the baby for an expedited passport. He said she'd need one in case we decided to take a few days off and go to the Bahamas. And as a beneficiary of the trust, Sean would gain full control over Mia's share. The passport arrived a week before I gave Mia to Lyssa."

"Did anyone but Sean know about the passport?"

Darby shrugged. "Peggy was there when I put it in the safe."

"Does Peggy know the combination?"

Darby let out a slow breath. "Yes. I gave her the code when she came to see me right after Mia was born. Carl. He needed some of that information for the bookkeeper."

"Anything else in the safe?" he pressed.

"A file."

"What kind of file?"

"The patient who has Mia."

"Shit," Jack muttered between clenched teeth.

"What?"

He heard panic in her voice and tried to adjust his tone to keep her calm. After all, he only had a theory. "The alarm went off at your office and was logged in at 10:01 by the police dispatch."

"Okay."

"No, not okay," Jack countered. For some reason he reached out and covered her hand with his. He felt a slight tremor and the fear she must be feeling was evident in her eyes. She was sleep deprived and he couldn't imagine the level of separation anxiety warring inside her. He'd seen his sister-in-law with her little boy and she never let the little guy out of her sight.

"Peggy was there in five minutes. I got there a few minutes later, and the police arrived at ten-seventeen."

She raked her hand through her hair. "Was the door forced or the lock tampered with?"

"No."

"Then how did they get in, get the petty cash *and* empty a locked safe, and be out of there in under five minutes?" Darby absently twisted her hair up into a bun. Jack tried not to notice the gentle slope of her neck, or the temptation it inspired. He tried, but he failed.

"Are you saying…?"

"W-what?" Jack asked, returning to the present.

"You think someone staged the robbery for a hundred dollars and some paperwork?"

"You just told me the paperwork had the name and information on the woman who has Mia."

"It does, but I wrote 'relocated' on the outside of the folder and I don't normally put folders in my safe. That was a bonus. The person had to be after the paperwork. And the only person who would want it would be Sean except that Sean thinks Mia is dead, so he'd have no reason to need her passport or go looking for her." Darby blanched. "Unless he's figured it out."

He reached across the cool metal table and took her hands. "That's what I was thinking. So while I understand the reason you did what you did, Darby, it's time to tell the truth. I know the State's Attorney assigned to your case. He's tough but he's a good guy. All we have to do is have Lyssa bring the baby back."

Darby vehemently shook her head. "I can't risk it. Sean killed my parents. Even though Mia is his flesh and blood, he'd kill her just to punish me."

"I think I may have a way around that," Jack said, still clutching her hands. They were soft and seemed so small compared to his own. "I went up into the attic of your house." He told her about the DVR he'd found and that he had a friend. "Big Tony should have discs to me by tomorrow."

Darby squeezed her eyes closed and pulled away from Jack.

"Assuming they show Sean beating you, we can get a judge to issue a protective order for both you and the baby."

Darby shook her head. "You don't know Sean. An order won't do anything to deter him."

"But Declan will."

"Who is Declan?" she asked.

"My older brother. He's a private detective in West Palm Beach. After college I went to law school. He went to the gym. Trust me, once you get a look at Declan, you'll feel totally safe."

"So, how would this work?" Darby asked.

"We have to get Lyssa back. Give me her number."

Darby met his gaze as his pen hung in the air. "I can't."

"What?"

She sighed and raked her fingers through her hair. "I went to a gas station and bought two throwaway phones. I gave one to Lyssa and kept one for myself. She is supposed to call me when she gets settled."

"But you don't remember the number?"

"It was on a piece of paper in my office safe."

"Did *anyone* know about that?"

"No."

"Where is your throwaway?"

"In the pocket of the black dress I was wearing when I got arrested. Lyssa's number is already saved into the contacts."

Jack seemed to relax. "Good, because your personal belongings are transferred with you, so the phone is close by."

"How do I get it?" Darby asked.

"You can't, but as your attorney, I can. But you'll need to do something first."

"Anything."

"Fire Greer."

"Will you be here for the second psychiatrist appointment?" she asked, hearing the panic in her own voice.

"Yes, and as soon as you finish that session, I'll get in touch with Lyssa and—"

"She'll hang up on you," Darby insisted. "I was very emphatic about her not speaking to anyone except to me directly."

"We can get around that. As soon as the meeting with the psychiatrist is over, I'll go down and get your belongings and meet you back here. I've got to write a motion to the court requesting that the items be turned over to me. You just have to sign it." He stood. "I'll be back in about an hour or so. What time is your appointment?"

"Three o'clock-ish. Being on time isn't a big thing here."

He started for the door and Darby jumped up and threw her arms around his neck. "Thank you." His hand went to the small of her back and he applied just a touch of pressure. It didn't last long, but it was long enough to make her heart rate fluctuate. She tried to tell herself she was just grateful, but in truth she was feeling something far stronger. Jack was more than an attorney and confidant. He was the only person she trusted.

* * *

On the short trip to his office, Jack called Declan and asked him to meet him there. And as requested, Declan was out in front of the building, massive arms crossed against his chest. Jack could go to the gym every day for the rest of his life and he'd never be buff like Declan. Declan was a freak of nature. Or at least a freak of the dysfunctional Kavanagh family. He was six feet, four inches with jet black hair and bright blue eyes. He was a health nut and when it came to his work, he was like a dog with a bone. Jack had yet to find the task Declan couldn't resolve.

Darby's case was important. And not just because a mother and baby were in jeopardy. No, he thought as he circled the block for a second time looking for an open spot. Not an easy task in the tiny city of Stuart.

He got lucky on the third circle. He and Declan greeted each other with a fist bump and a resounding pat on the back. "You look like shit, little brother," Declan said.

"This is a tough one," he admitted as he unlocked the door. Once they were inside he relocked it and turned the sign to read OUT OF OFFICE FOR THE DAY since he didn't know exactly how long he would be gone.

Ignoring the blinking light on his voicemail button, he sat behind his desk with Declan across from him and shared what he knew about Darby and her crazy scheme to save her baby from the wrath of her abusive husband.

"No way to get him on the parents' murder?" Declan asked.

"Already ruled accidental by the medical examiner. It would take a complete confession from Sean in order to get an ME to change the manner of death. We have to focus on getting the baby back so I can get her out of Green Haven and then—and this is where you come in—I need you at her side twenty-four-seven until I can get a restraining order."

Jack turned on his computer and began to type.

"Is this the woman from Sewell's Point you called me about a while back?"

"Yep."

"Well, at least you have a paying client."

Jack stopped typing for a minute and met his brother's gaze. "She's more than that," he admitted. "I saw the bruises."

"And she's pretty, right?"

"Absolutely," Jack said.

"You can't go back fifteen years and change what happened," Declan warned. "She isn't Mom. Try not to get too attached."

"Who said I was attached?"

"I'm your brother. I know you."

"I empathize with her. He's been beating her for years. She's practically afraid of her own shadow."

"Well, that has the beginnings of a healthy relationship."

"I hate you."

Declan laughed. "You can't hate me, you need me."

"Then remind me to hate you when this is all over."

* * *

"Grisom?"

This time when the guard called her name Darby was in the sunroom trying to blend in with the furniture. It had been an eventful day. As excited as she was by the prospect of having Mia with her again, she couldn't celebrate in her current surroundings. Not when the yellow alarm lights kept dropping from the ceiling. She learned quickly that that meant stop what you're doing and stand with your face looking straight ahead and your hands flat against the cement wall. In a matter of seconds, a small contingent of officers would enter the locked facility, tasers drawn.

One particular crisis concerned a young man who wanted to use the telephone during non-telephone hours. When informed he'd have to wait until after dinner, he attempted to rip the phone from the wall. He was yelling and cursing and as soon as he saw the guards, his level of irritation seemed to increase tenfold.

The inmate's cursing was creative and loud. The guards gave him one chance to stop banging the industrial-strength metal receiver. When he failed to comply, he was tasered. After wetting himself, he fell to the floor, writhing and yelling "Okay! Okay!"

He was placed in zip ties and the guards took him to the segregation cell, the one the regulars called a punishment cell. Darby hadn't ever seen one, but she'd heard about them during the first half of her court-ordered stay. Apparently it was padded and the inmate was made to strip, then a dress-like garment was velcroed on and the inmate was left in there until medical arrived to make sure the tasering hadn't caused any permanent damage. The reason for the dress was that it was made from rip-resistant fabric, just in case the inmate was suicidal.

Enough time in Green Haven and Darby was pretty sure she might become suicidal. The clock was ticking very slowly as it neared three o'clock. And still no Jack. Her anxiety level was off the charts. She kept mentally reminding herself that she could be mere hours away from reuniting with her sweet baby as the guards gave the all-clear for the patients to go on about their business.

"Grisom?"

Darby offered a weak smile to the female guard, then followed her down the corridor that led to the visiting areas. She prayed it was Jack; she didn't relish the idea of Greer or even worse, Sean, waiting for her behind the reinforced glass wall.

Only one half of her fears came true. Seated in a perfectly pressed, designer suit, Sean was over by the window. The guard practically had to shove Darby inside the room.

"What do you want?" Darby asked.

Sean tilted his head to one side. Obviously he'd taken notice of her change in tone. "No kiss for your devoted husband?"

He stood and stepped toward her and she instinctively recoiled. Sean stopped, raising his hands in mock surrender. "My hat is off to you, Darby. I never would have guessed you had it in you."

"Guessed what?" she asked, watching his every move like a trapped animal tracking its predator.

"I know you," he taunted. When she said nothing, he continued, "You don't have it in you to kill your own child. Greer told me you tanked your interview yesterday. Apparently the staff shrink didn't think you were being honest."

"That's one shrink," Darby countered. "Fran believes me, so today's appointment is the only one that matters. All I need is a majority of three doctors."

He reached for a manila envelope on the table and took out the newspaper from this morning. "Which won't happen because you are and always have been a shitty liar. You'll stand trial for Mia's murder. I'll play the role of the tortured father whose infant daughter was murdered by his jealous wife in retaliation for his affair."

Darby felt a tight knot in her stomach.

"When I finish, everyone within the sound of my voice will want your head on a pike. Read the paper, Darby. Everyone hates a baby killer."

"They hate wife beaters, too."

Sean made a *tsk* sound with his mouth as he shook his head from side to side. "Like you'll ever be able to prove that. Greer doesn't think you have a chance in hell, so, I hired another attorney and this requires your signature." He handed the manila envelope over to her.

Sighing in disgust, Darby pulled the pages out and began to read. She flipped to the second page and by the third paragraph, she was seething. "You have to be kidding me."

"I'm just going with the story you're telling. Just sign the papers and we'll be divorced in a month or two."

"I'm fine with that," she said in clipped tones. "But you're nuts if you think I'm going to give you one-point-three million dollars. And if you're so sure I didn't kill Mia, why aren't you asking for custody?"

"You can afford the money and if I asked for custody I'd be admitting that she's still alive," Sean countered. "Either agree to my terms or I'll become the state of Florida's primo witness when they charge you with first degree murder."

"Go screw yourself," she said as she turned and pounded on the door. "Guard!"

CHAPTER ELEVEN

Is there a problem?" the guard asked as she eyed both of them.

"I'd like to return to the pod," Darby said.

"Don't forget these," Sean said, slapping the envelope and the newspaper against her midsection.

Her hands were shaking and she was drowning in her own fury. Once she'd returned to the day room, she fell into a chair and stuffed the newspaper inside the envelope and tortured herself by reading the Petition for Dissolution of Marriage from cover to cover. Sean's greed knew no bounds.

Not only did he want the cash, he wanted the house, his car, and the beachfront cottage Darby owned in the Bahamas. She'd bought that little getaway long before marrying Sean. But something was bugging her. "Why?" she wondered aloud. "No mention of the baby? If Sean really believed the baby was alive, he would be making a play for her." That was Sean. Everything, including people, belonged to him and she'd never seen him walk away from anything in the time they'd been together.

Especially his own flesh and blood. She was missing something.

"Grisom?"

Darby looked up and then followed the guard back to the visiting area. Much to her relief, Jack was waiting for her. He was pacing in the small room and Darby was instantly on the alert.

"Hi," he greeted her.

"Hi," she returned as she rolled the envelope and the newspaper into a twist. "Sean was just here."

Jack took her hand and led her to the table. They sat next to one another. His dark eyes scanned her face and she wondered what she must look like. The only grooming products she'd been given were a bottle of harsh shampoo and a small, black barber's comb. She was suddenly keenly aware of her appearance. Most of the fury she had clenched in her stomach evaporated, replaced by silly, girlish thoughts of her appearance—or more accurately, what Jack must think of her appearance. It didn't help that he was looking at her with those intense eyes.

"What did he want?" Jack asked.

"This." She handed him the now-crumpled petition, then placed the newspaper with her mugshot on the front page inside the envelope. "He's up to something," Darby insisted.

"This could be your ticket out of here," Jack said. "All you have to do is confess to the hoax and produce the baby. You might get fined for filing a false police report, but other than that…Can you afford the terms he's asking for in the divorce?"

"I can afford it, but I don't think Sean has any intention of just walking away from me or his daughter. He doesn't walk away from fights. He has to win. It's coded in his DNA."

Jack sighed. "Are you willing to give him what he's asking for?"

"To get my daughter back?" she scoffed. "I'd give him everything. But Sean never does anything that isn't to Sean's gain. And he wouldn't walk away from his daughter. Not when he can use her to make my life miserable. I honestly think I could give him everything on his list and the first time he had the opportunity, he'd take her and run."

"Because?"

"Because he'd never turn down an opportunity to hurt me. If you could have seen the hatred in his eyes when he was here…"

"He can't hurt you in here."

Darby raked her fingers through her hair. "But he would if he could," she insisted. "That's why I don't think I can take those divorce papers at face value. He's planning something."

"Well, for now, let's focus on this." He reached into his briefcase and took out a sheet of paper. "Sign the substitution of counsel form right here and I'll run over to the courthouse and get it signed by the judge, then I'll meet you back here with the stuff you were wearing when you were arrested."

Darby smiled and tears welled in her eyes. "Please hurry. I want my baby back."

True to his word, Darby was summoned to visiting area again in just over thirty minutes. Jack's brow was damp, probably from racing around in the Florida heat. But it was the look in his eyes that caused an instant rock to form in her gut. "What?"

"Your attorney already picked up your belongings."

"What? How?" Her heart sunk to her feet.

"Did you sign a request for Greer?"

Darby pressed her fingers to her forehead. "He had me sign a whole bunch of things before court the day before yesterday. I don't specifically recall that form, but I wasn't exactly at my best." She stood and slapped the envelope against the desk. "Damn it! Something is really wrong, Jack. Greer didn't say a word to me yesterday about taking my things out of police custody. Can he even do that? I mean, aren't my clothes or the disposable phone evidence or something?"

"He probably did the same thig I did, which was to ask a magistrate to take judicial notice of the items, then release them to the defense for private testing and investigation. In your confession you said you'd been wearing something else when you killed your daughter, and those items are in state custody pending testing since you told them there might be some blood on the top." Jack was now pacing as well. "All I got was this," he reached into his briefcase and pulled out a flimsy half-page document.

She scanned the copy of the list they'd had her sign when she turned her belongings over to the police while she was being booked. "I need that phone to find Lyssa," Darby said as tears streamed down her cheeks.

Jack reached out and brushed them aside with the pads of his thumbs. "Don't panic just yet," he said. "Did you buy them with cash or a credit card?"

"I used my business American Express. Why?"

Jack smiled as his finger looped under her chin. "Then we might not need the actual phone to find her."

He checked his watch and in doing so, lowered his hand so

that he was no longer touching her. Darby wanted to grab it back. Somehow the human touch was comforting to the panic knotting her gut.

"Let me make a call."

"To who?"

"The state's attorney," he said as he took out his cell. "Is he in? Jack Kavanaugh calling. It's important." There was a brief silence, then Jack asked, "Matt, I need you to come to Green Haven. I want you to sit in on the psych session with Darby Grisom." Jack was quiet while the state's attorney responded.

"Greer is about to be fired and I promise you, you'll want to hear this Besides, Green Haven is a five minute drive for you." There was another short pause on their end. "Thanks. I owe you."

No sooner did Jack end the call than Greer was standing at the door, waiting for the guard to open the lock. He seemed uninterested in Darby but very interested in Jack.

"Kavanaugh, right?" He extended his hand.

Darby wasn't in the mood for niceties. "Where are my things?" she demanded. "The stuff you signed out of the property room?"

Greer seemed taken aback. "Sean said your act was all a front," Greer said. "I guess a few days in here has cured you of your depression?"

"Let's take a second," Jack inserted. "Mrs. Grisom and I have a previous relationship and she's decided to have me represent her in this matter. So, your services will no longer be needed but I will need the items you took."

"Good luck," Greer said. "Right now she's probably the

most hated woman in the county." He turned to Darby. "I think some sort of diminished capacity is your only hope but your behavior yesterday and today is going to make that difficult. I know Fran believes your postpartum psychosis is why you killed your baby but the doctor who interviewed you yesterday found you evasive and less than honest." He turned back to Jack. "My office will send over my files."

"And my items," Darby added.

"I gave those to Sean," he said.

Darby's knees nearly buckled. "Why would you give my things to him when I'm your client?"

"He said he was going to take the dress to the cleaners for your court appointment tomorrow."

"Jesus Christ," Darby muttered. "You have no idea what you've done." Greer looked at her with a bland expression, which only piled fuel on her fiery anger. "Just go. I can't look at you anymore."

Greer walked out of the room without so much as a backward glance.

"Now what?" Darby said with a hitch of emotion in her throat. "I knew Sean was up to something."

"Will Lyssa talk to him if he calls her?"

Darby shook her head.

"Grisom?" the guard opened the door. "Time for your session."

"What do I do?" she asked Jack.

"Just be honest."

Darby was struggling to keep from crying as she and Jack were taken to a conference room. Unlike the interview room from the day before, this was a larger room and it was already half full. Fran was there and she offered a compassionate smile. Matt Johnson, the state's attorney, was there, and seated next to him was a stenographer. There was also a heavyset man with a bad combover she assumed was the third psychiatrist she was supposed to convince she wasn't crazy. He introduced himself as Dr. Rawlings, then everyone went around the room for the benefit of the stenographer and identified themselves for the record.

Jack stood and said, "Thank you all for coming, but the reason for this session has changed. Mrs. Grisom is going to tell you a story. Her story. Darby?"

She remained seated. "Where do I start?"

"With your marriage," Jack advised.

She couldn't look anyone in the eye, so she focused on the design of the wood grain on the tabletop, tracing it with her fingertip as she spoke. "I met and married my husband in six weeks. At first, he was the perfect husband. Kind, considerate, fun. But by the second week of our marriage a different side started to show. Sean got very possessive of my time. He even resented the time I spent walking my dog. I was very close to my parents but he somehow managed to isolate me from them as well as my other friends." Having to talk about this now made Darby truly realize how calculating Sean had been, but at the beginning it had felt like he was just too in love with her to be apart for any length of time. She felt like a fool for not seeing it sooner.

"The first incident was when I came home from work and found my dog dead in the garage. There was anti-freeze on the floor. Sean insisted it was just a fluke accident, that one of the cars must have leaked. I think I believed that because I wanted to. Or rather I didn't want to think the alternative was possible.

"I'm a veterinarian but I also have family money and shortly after my dog died, Sean came to me with the idea of opening a restaurant. He's worked in fine dining his whole adult life, and he was my husband. I fronted the cash and he took over an existing space and opened the Tilefish Grille in less than three months.

"Sean became very quick to anger after that. I assumed it was because I worked days and he worked nights and we weren't spending enough time together. So we worked out a plan where he would come home for dinner each night, then go back to the restaurant. The first night I accidently burned the rolls and that was the first time he shoved me." Darby hated saying all this to virtual strangers and she especially hated admitting it in front of Jack. Darby wondered how long she'd feel guilty for being so blind and stupid.

"Did you call the police?" the state's attorney asked.

Darby shook her head. "I was embarrassed and I knew he was under a lot of pressure to get the restaurant going so I let it go. Even though he promised it would never happen again, it did. And it escalated. I was terrified of my husband. And then I got pregnant. At first I was excited and I hoped the baby would bring us together as a family."

"Did it?" Fran asked.

"For a few days. No slaps, no choking me over some perceived slight. I knew he was cheating with another woman but by that point, I didn't really care. Then two months ago I broke one of his cardinal rules. I burned something on the stove and when he came home, he caught me off guard and beat me. I was eight months pregnant and cowering on the floor and he was throwing plates and food and kicking me and I was terrified for my baby. As soon as Sean went back to the restaurant, I called my parents and told them everything that was going on." She closed her eyes and tears ran down her cheeks. "If only I would have taken them up on their offer to come over immediately. If I would have gone there, they would still be alive."

"Are you claiming your husband killed your parents?" the state's attorney asked.

"I know he did. He taunted me with it. I can't even count how many times after that that he threatened to kill me and the baby. I felt trapped. So I came up with an idea."

"I think this is where I come in," Fran acknowledged.

Darby lifted her eyes and looked at her doctor. "I'm sorry. I went on the computer and learned all about postpartum depression. Then I regurgitated what I'd learned to you. I didn't have any options."

"You could have gotten a restraining order," the state's attorney interjected.

"Sean would have ignored that and it would have made things worse. The last time I reached out for help he killed my parents."

The state's attorney shuffled through some papers. "Their deaths were ruled accidental."

Darby felt a small resurgence of her anger. "I know my father did not leave his car on in the garage."

The state's attorney pressed, "It happens with those new push-button ignitions."

"And my father knew that. There was a post-it note by the alarm pad to remind him."

"But the alarm never went off that night."

"Because Sean knew the codes. The one for the side door and the one to kill the alarm from inside the garage. My parents never, and I mean *never*, went to bed without setting the alarm."

The state's attorney seemed unimpressed. "Did you tell all this to the responding officers?"

"Yes. They dismissed me as some hormonal nut job and sent me home with my husband who choked me into unconsciousness as soon as we were in the door. With all due respect, Mr. Johnson, the police were useless."

"So, you…?"

"I just wanted my baby to be safe. And the only way I knew she would be safe was to send her away."

"Away where?"

Jack reached out and touched her forearm. "That's a bit of a problem. She gave the baby to one of her clients and they were supposed to stay in touch via drop phones. However, previous counsel gave the cell phone to Mr. Grisom yesterday."

"And today he came by and dropped these in my lap," Darby said, taking the divorce papers out of the envelope. "He basically told me that if I didn't give him what he wants, he'll somehow make up some story to make it look like I really did kill Mia."

Dr. Rawlings said, "Without commenting on your guilt or innocence, Mrs. Grisom, I can tell you right now that I'm not seeing any signs of any underlying pathology. Doctor?" he looked at Fran.

"While I may not see postpartum psychosis after listening to her story, I personally saw choke marks on Mrs. Grisom at one of our sessions, which leads me to believe she very well could have acted out of a genuine fear for herself and/or her daughter."

"Which is not a defense," the state's attorney said. "Jack? Got a minute?"

As Jack stood, he noticed Darby had almost twisted the divorce papers and the newspaper into a knot. Hopefully her truthful recitation of the facts would earn her some points with the state's attorney.

He followed Matt out into the hallway. At first, Matt just looked at him, his expression impossible to read. "Is this for real?"

Jack nodded. "I met her when she was pregnant. She had me draw up a new Trust for her, making Lyssa Chandler the Alternate Trustee."

"Since when do you do Trusts?" Matt asked.

Jack shrugged.

"Oh please," Matt said on an accusatory breath. "You let the fact that she's hot influence you?"

"She's also rich," Jack said with a straight face. "Okay. I was going to do the Trust for her because she was hot and rich but then I saw the bruises. You know how that kind of thing makes me crazy."

Matt's expression immediately grew serious. "You can't change what happened fifteen years ago."

"I know." Jack brushed his hair off his forehead. "Listen, the bottom line is the baby isn't dead and Darby only did what she did to protect her daughter."

"Except you can't produce the daughter, right?"

"Give me twenty-four hours," Jack pleaded.

Matt shrugged. "I'll give you months," he said.

Jack was elated, then he read the blank expression on Matt's face as he said, "Tomorrow morning I'm charging her with second-degree murder."

CHAPTER TWELVE

Darby felt a little more like herself as she stepped into the court room in real clothes. Thanks to Peggy, she was wearing a floral lace sheath dress and nude heeled sandals. Her hair was caught up in a clip and she had on a touch of blush and a little mascara.

She'd been on pins and needles ever since Jack had brought her the clothes and then went over what would happen. Unfortunately, he didn't think it would be a cakewalk to get the judge to intervene. Not in a case this high profile.

And just how high profile it was was instantly apparent as she was led into the court room. The gallery was filled. She recognized a few of the local reporters, and Peggy was there in the second row. She smiled and gave Darby a discreet thumbs up. Sean was nowhere to be found. Darby didn't know if that was good or bad.

She joined Jack at the defendant's table. "Is it always like this?" she whispered.

"Word has already leaked out that something noteworthy will happen here today. Probably a move by Matt to help him run for office next Fall."

"How do you know so much about him?" Darby asked.

"I worked for him for ten years."

Darby's stomach clenched. "Please tell me you parted on good terms?"

Jack patted the small of her back. "I'll be happy to tell you that."

"Thank you for arranging for the clothes."

"You're welcome, except it wasn't my doing. Peggy was here on the courthouse steps when I arrived."

Darby turned around and mouthed 'thank you.' She didn't have an opportunity to see her friend's response because the clerk announced the arrival of the judge.

It was the same judge who had presided over her first hearing. He didn't make eye contact with Darby but instead he looked at Matt.

The prosecutor buttoned his jacket as he stood. "State versus Darby Hayes Grisom."

"And Mr. Kavanaugh?" the judge asked. "I see I have a motion here for replacement counsel?"

"Yes, sir."

"Fine then, let's get through this stack of motions. Mr. Johnson?"

"The State wishes to amend the charge to murder in the second degree."

"Mr. Kavanaugh, how does your client plead?"

"If I may, Your Honor," Jack said as he rose. "I provided the court with a transcript of a meeting yesterday attended by two psychiatrists and the state's attorney. Based on that meeting, I have asked that all charges be dismissed as no crime has been committed by my client."

"Mr. Johnson?"

"The State is sensitive to the defendant's situation. However, we have been unable to locate the person whom the defendant claims has custody of the infant. Further, we have a notarized statement from the defendant's husband swearing his belief that his wife is and was fully capable of murdering their minor child."

"Prick," Darby muttered under her breath.

"Further," the prosecutor said, "we have preliminary lab results indicating that the baby's blood was on the defendant's clothing. The same clothing she was wearing as she was seen on videotape carrying a bundle to the canal behind the convenience store."

"Thanks for the case preview," Jack said as he braced his fingertips on the top of the scarred table.

"Mr. Kavanaugh, please direct your remarks to the bench."

"I'm sorry, Your Honor. My client explained in graphic detail all of the things she did to make it appear as if she hurt her daughter but the truth of the matter is there is no body and no one saw the defendant do anything harmful to her child. This case actually boils down to a horribly abused woman doing something drastic to protect her child."

"The child she can't produce?" the judge asked.

Darby didn't like her chances. She had a sense of foreboding that made her stomach drop to the floor. She could produce Mia if she could get the drop phone back from Sean. But something told her Sean had already guessed the importance of the phone and had dropped it into the ocean.

Jack went through the elaborate steps Darby had taken to make her plan work. The judge seemed to be listening intently. At times he even leaned forward, which Darby assumed was a sign that he was finally coming around.

She was wrong.

"Motion denied, Mr. Kavanaugh. How does your client plead?"

"Not guilty."

"Fine." The judge checked something on his desk. "Bail?"

The prosecutor leapt to his feet. "No bail, Your Honor. The State believes Mrs. Grisom is a danger to society."

"Mrs. Grisom hasn't even so much as had a traffic ticket," Jack argued. "She's a veteran who served two tours in Iraq. She owns her own business and also oversees Hayes Groves in Palm City. She has deep ties to the community and no reason to be considered a flight risk."

"No reason?" the prosecutor mocked. "Look at the amount of planning that went into the crime."

"A crime you wouldn't have known about if she hadn't confessed. And she only did that because she's terrified of her husband. She would rather be in jail than suffer another beating."

"Gentlemen," the judge interrupted in one terse word. "This is neither the time nor the place to try your case. Mr. Johnson, I want a number."

"You're granting her bail?" Johnson scoffed.

"Either give me a number or I'll come up with one I don't think you'll like."

The prosecutor sighed, then dropped his head, then lifted it and calmly said, "One million dollars. Cash. No Bond."

"That's a ridiculous amount," Jack insisted.

Darby's heart was pounding in her ears. She reached over and closed her hand over Jack's and gave it a squeeze.

"Fine," Jack amended.

The judge raised his gavel. "One million cash no bond—"

"And she surrenders her passport to the court," the prosecutor said.

"And she surrenders her passport," the judge finished, then pounded his gavel.

Darby was so excited she slipped her arms around Jack's neck and pulled him close. His cologne was subtle but kind of woodsy. She could feel the outline of his body. He was definitely in shape, but not one of those freaky muscle-bound guys she didn't find attractive. Which meant she did find Jack attractive. That little realization had her leap back from him. The last time she had acted upon attraction she'd ended up married to a sadist.

Jack was looking at her with a touch of confusion. "I-I'm sorry. I just can't believe I can get out of here."

"I can't either," he admitted with a very sexy half-smile that Darby felt all the way down to her toes.

Get a grip! "Can we do something legal that will allow you to access my money market account?"

"Not a problem."

"What do I do until you pay my bail?"

"Unfortunately, you go back to jail."

"Then let's be quick."

* * *

Darby thought sitting in a jail cell with nothing but the divorce papers and a newspaper to read for four hours would be unpleasant but it was nothing compared to the gaggle of press who descended on her as she left the courthouse.

"Is the baby dead?"

"Who has the baby?"

"Why won't you tell police where to find the baby?"

"Where is your husband?"

Darby was so happy when Jack put her inside his car and the two of them drove away from the small courthouse just a few blocks from his office.

"Will you take me home?" she asked.

"Not a problem. Sean was served with an Order of Protection a few hours ago. He can't come within 500 yards of your place. But," Jack hesitated.

"What?"

"There may be press there," he warned.

"It's a gated community. You have to know the code or the guard or you can't get in."

They arrived in twenty minutes and as predicted, there was a small contingent of reporters on the curb across from the entrance to her community. Her neighbors were going to love her. Who was she kidding? Her neighbors were probably already asking the HOA if there was a way to get her out of the neighborhood. It wouldn't matter. The only reason she wanted to go home was to shower, wash her hair, and get to work finding Lyssa.

Darby got out and used the keypad on the garage door to open it. Jack was at her side just in case Sean was defying the Order and was inside. His car was gone. Her car was where she'd left it on the day of her arrest, only now it was covered in fingerprint dust and several sections of carpet and seat cushions had been cut out. "What a mess."

The door leading into the house was open, which was normal. What wasn't normal was the disarray. "Do they always trash a house like this?" she asked.

"Yes."

She put the cushions back on the sofas as she made her way to the back of the house. She paused when she got to Mia's room. It had been violated in the search. A lot of her little things had been tossed to the carpet. The crib was empty and it drew her inside the room. On automatic pilot, she replaced the fitted sheet on the mattress and re-tied the bumpers. The room smelled like Mia. Darby started to cry—softly at first, then gut-wrenching sobs rocked her whole body as she slid down to the floor.

Jack gently picked her up and helped her into her bedroom. He sat her on the bed then knelt in front of her. He wiped her tears away. She could feel his breath on her face and that was oddly soothing. Darby shuddered a couple of times, then managed to regain her composure. "I'm sorry."

"Don't be. I'm impressed that you manage to keep it together as well as you do."

"I've had a lot of practice pretending everything is fine and dandy." Darby lowered her eyes and again wondered how she could have allowed Sean to steal her life from her. It was both sad and maddening. He had alienated her friends and family from her, and for some unknown reason she had allowed it to happen. And now it had cost her her daughter. Her heart literally ached in her chest.

He met and held her gaze. "You don't have to do that with me."

Without really thinking about it, Darby reached out and pushed the dark hair off his forehead. The action, or rather her reaction to touching him, filled her with confusion. How on earth could she be in the middle of the worst crisis of her life and yet still have such an awareness of a man who was a virtual stranger?

"Tell me something about you," Darby asked.

"Like what?"

"Ever married?"

He shook his head. "Nope. But I have had the same dog for almost eight years. So I'm loyal."

She laughed. "What kind of dog?"

"Mutt. I like to run along Stuart beach in the morning. So one morning this mutt comes out of the dunes and follows me. Then he did the same thing for two more mornings, so I decided to take him home. He was in pretty bad shape. But he's a good dog."

"What's his name?"

"Dog."

"That's original."

"That's what I called him on those mornings on the beach, so it kinda stuck. Before I forget, my brother is on his way over here."

"Why?"

"He's going to keep an eye on you in case Sean happens to show up."

"What about you?"

He chuckled. "Trust me, when you have a chance to see Declan and me next to each other, you'll pick Declan every day. I've got a couple of errands to run and then I'll bring back dinner. Any preferences?"

"There's a decent Greek place right around the corner." She struggled to keep the disappointment out of her voice. "I'm going to take a shower," Darby said. "I need to wash the incarceration off me."

"I'll be in the kitchen," he said as he stood.

Darby was alone in her master bath. It felt as if it had been a lifetime since she was alone. No guards, no inmates, no patients. No daughter.

She stripped off her dress, stepped into the shower and had a good cry. Then she washed her hair and scrubbed her body raw with the loofah before stepping from the shower and wrapping herself in one towel and making a turban out of another. Her first instinct was to stand on the bath mat until she was dry. Sean hated a wet floor. Then she shook it off and promised herself Sean could rot in hell. She didn't have to fear his wrath or to adhere to his strict standards around the house. The first inklings of freedom started to replace the eighteen months of violent outbursts.

She dried her hair and pulled on some yoga pants and a top and went back to the kitchen. Jack wasn't alone. He was standing next to a tall, dark, intimidating man with barrels for arms and thighs that looked as if they'd split his jeans with very little effort.

"Declan, this is Darby."

"Ma'am," he said as he offered a beefy hand.

"Darby," she corrected. Then she glanced over at Jack, who was smiling. "I see your point," she acknowledged. "Thank you for coming over to babysit."

Now Declan smiled, making him seem far less intimidating. "He's paying me."

"Technically," Jack said, "*she's* paying you."

"In all seriousness," Darby said, "my husband is a very dangerous man."

Declan reached behind himself and pulled out two Glocks. "I've also got a knife strapped to my ankle. Is he Iron Man?"

She shook her head. "The authorities took all of my guns," Darby said. "Or Sean took them. Who knows?"

The phone rang and Darby's heart leapt in her chest. She grabbed it off the hook before the first ring ended. "Hello?"

"Hi, it's Peggy."

"Hi. And before I forget, thank you for the clothes."

"It was the least I could do. Listen, may I come over?"

"Sure. We're going to have dinner in about an hour," she looked to Jack for confirmation. "Why don't you join us?"

"I'd rather just talk to you."

"Sorry, my friend, but so long as Sean is in the wind, I have a keeper. Besides, it's my attorney and my private detective who doubles as my personal assassin."

"I guess I don't have a choice, huh?"

"Nope."

"See you in an hour."

Jack left as soon as she got off the phone. Declan got busy helping her put things back in their places. She realized he wasn't much of a talker. "Tell me about Jack. Is he a good attorney?"

"Yep."

"Are you older or younger?"

"Older."

"Married?"

"No."

"Kids?"

"No."

"Pets?"

"No."

"Hey, Declan? You're making me work really hard here. I've just spent three days locked up in virtual solitude, so talk to me."

"What's your deal with Jack?"

"Deal?"

"I don't want to see him hurt."

Darby was astonished. "Hurt? How could I possibly hurt him? My priority is finding my daughter. Period." She crossed her arms in front of her. "Yes, I'm grateful to Jack for all he's done so far, but it's not like I'm taking advantage of him. I'm paying him."

Declan shrugged. "Yeah, I got pretty much the same answer from him."

"Then why would you even ask?"

"He's my kid brother and I know him. I know when he's in over his head."

"You don't think he can help me find Mia?"

Declan shook his head. "Just the opposite. I think he'll move hell and high water to help you find your daughter. So will I."

"But you think I'm somehow scamming him? You think I'll stiff him on the bill or something?"

"Nope. I think you're in the middle of a shit storm and Jack is in it with you. You remind him of someone he loved dearly, our mother. Good old Dad used to beat her all the time. Then fifteen years ago, our oldest brother, Michael, intervened and there was a shooting. Mike was arrested and convicted of first degree manslaughter. That's the whole reason Jack went to law school. He wanted to find a way to get Michael out of prison. So, I don't think he's doing it for the money. I think he's falling for you fast. I just can't tell whether it's you or the memory of our mother that has him so intrigued."

"Th-that's crazy," Darby argued. "And it's wrong. Jack and I have a professional relationship. I'm not stupid, Declan. The last time I leapt into a relationship I ended up getting the crap beat out of me on a regular basis. I'm still married, by the way."

"Not in any real way that counts," Declan said. Then he let out a low sigh. "Look, I'm sorry for sounding accusatory; I'm not. It's just that he's my brother and I see the way he watches you when you aren't looking. I don't want to see him hurt again."

"You don't have to worry."

"I won't," Declan said. "So where do you think Sean has gone?"

"Hand me the phone and I'll call the restaurant."

Darby pressed the numbers, then listened as the machine

picked up. She glanced up at the clock. It should be the middle of the dinner rush. "That's weird. No one is there." She felt a pang of fear in her gut. "Do you think he's around here?"

Declan shook his head. "Too hot. He'd have to get past the guard house and the reporters in order to get here."

"He could walk in," Darby offered, then quickly changed her mind. "No, he'd never do that. He's terrified of snakes and creepy crawlers. He'd need a handful of Xanax to walk through a Florida wetland without me at his side."

"What are you, a snake whisperer?"

She shook her head. "No, but I'm a great shot and if I can see it I can kill it."

"Where did a fancy lady like you learn to shoot?"

"The United States Army."

Declan, like many before him, looked at her with shock in his eyes. "I thought you came from money."

"I do, but every generation of my family has volunteered for duty dating back to the Revolutionary War. I would have been a great asset if they hadn't had a ban on women in combat when I was on active duty."

"Did they have you in the mess?" Declan asked.

"I trained dogs to search for IEDs."

"Like it?"

"Yeah. They have some amazing animals in the program."

"Why don't you have any pets?" Declan asked. "I would guess a veterinarian would have a whole houseful of critters."

She shared the story of the untimely demise of her dog. "Sean didn't like anything that took me away from him."

"If you're such a good shot, why didn't you just shoot him?"

Darby contemplated the question for a few minutes. "I…because I was embarrassed. Here I was on the ugly side of thirty. I'd done my two tours. Gone to vet school. Established my own business. I just couldn't dream of letting anyone know what was really going on. I knew Sean was cheating on me from the time we came back from our honeymoon. It reached a point where I didn't care. Even when he wouldn't come home at night. I was actually happy when that happened. Then I had to think about my daughter. I didn't want her to end up in foster care because Dad was dead and Mom was in prison. I'm not one hundred percent sure I could kill another human being. But mostly, if I shot him, I'd be just like him. I don't know. I guess I just couldn't bring myself to admit that I was such a fool."

"Why are you a fool?" Jack asked as he came through the garage door carrying an armload of takeout.

Darby shrugged. "Never mind." She watched him place the food on the kitchen table—the new one she'd had to buy after Sean had broken the glass one.

"I stopped by Big Tony's place and got these," he said as he pulled two jewel cases out of his jacket pocket. "They're the DVDs he burned off the DVR I found in your attic. Plates and utensils?"

Darby got out a service for four since she was expecting Peggy at any moment. It wasn't until she recalled replacing the items into their rightful places that a thought grabbed her. "This place should have been cleaned up."

Jack was opening Styrofoam boxes and plastic containers. "The cops are notorious for trashing a house during a search."

"But Consuela should have cleaned it all up yesterday."

Jack lifted his head. "Consuela?"

"My cleaning lady. She comes twice a week and there's no way she would have left this place like we found it." Darby grabbed the phone, dialed the number and then listened. "It's going straight to voicemail." Darby left an urgent message.

"Is that normal?" Jack asked.

"She almost always answers."

Declan asked, "Where does she live?"

Darby gave him the address.

Declan grabbed an olive and put it in his mouth, then said, "I'll go over there now. Save me some food."

Just as Declan was leaving, Peggy arrived. She came over and gave Darby a tight hug. "I'm so glad you're out of that place."

"Me too. Come sit down and have some dinner with us."

Peggy dropped her hands to her sides and squeezed her eyes closed tightly for a second. "I don't think you'll want me to eat with you when I tell you what I did."

"She slept with your husband," Jack said matter-of-factly.

Darby offered a compassionate smile. "You weren't the first or the last."

"But it gets worse."

"How?" Darby asked, bracing herself.

"Sean came to me two days ago and asked me to do something for him."

"Fake the break in at Darby's office?" Jack asked.

"Yes. But there was more."

"Did he have Mia with him?" Darby asked in a panic.

"No, but he said if I didn't help him, he'd tell you about our affair and I didn't want you to hate me—"

"I don't hate you. What did you do?"

"I opened the safe and showed him Lyssa's file. Sean handed me a phone and had me call her and pretend I was calling on your behalf. Lyssa wouldn't tell me exactly where she was, just that she was settling in."

Darby started to cry. "Think, Peggy! Did you hear anything in the background? Any voices, names, anything?"

"She mentioned that she had visited with her mother, then she seemed to get a little spooked and she practically hung up on me."

"What happened to the phone and the file?" Darby's nerves were beginning to fray. All she could think about was Mia. Was she hungry? Scared? God, her heart was squeezing her chest.

"Sean kept the file. I have the phone," she fished inside her purse and pulled out the disposable cell. "I'm so sorry, I—"

Darby was elated. Finally, a direct link to her baby. Quickly, she dialed the number. She listened to the first ring. Then three more rings, then the phone was answered.

"Hello, sweetheart."

"Sean!" she could hear the baby fussing in the background. "I'll give you whatever you want, just bring the baby home."

"I gave you that option two days ago. You weren't very polite as I recall."

"Name it, Sean. Give me a number, any amount, and we'll agree to meet for an exchange."

"I'll have to think about it. Right now I'm bonding with my daughter."

"Sean?" Darby's voice was a plea. "Don't do this. You don't really want Mia; you want me to suffer. Well, I've suffered. Bring me my baby, please?"

"Not yet, Darby. I don't hear enough remorse in your voice."

"I'm sorry," she insisted. And that was no lie. Her gut hurt, her heart was in tatters and she hated Sean at that moment like she had never hated him before. Her personal fear was abating but her fear for her child was so much more palpable. If Sean hurt a fuzz on that baby's hair, Darby silently vowed to track Sean down and blow his brains out.

Odd that two days ago she had rationalized her way out of hurting Sean yet now she was ready to mow him down without remorse. But she had to be strong and play his game. He had all the balls in his court. She'd have to make him think that she was still afraid of him to make this work.

Sean laughed. "Not very convincing. I'm not sure you even know what you should be sorry for."

"Does it matter?"

"You had no reason to turn on me."

"I'm sorry I let you down." The baby let out a strong wail. "Please, Sean?"

"Not yet, Darby. You'll get her back on my terms, not yours. Or maybe not at all."

The line went dead.

CHAPTER THIRTEEN

Darby cried for several minutes. Her tears were fueled in part by anger but mostly because of the heavy burden of knowing Sean had her daughter. "He wants to toy with me," Darby said once she'd composed herself.

"Did you get any clue as to where he might be holding the baby?"

She shook her head. "I was too distracted by hearing the baby cry in the background." Darby redialed, but her call went straight to voicemail. "He turned the phone off." She looked at Jack. "Can a throwaway phone be traced like a regular cell?"

"I'll ask Declan when he comes back."

"I'm so sorry," Peggy said. "I'll finish out the week with Carl and then—"

"That isn't necessary," Darby interrupted. "You kept the phone, so at least I got to hear Mia."

"But the affair…"

"I stopped caring about Sean's bed buddies months ago," Darby insisted. "I'm guessing you got jettisoned when Roxanne came into the picture."

"Your husband has a thing for redheads."

"Can we call him something other than my *husband*? I don't feel married."

"Speaking of which," Jack went to his briefcase and took out a half-inch-thick document. "You need to sign this and we'll file it with the court."

Darby glanced at the document, a response to his petition for divorce and a counter-claim by her of adultery. "Why am I worrying about this now? He made it very clear it was going to cost me a lot more now."

Jack reached out and patted her hand. The touch was electric and Darby wondered if Declan's assessment of Jack's feelings might be spot on. "If you ignore it for more than thirty days he'll get a default judgment, granting him everything except Mia. Your counter-claim basically says to the court that he left out some major things in his petition, namely his adultery and the minor child, and that you want sole custody of the baby."

"Can I do an affidavit or something?" Peggy asked. "I'd be happy to tell a judge about our brief affair and all the times you came into work with bruises, or makeup trying to cover your bruises. I should have come to you sooner. I thought he might be hitting you but I didn't bring it up because I was afraid if I did, Sean would tell you about the affair."

"That would be great," Jack said. "Where's your laptop?" he asked Darby.

"Police took it. Or Sean did."

"Not a problem," Jack said. "My laptop is in the car. I'll go get it."

Peggy sat down and said, "I really am sorry, Darby. I don't know how I let it happen."

Darby patted her hand. "Sean can pile on the charm."

"It started really innocently. I came out of work and was walking to the Tri-rail station in the pouring rain and then suddenly Sean appeared and offered me a ride home."

"You don't have to explain yourself to me," Darby insisted. "In fact, let's agree just to put the whole thing behind us."

Peggy's eyes welled with tears. "Thank you."

Jack returned with Declan on his heels. Jack was carrying his laptop and Declan made a beeline for the food. In between bites, Peggy and Jack crafted an affidavit for the court. Darby focused on her food and then on clearing the table, because she really didn't like hearing that her entire staff had suspected Darby was being battered but no one had known how to approach her.

Jack printed the affidavit, had her sign it, then Peggy left.

"Do you have a DVD player?" Jack asked.

"In the media room," she said. "Why?"

"I want to see what's on these discs before I attach a copy to the divorce petition."

"Follow me," Darby said as she led Jack and Declan down the hall to the media room. It wasn't a large room, but it did have two rows of stadium-style seating, a large screen and surround sound. The room darkening shades kept the space pitch black. "Give me the DVD."

After a few seconds, the screen came to life in the shape of a tic-tac-toe board. There were nine images in the boxes, covering almost every room in the house. "This was in the attic?" she asked.

"Yes," Jack said. "According to Big Tony I can select any one of the individual small screens and open it as a full screen. This is pretty advanced stuff."

"Sean does like his toys."

She reached behind her and took a throw off the back of her chair. She was seated next to Jack and right beneath the air conditioning vent, so she was cold in no time. Declan was in front of Jack, leaning forward as the disc rolled on.

The first twenty minutes or so was just Darby doing various things around the house. She was very pregnant and her recollection of what was about to happen was very vivid. So vivid that she couldn't bear to watch. "You'll have to excuse me," she said as she left the room.

Jack used the arrow buttons on the remote to select the kitchen as soon as he saw Sean come into the frame. He also turned up the volume.

Sean took off his suit coat and carefully hung it on the back of one of the chairs. "Why isn't dinner on the table?" he asked in a low voice.

"Two minutes," Darby replied.

Jack could hear the fear in her tone as she donned a pair of oven mitts and started to walk past him. She took maybe two steps before Sean backhanded her, sending her spinning to the floor. She struggled to get the mitts off her hands as Sean grabbed her by the throat and dragged her to her feet.

"How hard is it to get dinner on the table on time?" he growled. "I can't be away from the restaurant forever while you dawdle around like a moron."

"Sean! Please?" Darby was clawing at his steely grip. "You're hurting me."

He slapped her. "I haven't started hurting you yet," he threatened.

A trickle of blood fell from her quivering lip. "I'm sorry."

Sean let her go with a shove. Then he let loose with a long string of complaints and perceived slights. Jack felt his blood boiling. And naturally the memories came flooding back. "I want about five minutes alone with this jerkoff."

"Me first," Declan said. "Oh shit. Where's he taking her?"

Jack switched back to the multi-camera view. Sean was pulling Darby through the house by her hair. When he took her into the master bedroom, Jack felt his stomach clench along with his jaw. There was no camera trained on the bed but it was clear by the sounds that Sean had done the unthinkable. Darby reappeared about fifteen minutes later wearing a robe, and her right eye was already puffy and purple. Her lip was a little swollen but it was the look in her eyes that haunted him.

"That man needs a good asskicking," Declan said. "How long did she stay with this bozo?"

"A little over two years," Jack answered. "I don't think I can watch any more of it."

"I'll take over," Declan offered. "Just tell me what to do."

"Just keep a log of any scenes of violence, verbal or physical. Just note the time and date stamp." He handed him a notepad and pen. "Thanks, man."

Jack found Darby in the living room hugging a cup of coffee. "Want some?" she asked.

"That would be great. But you sit. I'm perfectly capable of getting my own."

"The phone is still turned off," she said as she waved the throwaway in the air. "Sean is probably loving this. Where's Declan?"

Jack joined her on the sofa. "He's still watching the DVD."

She appeared to wince. "How bad is it?"

Jack sat his mug on the coffee table. "Bad."

She blew out a slow breath. "I'm really embarrassed."

"You?" he asked. "Why? The guy is a total ass."

"Of course. Can you imagine that kind of abuse going on and there's no one you can turn to? Then you finally get up the nerve and it results in having your parents murdered. Especially when your abusive husband can charm the white off rice. Ask anyone, Jack, they'll tell you Sean is a wonderful man. So devoted to his wife. We put up a good front. I don't know why he did, but I did it because I was humiliated."

"Why?"

"I picked him. I brought him into my life. Forget what he did to me; I got my parents killed and now my daughter is God knows where. Helpless."

He reached out and tucked a lock of her hair behind her ear. "I know a little something about your situation and what I know is one hundred percent of the blame is on Sean."

"You've had a client like me before?"

He shook his head, then his expression grew serious. "My father was a lot like Sean," he admitted. "My mother had five sons and she did everything possible to shield us from his violence."

"I'm sorry," Darby said.

"It got worse and worse until my oldest brother, Michael, stepped in."

"That was brave of him."

"He wasn't going to let my mother take another beating."

"What did he do?"

"The next time my father got drunk and in a rage, Mike went for the shotgun. The two of them struggled and the gun went off." Jack stopped for a moment to collect himself. "Several of us went running into the living room, expecting Mike or Dad to be dead on the floor."

"But?"

"In a cruel twist the shotgun blast hit my mother, who was trying to separate the two of them, in the chest. She died instantly."

"I'm so sorry," Darby said. She reached out and patted his hand. "That must have been horrible for your family."

"It got worse."

"How?"

"Mike ended up with the gun and he shot our father."

"That's terrible."

"He just reacted, but the courts didn't see it that way."

"What do you mean?"

"He was tried and convicted of first degree manslaughter for the murders and was sentenced to fifteen to life. He's been inside for sixteen years now."

"Is that why you became a lawyer?"

Jack nodded. "I thought I could pass the bar and miraculously get his conviction overturned in a week. So far, nothing I've tried has worked."

"I'm sure he knows you're trying."

There was a long moment of silence and Jack felt a certain tension straining between them. Without analyzing it too much, he reached out and cupped Darby's cheek in his palm. He ran his thumb along her jawline as his eyes fixed on her slightly parted lips. He felt her warm breath on the back of his hand and he watched mesmerized as her breathing became erratic. He scooted a little closer and wrapped one arm around her slender shoulders as he continued to explore the soft lines of her face.

His own heart was pounding in his ears as he reached up and gently clasped her neck, urging her closer. Dipping his head, he took a slow, almost cautious approach to the kiss. Her lips were soft and pliant. Her palms flattened against his chest and for a second he was afraid she would push him away. Instead, she took fistfuls of his shirt and pulled him to her.

She tasted of coffee and her small hands began to explore the contours of his body. First his chest, then she ran her palms along his sides and he let out a low groan as she trailed her fingers along his spine. Jack needed no encouragement, he deepened the kiss and did a little exploring of his own. Her hair was silky and he ran his fingers through it as he worked his way down to her waist. She made this little noise that thrilled him as he slipped one finger beneath the hem of her shirt. Her skin was hot and smooth and after making a few tentative motions with his fingers, he slipped his entire hand up the back of her top.

"'Scuse me," Declan said after loudly clearing his throat.

Darby and Jack separated like two teenagers caught by their parents with the lights off. Darby felt abandoned and cheated as she willed her heart rate back to normal. Nervously, she raked her hair into place and gave her top a little tug.

"Yeah?" Jack replied in a voice that didn't betray a single lingering second of what had just transpired.

"Disc," he said, holding up one hand, then, "notations," as he held up the notepad.

"Put them with the divorce stuff over by my briefcase."

He did, passing a red-faced Darby on his way. "Declan, is there any way to trace the throwaway phone like you can track a regular cell?"

"If you have the codes, yes."

"How do you get the codes?" Darby asked.

"Off the receipt. How did you pay for them?"

"My business Amex."

"Can you get a copy of the receipt?"

"Let me call the help desk," Darby said. She went to the kitchen and got her credit card out of her purse, then dialed the number off the back of the card. She was placed on hold and so she leaned against the counter waiting for the next available representative and listening to really bad music. Her eyes fixed on the items on her counter. A divorce pile, Jack's briefcase and laptop. The mangled envelope Sean had given her just two days earlier. Still waiting, she pulled out the newspaper and tortured herself with the picture of her arrest splashed on the front page. God, had this plan gone horribly wrong. She flipped open the paper, torturing herself with the story, but there was a problem.

"Hey, Jack?"

"Yes?"

"Come look at this," she said as she smoothed the page.

"What?" he asked as he came up behind her.

"This," she began as she flipped back to the front page, "is the front page of the *Palm Beach Post* but the interior pages are the *Charleston Post and Courier*."

"Does that mean anything to you?" he asked.

"Consuela's oldest daughter lives in South Carolina. The younger one is in Stuart."

"Your housekeeper?"

"Yes. Do you know how to get in touch with her?"

Darby shook her head. "All I know is her first name is Maria. She's married and has a couple of children."

"What was her maiden name?" Declan asked.

Darby answered, "Ruiz."

"Let's go to my office and I'll see if I can track her on any of my databases."

"Do I stay on the line with American Express?"

"Yes," Jack said. "Get the transaction information, preferably a faxed receipt, and we'll work out of Declan's place tonight."

"Give me the fax number," Darby said.

Jack wrote it on the top of the newspaper's banner.

Declan and Jack were talking in a quiet whisper as Darby took care of handling the receipt for her purchase. She felt buoyed for the first time in days. If she could find Consuela, maybe she might know where Sean had the baby. And what about Lyssa? Darby felt a terrible lump in her throat. If Sean had the baby and the phone, what had he done to Lyssa? Darby was terrified to even think of the possibilities and her own responsibility. It was like her parents all over again. Had she involved someone and gotten them killed, too?

"Are we ready to head out?" Jack asked.

"Give me five minutes to change," Darby said.

True to her word, she switched to a pair of capris and a top in a matter of minutes. She sat in the back of Declan's SUV. Well, she wasn't sitting so much as she was crouched behind the front seats in case the press was still outside the gate.

"Can we swing by the restaurant to see if Sean left any clues as to where he might be?" Darby asked.

"I thought you said it was closed."

"It is, but I have a key and the alarm code. And if you want to get super technical, I own the place." Darby explained to Declan.

"Then let's have a look around," Declan agreed.

The restaurant was dark when they arrived. Even the outdoor sign was off. Darby used her key and killed the alarm, then switched on the lights. The place was eerily empty. Normally the tables were set for the next business day but now they were bare.

"Follow me," she said. With both men on her heels, she went through the deserted kitchen to Sean's office. The door was locked. Darby didn't have a key. "Damn it."

"Move away," Declan said.

He reared back and kicked the door right near the lock and

it splintered, then slammed open. They were immediately assaulted by a foul odor.

Declan let out a muffled curse. Darby peered around him and found herself staring into the lifeless eyes of Consuela.

CHAPTER FOURTEEN

An hour later, Darcy found herself in an interview room at the Martin County Sheriff's Department. She rubbed her exposed arms against the chill in the room and wondered how much longer she was going to have to wait.

The scent of stale coffee was strong but she would have loved a cup to ward off the chill. Florida was nothing if not air conditioned.

A female deputy opened the door. As if reading Darby's mind, she was balancing two paper cups of coffee on her binder. "I'm Detective Melody Younger," she introduced herself as she placed one of the cups in Darby's direction. "Cream or sugar?"

"No, thank you. Where is Jack?" she asked.

"Mr. Kavanaugh is being interviewed by another deputy."

"But shouldn't he be in here with me? He's my lawyer."

The pretty blonde smiled and shrugged. "You can refuse to talk to me. That's your right. But from what I understand the deceased may have been involved in the kidnapping of your daughter."

Darby relaxed a little. "You mean you aren't going to accuse me of killing my baby *and* Consuela?"

"The woman at the scene has been dead for at least two days," the deputy explained. "You were in custody at that time."

Detective Younger slid out a chair and took her seat. She flipped open the leather binder and then thumbed through some notes Darby couldn't read until she got to a blank page. "Can you tell me what happened?"

"I honestly don't know," Darby replied. "Was she strangled?"

The deputy nodded.

"Have you found any evidence of where Sean might have gone afterward? He has my baby." Darby recounted the phone call and the threats and the more she talked the more she felt tears burn at the back of her eyes. "I know I've been charged with killing Mia but I didn't do that. I couldn't. I was just trying to get her away from Sean and I couldn't think of a safer place for myself than jail."

"The deceased was your maid?"

"More like a helper. She came twice a week to help me keep the house clean and tidy because my husband would literally beat me if the place wasn't perfect. With Sean, *everything* had to be perfect. The house, the cars, the baby. *Me.*"

"Yet you never called the police?"

"I was afraid and embarrassed," she admitted. "And I was fairly sure Sean could have talked his way out of everything. I didn't have any real proof of the abuse until recently, when it escalated on practically a daily basis. I didn't know until after Mia was born that Sean had wired the house for video. He was watching my every move. There's a DVD back at my house that, much as it pains me to say, if you watch it you'll get a flavor of what my life was like with that lunatic. Then he killed my parents, and now poor Consuela."

"Why do you think he killed her and left her at the restaurant?"

"Probably to buy some time. I'm sure with the publicity my case was getting he couldn't keep a body in our house. Or he may have lured her to the restaurant for some reason. Probably to take care of Mia. Consuela was wonderful with the baby. But I'm guessing that once Consuela saw the baby was alive, she would have gone straight to the authorities to get me out of jail."

"Did she have family? Do you know why no one has reported her missing?"

Darby hung her head. "Consuela wasn't legal but she has a daughter who is. Maria Something. Garcia? We were on our way to try to track her down when we stopped at the office and found Consuela's b-body."

"You thought she might be at your husband's restaurant?" the deputy asked.

Darby shook her head. "No. I just wanted to look around to see if Sean left any clues behind to help me find him. If I can find Sean, I can find my daughter."

"Can you think of anyone else Sean might have confided in or talked to before disappearing?"

"Not really. Greg, the bartender, is the closest thing he has to an assistant manager. Oh, and he's screwing his hostess, Roxanne Kolkina."

The deputy was furiously taking notes as Darby talked. "I don't know how to contact either of them but their numbers should be in Sean's office. There's a phone list taped to the wall just above the vendor directory."

Deputy Younger took out her cell phone and from what Darby could gather, she was asking the person on the opposite end of the phone to retrieve the numbers. "Thank you," she said, then she disconnected and placed her phone on the well-worn table.

There was a knock at the door and then Jack, accompanied by State's Attorney Matt Johnson, stepped into the room. Darby's heart skipped a beat. Johnson's presence made her nervous. He believed she was a baby killer, so she fully expected the accusations to fly.

Jack came around and sat next to her in the hard wooden chair. Johnson stood, his back braced against the opened doorjamb. "Declan is going back to your place for the DVD," Jack explained.

Darby hated that another person was going to watch her humiliation. "Okay. Can we leave now?" she asked.

"Not yet," Johnson said.

Darby began to shake and Jack reached out and covered her tremulous hands with one of his own. "It's nothing bad," he promised. "Matt?"

"In light of the discovery of your maid's body, I'm going to ask the court to dismiss the charges against you."

She looked up at him as if he was speaking in tongues. "Seriously?"

"I had one of my investigators look into your husband after court. It seems he has a pretty unsavory history."

"Define 'unsavory,'" she said quietly, not knowing how much he actually knew about her past with Sean—the rapes, the beatings, the deaths of her parents and her housekeeper. "He has my daughter."

"Seven years ago he was dating a woman in Michigan. The woman was last seen leaving a bar with Sean and getting into his car. He claimed she stormed out in a huff after a brief argument. Only it was February and she didn't take her coat or her purse or her keys."

"Is she dead?" Darby asked.

"Never found a body, so the case is still open, and Sean is the only person of interest in that one. Then there's Texas."

Darby was feeling stupider and more scared by the second. "What happened in Texas?"

"According to a young woman he was dating, he beat her so badly her jaw and orbital bones were broken."

"Why wasn't he put in jail?" Jack asked.

"The victim backed out. Said she was drinking heavily that night and had no memory of how she got hurt. Even tried to claim she'd fallen down the stairs and that's what caused her injuries."

Darby looked down at Jack's hand covering hers and squeezed his fingers. "I'm sure Sean talked her out of pursuing the case. He can be pretty convincing and intimidating."

"And you have no idea where he might be?"

Darby shook her head. "If I can get to a laptop I can tell you if he has taken any money out of our accounts or used any of our credit cards."

Matt nodded and Darby was taken to an open cubicle where

she sat in front of a desktop. The area around the machine was devoid of personal items, so she figured this was just an extra terminal.

It took her about five minutes to access her bank and money market accounts. Sean had been a busy boy. "He's taken about twenty-two thousand dollars out of the bank. Let me check the credit cards." Darby dialed the customer service numbers on the backs of both cards and learned a charge had been made on the last day Sean was seen in the amount of $1,257 on one card, and a charge of $439 had been made on a second card. "I'll have to wait until morning to speak to a rep who can tell me where he spent the money, and to cut him off."

"Don't do that," Matt and Jack said in unison.

Jack continued. "We might be able to track him by the credit cards."

"Okay." That tiny tidbit gave her a glimmer of hope. "But isn't he going to find out that the charges against me have been dropped?"

"That could push him farther underground," Matt agreed. "Okay, for now I'll let the charges stand."

"Thank you," Darby said. How surreal had her life become that she was *thanking* a state's attorney for not dropping murder charges against her?

"You said your husband has a mistress?" Matt asked.

"Roxanne Kolkina," Darby answered. "She's worked at the restaurant for about three months."

"Sean has naked pictures on his office computer," Jack interjected. Then he explained about Peggy and what Sean had had her do before vanishing.

"You have no idea where this Lyssa person might be?"

Darby shook her head and rubbed her arms as cold fear trickled down her spine. "Her parents are dead, but—" Darby's mouth snapped closed and she looked up at the two men and one woman staring at her. "But she told Peggy she had visited with her mother. Remember? I think Peggy was trying to throw Sean off track. But Sean has Mia and I'm afraid that the only way he'd have gotten her was to kill Lyssa as well. Maybe she spoke to Peggy before Sean found her?" Darby guessed. "But Lyssa's mother is dead." She sighed heavily. "This is so confusing."

Jack nodded. "So how could she have visited with her mother?"

"Gravesite?" Darby suggested.

"Any idea where her parents are buried?"

Darby started to shake her head, then she froze. "Charleston," she said just above a whisper.

"South Carolina or West Virginia?" Matt asked.

"The damned paper," Jack said as he pounded his hand on the desktop. "He gave Darby divorce papers and a newspaper, but it was just the front page of the *Palm Beach Post*. The interior pages were all from the *Charleston Post Courier*. He's known where Lyssa was since before you formally charged her with the baby's murder."

Darby practically leapt from her seat. "I have to get to Charleston." She started to push past the two men but Jack stopped her by bracketing her shoulders in his hands.

"We have to make a plan," he cautioned. "Sean has obviously put a lot of time and thought into this so we can't just go charging up there without knowing what we're up against. Not if we want to make sure Mia stays safe."

"Can we call South Carolina and ask the police to look for them?" Darby asked.

"We're going to need something more than just the name of a city and physical descriptions," Matt explained. "Does your husband have any habits or vices?"

"He likes going first class. Especially when it's on me," Darby scoffed. "Like renting a car. He's probably not going to use Budget."

"Same with hotels?" Jack asked.

Darby nodded. "Yes. He's grown accustomed to being served."

Detective Younger said, "Let me call the Charleston PD. Maybe they can canvass the better hotels for Sean, Roxanne, and the baby."

Darby's gut clenched. "Please make sure they understand that my baby is with them. I don't want a single hair on her head harmed."

"Got it. Do you have a recent picture of Mia?"

Darby went into her purse and took out her phone. "This was a week ago."

"Good. I can use DMV photos for Lyssa, Roxanne, and Sean." She disappeared down a hallway. Darby took the other phone out of her purse and tried the number again, but the call still went to voicemail. She was fighting back tears and feeling utterly useless. She wanted to go to Charleston herself and go door to door if necessary. Sitting around doing nothing only made her feel as if things were getting worse.

"What will they do if they find him?" she asked Matt.

"They'll hold him, either on custodial interference or in reference to Consuela's murder."

"What about Mia?"

"They'll place her in foster care until you can get to Charleston to pick her up."

"No, no, no," Darby insisted. "My daughter is absolutely not going to foster care. I'm going to Charleston tonight. I promise I won't get in the way of the Charleston P.D. but I'm not going to let anyone pass my baby around foster care even for one night."

"What if they've already left Charleston?" Matt asked.

Darby shrugged. "Then I'll fly or drive or *crawl* in whatever direction he's going with my baby."

It was Matt's turn to shrug. "I can't stop you, but I strongly advise against it. At least wait until morning when you can talk to your credit card companies. It could be that Sean has charged a hotel room to your Amex and then we'll know precisely where to find him."

Jack placed his hand on her shoulder. "It's almost three in the morning now," he suggested quietly. "We'll get a few hours of sleep, then deal with the credit cards and plan our next move. Okay?"

Declan joined them just then, handing a DVD over to Matt. "So what's the plan?" he asked.

All eyes were on her. As much as Darby wanted to go racing to Charleston, she had to admit that patience might just be the right approach. "Sleep, financials, and then we charter a flight to Charleston if it looks like Sean has spent so much as five minutes in that town."

Declan offered to go to Jack's place to take care of the dog, and then he wanted to go by his own office to work on some of the databases he subscribed to as a private investigator. With the police focused on Sean, Declan, Darby, and Jack thought it was a good idea if someone focused on Roxanne.

A very jittery Darby and Jack ended up alone together in her house. "Sorry. I think I have cop coffee syndrome," she joked. "My hands are shaking from drinking that stuff."

"Then you need to relax," Jack suggested. "Come here. I'll help you."

She joined him on the sofa. Initially his fingers molded the tense muscles at her neck. She knew he was just trying to help but her body was reacting in a completely different manner. Her skin warmed and tingled and she was acutely aware of the slight calluses on the pads of his thumbs as he ran them up and down the back of her neck. It felt so good that she couldn't help but let a small moan escape her lips.

Ever so gently, Jack picked her up, turned her over and laid her belly-down on the sofa. He straddled her backside as his hands molded her skin. Jack lifted her hair and pushed it to one side, baring one side of her throat. His hands slipped down so that just the ends of his fingertips brushed the sides of her breasts. He dipped his head and began to place tiny kisses against her warm skin.

Darby experienced an odd combination of relaxation and intense desire. There was a fire in the pit of her stomach and his kisses left a blazing trail on her skin. He nibbled her ear and she felt his hot breath on her. Darby managed to wriggle over onto her back and she immediately reached for the buttons of Jack's shirt. She was so full of need that her fingers refused to cooperate at first and she was half-tempted to just rip the damned thing off. But she fell into a rhythm and in no time, she was pushing the shirt from his shoulders and admiring his chiseled form.

Lifting her head, she was able to place kisses against the dark hair covering his chest. She put her fingers where her lips had been and traced the hair as it tapered, then disappeared inside his pants.

Her anxiety was forgotten and she was totally immersed in desire. She had forgotten this magical feeling. Forgotten what it was like to want a man more than you wanted your next breath. She wound her arms around him, stopping every now and again to feel the outline of his muscles. She pulled at him, desperate for the feel of his mouth against hers.

He glanced down at her through thick, inky lashes. "Do you think this is a good idea?"

"Yes. A very good one," she insisted as she snaked her fingers up past his collar and into his hair. Again she tugged and again she felt resistance.

"I need to know you're sure."

Hearing the hitch in his voice made her feel powerful and desirable. "I'm *very* sure."

Jack shifted his weight so he was next to her on the plush sofa, and he dipped his head forward and his lips touched hers. His touch was much less tentative this time. He tugged the hem of her top free and tried to unbutton its tiny pearl buttons. Darby giggled, then moved his hand aside and slowly unbuttoned her blouse. As she did so, she watched his smoldering gaze follow her every move and felt his hardness against her thigh.

He pushed back the shoulder of her shirt. He began his kisses on her mouth, then dipped lower until he was placing warm, urgent kisses against the swell of her breast above her demi-bra.

He tried to shift their position again but it didn't work. "Damn it," he cursed softly as he struggled to remove her top.

"How about we go into the bedroom?" Darby suggested.

"I thought you'd never ask," he said with a smile.

Somehow he managed to stand up and keep her in his arms at the same time. He kissed her partially open mouth as he carried her down the hallway to the master bedroom. Once they were on the bed, their frustration evolved into impatience. They became a tangle of arms, legs, hands, fingers…

Darby loved the feel of his body. He was beautifully built with just the right amount of muscle. And he was patient. Too patient. Darby was already nearing the edge when his mouth closed over her breast. She groaned and grabbed his head, half-tempted to push him away so that they could move on to the next step. But Jack was having none of it. He touched her and toyed with her until her brain was flooded with passion.

When she couldn't take it another minute, Darby surprised him by quickly changing their positions. She was now on top and in control.

In one smooth motion, he was inside of her. Jack moaned at the sensations coursing through him. He'd never been so patient and he wasn't sure how much longer he could contain himself. But he knew this had to be at her pace. After everything she'd been through, she had to feel safe with him. And based upon her actions, she was just fine in that department. She was kissing his nipples as she slowly increased the rhythm of their bodies.

Jack knew he couldn't wait forever, so he reached between them and smiled when she made this sexy little sound. Touching her until she could no longer hold back, Jack waited until she was at the crest of the wave before he allowed his release. Hers came a second later.

They lay there, a tangle of body parts, breathing heavy and each wearing a sheen of perspiration. Darby was making a tiny circle with her fingertip around his nipple as she cuddled against him.

Jack rolled onto his side and met her gaze. Darby's heart stopped when she saw the flicker of regret in his eyes. She stopped touching him, suddenly feeling naked and vulnerable.

"That shouldn't have happened," Jack said apologetically.

Darby's emotions twisted in her gut. Anger won out and she snapped, "You didn't seem to mind when it was happening." Yanking the sheet off the bed, she wrapped it around herself and started to get up.

Jack grabbed her arm. "Wait, please?"

She did, but she didn't turn and look at him. She was on the verge of tears. Several uncomfortable seconds ticked by, and with each one she felt more and more like a fool. Had this been pity sex for him? She didn't need or want any man's pity. Not after everything she'd been through. When he didn't speak, she asked, "What?"

"I think you need a lawyer and a friend more than you need a lover."

"Fine."

"Darby? Look at me."

Pride stiffened her spine. She turned halfway. "You're absolutely right. It shouldn't have happened and it won't happen again."

"You sound hurt," he said.

"I'm angry." It felt good to be able to vocalize her emotions without fear of repercussions.

"I'm sorry."

"Not at you," she insisted as she tucked the sheet tighter. "I'm mad at me for allowing myself to get caught up in the moment. The last time I did that I ended up married to a psycho killer husband. Who"—her voice was growing louder—"I am technically still married to, which is another reason why this…_this_ won't happen again."

"Don't get carried away," Jack warned. "Remember, I saw the DVDs. I'll bet you've just been going through the motions of being married for almost a year. And just because you had a whirlwind relationship with Sean that didn't work doesn't mean you have to cut yourself off from men in general."

"No, right now my only focus is on finding my daughter. Nothing is more important than that."

"I know," Jack said. "That was the point I was trying to make."

"Well, you did a crappy job of making it."

"All I'm trying to say is that you and I should probably put this part of our relationship on hold until after you have Mia back."

"Trust me, it's on hold."

"See? You're pissed. I'm just trying to do the right thing here."

"You should have thought about that an hour ago before we ended up here." Darby stubbornly stood her ground. She was not going to allow him to make her feel guilty.

"I did," he defended. "But I'm not Superman. You touched me and all I could think about was making love to you. You were the aggressor, not me." His voice rose an octave.

Darcy felt her cheeks grow warm and she turned away so he wouldn't see the humiliation on her face. "Let's just agree that it won't happen again." When would she learn how to read a man?

"For now."

"What does that mean?"

"That means that once we get your life in order, all bets are off."

CHAPTER FIFTEEN

Darby?"

She felt a gentle shaking and it took her a second to acclimate herself. She opened her eyes to find Jack standing over her bed.

"You have to wake up," he said.

"What time is it?" she asked.

"A few minutes before nine."

She sat up and rubbed her eyes, then shoved her hair off her face. "I fell asleep?" she mumbled.

"You needed it," Jack said. "I wouldn't have bothered you but you need to get on the phone with your credit card companies."

She looked at him and realized he had showered and was wearing fresh clothing. "Did you go home?"

He nodded. "Declan was here. I had to make arrangements for my neighbor to take care of the dog. I hope you don't mind, but I packed a bag just in case we have to go to Charleston."

Just the thought of her daughter propelled her from the bed. She quickly showered and grabbed a pair of slacks and a blouse. Darby used the dryer just long enough so that her hair wouldn't soak the back of her shirt. For the first time in days, she stood in front of the mirror and applied a small amount of makeup. The few hours of rest had done wonders. She didn't have that brain fog from sleep deprivation anymore.

She hesitated for a minute, her mind replaying the passionate encounter with Jack. He was right, she acknowledged with a twinge of sadness. The sex may have been great, but it couldn't keep happening. She needed him to help her find Mia, and sleeping with him had made her feel like a woman for the first time in a very long time, but it was too soon. Hell, she was still married to a murderer.

Darby shook her head. She did full background checks on all her employees, and yet she had managed to marry a man with a dangerous and checkered past. She thought about the women in Sean's past, especially the one who was still missing. Darby knew nothing of the case save for what the state's attorney had told her, but she knew in her gut that Sean had probably killed her. Just as he had killed her parents. "And now he has Mia," she whispered as tears threatened her recently applied mascara.

Darby made her way back to the kitchen area by following the scent of coffee. She acknowledged Declan, who was seated at the table working on his laptop. Jack was next to him, reading the newspaper pages Sean had given her on his visit to the jail.

After pouring herself a cup of coffee, Darby took her credit cards out of her purse and dialed the first customer service line, finding herself in the maze of automatic routing. She was vaguely aware of the music playing in her ear as she waited for a representative. She was more aware of the man with his back to her. The knit polo shirt he was wearing was a pale green and complimented his black hair and dark eyes. A shiver of desire danced along her spine as she thought about having sex with him only hours before. It was a warmth that started in her groin, then moved to her belly before finally forming a knot of desire that seemed to capture her whole body.

She realized that Declan was staring at her and immediately felt her cheeks burn. His only response was a slightly crooked smile, then he went back to the computer.

"…May I help you?"

"Yes, thank you. I need to know about the recent activity on my card," she explained.

"Has the card been lost or stolen?"

"No," Darby answered.

"Before I can do that I'll need to get some information from you."

Darby provided her name, address, birthdate, and then answered the special security question before the rep asked, "What transactions are you concerned about?"

"I need everything from the last four days." Darby grabbed the pad and pen she kept on the counter. Pen poised, she waited impatiently for the representative.

"I'm showing a charge in the amount of one-thousand-fifty-seven dollars to Jet Blue. I have a second charge to Extraordinary car rentals in the amount of four-hundred-thirty-nine dollars."

"Where was that charge made?" Darby asked.

"All I have is the billing memo from the home office in Atlanta, Georgia."

"Anything else?"

"Yes, I have a charge in the amount of two-hundred-fifteen dollars and seventy-one cents to Babies-R-Us."

"Do you know where that purchase was made?"

"Vero Beach, Florida," she answered.

"And when was it made?"

"Four days ago."

"Anything else?"

"A cash advance in the amount of fifteen thousand dollars."

Darby sighed, thanked the woman, then hung up and turned to the Kavanaghs. She recounted the conversation.

"You two go to Vero," Declan suggested. "It's only about an hour north. They might have video, or maybe a clerk will remember him. I'll stay here and try to pick up a lead on Lyssa."

Darby grabbed up her purse and shoved her wallet back inside. She felt nervous, jittery—feelings that only got worse when Jack placed his hand at the small of her back on the way out the garage door. His fingers splayed and she felt warmth spread from the epicenter of his touch out along every one of her nerve endings. *Stop!* she silently chided herself.

As they drove north on I-95, Darby tried the disposable phone again. Still it went directly to voicemail. She was frustrated beyond belief. "I'm sure Sean is enjoying this to no end," she said, then blew out a breath.

Jack patted her knee and said, "Hang in there. Declan has the cell phone number and as soon as Sean turns it on, he thinks he can get a GPS location on it."

"I hope so," Darby said. "It terrifies me to think he's alone with my baby."

"Hey," Jack squeezed her knee. "I know this is hard but you have to hang in there. Sean can't hide forever, especially now that he's the number one suspect in Consuela's death."

"I can't believe I married him," Darby mused. "I know it sounds naive but I really didn't see it. Not in the beginning. He literally swept me off my feet. He was kind and attentive and sweet. It wasn't until after our honeymoon that things went south. Little stuff at first. Like I used to have dinner with my parents every Friday night. Sean came up with all sorts of excuses to nix that. He had me believing that he couldn't bear to be away from me and he even solicited some sympathy from me by claiming he was intimidated by my father.

"Slowly he cut me off from my friends and before I realized it was happening, I was completely isolated. That's when the abuse really started. Verbal at first. Ugly. But not as bad as when he got physical. By the time that happened, I was too embarrassed to tell my parents and I was pregnant and...well, I just felt stuck."

"That's how men like Sean operate. They start out charming as hell and then slowly alienate the woman from her friends and family. Then the violence begins and escalates, and it's basically all about control."

"But what happens if Mia gets on his last nerve?" Darby asked. "She's barely seven weeks old. She's totally helpless."

"She is part of him," Jack reminded her. "That will probably prevent him from harming her."

"*Probably* isn't very reassuring."

The GPS in Jack's SUV told them where to get off the highway and then announced they had reached their destination. The baby store anchored a strip mall on the busy street.

They parked and went inside the massive store. Darby was reminded of her many trips to the same chain store in West Palm as she put together Mia's nursery. The place was quiet save for the sound of a baby crying nearby. Darby longed to hear the cry of her own sweet daughter but she had to keep her act together.

"May I help you?" a young girl asked when they were just steps inside.

Jack handed her his business card and asked, "May we see the manager?"

"I'll get her for you," the girl said before she went to the back of the store.

Darby stepped over to the car seats and found the deluxe Peg Perego Primo car seat she'd purchased for Mia. She ran her fingers over the soft cushion and smiled as she remembered how she had struggled to put the seat in the car. She was torn. The police had taken Mia's car seat after she'd falsely admitted to killing her daughter and transporting the body to the nearby canal. Given that they had cut up her car, she assumed she'd get the car seat back in similar shape.

"May I help you?" a middle-aged woman in an attractive Lilly Pulitzer shift dress said as she extended her hand in greeting. "I'm Karen Jennings, the manager."

Jack explained the situation. "So we're hoping you have some sort of record of the sale and hopefully some videotape?"

Karen smiled. "We have video and I can pull the sales receipt if you have a transaction number."

"I do," Darby said. "And thank you."

The woman reached out and gave Darby's hand a squeeze. "I can't imagine how worried you must be. My ex-husband and I had a pretty ugly divorce but thankfully we kept the kids out of it. How old is your baby?"

"She'll be seven weeks tomorrow," Darby replied.

"You poor dear. Follow me."

Following Karen, they went back through the warehouse section of the store, then into a small, cluttered office that smelled of coffee and a sandalwood air freshener.

Darby reached into her purse and pulled out the notes she had taken when she'd spoke to the representative from American Express earlier. Karen sat at her computer terminal and in a matter of seconds, she had an invoice on the screen. "Let me print this," she said. "Now, using the time stamp on the invoice, I can pull up surveillance video from that date and time. You're lucky, by the way. Our system tapes over itself every seven days. If you hadn't discovered the charge in time, there's nothing I could've done to help you."

The video was remarkably clear. Darby glanced over one of Karen's shoulders while Jack watched over the other. Maybe two minutes later one of the cameras captured Sean and Roxanne walking into the store.

Darby's heart ached when she saw no trace of Mia. Had they left her alone in a hot car? She fumed silently as she watched Sean and Roxanne fill a cart with baby items. From the invoice she realized that Sean had to have left the jail, collected Roxanne and gone to the baby store. Which meant he had somehow figured out where Lyssa had taken the baby. But how?

Surely not from the phone call he'd made Peggy make the night before he'd come to the jail.

"So what did he find out?" Darby thought aloud.

"There has to be something that led him to Lyssa. Are you sure nothing comes to mind?" Jack asked.

No matter how hard she tried, Darby couldn't think of how Sean had located Lyssa. "I don't even know where to look."

"Maybe Declan has had better luck."

They drove back to Sewell's Point. Declan was still at the computer when they arrived with food. "Anything?" Jack asked as he handed his brother a sub.

"Maybe," Declan said.

Jack asked, "What?"

"Sean rented a Mercedes in West Palm Beach three days ago."

Darby felt a surge of excitement. "Don't they put GPS trackers in pricey rentals?"

Declan nodded. "In this case they didn't have to. The car was found abandoned in Kiawah Island, South Carolina yesterday."

"Should I call my credit card company to see if he's rented a new car?" Darby asked.

"Can't hurt."

Darby quickly made the call, but after a five-minute wait, she was informed that no new transactions had been billed to the card.

Jack stroked his chin for a moment, then asked, "Did Lyssa know Consuela?"

"They met a few times," Darby said. "Lyssa would come by here on the weekends so I could give her cat its shots."

"Would Lyssa trust her?"

"Yes. No. Maybe," Darby vacillated. "I warned Lyssa not to talk to anyone but I can't be sure."

"Does Consuela have a cell phone?" Declan asked.

Darby told him the number from memory. He entered some information into his laptop and asked, "Did Consuela have any friends or family in South Carolina?"

"No," Darby said. "She just has two daughters and one lives in Stuart, I think."

"I found one daughter," Declan said. "Maria Ruiz. According to my friend on the police force, she took the news of her mother's death hard."

"I can imagine," Darby said, still feeling the loss of her own mother and father. "Do you think she might talk to me?"

"I think she might know something," Declan said. "Consuela made a call to South Carolina on her cell. Then five minutes later she made a forty-second call to her daughter. That was the last time her phone was used."

"You think Consuela told her daughter where to find my baby?"

"It's worth asking her."

"Great. I'll head over there now."

"No," Jack contradicted. "You'll eat first. You have to stay healthy if you want to find your daughter. Declan can keep digging around his databases and you and I can go talk to the daughter. After you have some lunch."

Darby picked at her sandwich but ate enough to get Jack off her back.

"What if she slams the door in my face?" Darby asked as

they neared the front entrance of her community. She was about to duck down but for some reason the press was no longer camped on the roadside.

"I don't think that will happen. After all, Sean killed your parents, too. You have something to bond over."

"How did this become my life?" she said on a rush of breath.

Jack reached out and stroked her cheek with the back of his hand. "Don't give up on me now."

"I'm not giving up; I just feel so responsible for everything. My parents, Consuela, and my precious daughter. Not to mention Lyssa. I doubt he didn't just sit back and ask nicely to have the baby. There it is," Darby said, pointing to a modest Florida-style, single-story home with a tidy tiled roof.

The yard was neatly manicured, with colorful bushes in bloom against the bright yellow stucco. The air smelled of peppers and onions and in the distance, Spanish music played softly. Darby moved aside a tricycle as she and Jack went up the steps and knocked on the door. It was answered by a little boy Darby guessed was about five years old. A second later, a man appeared. "Yes?"

"My name is Darby Grisom. Consuela worked for me."

His dark eyes grew darker. "I know who you are."

"I know this is a difficult time, but could I please speak to Maria?"

He shook his head. "She's crying her eyes out. Thanks to your husband, she no longer has her mother. Our children have lost their grandmother. You got her—"

"It's okay, Manuel," came a female voice from inside. "Let her inside."

Darby and Jack stepped inside and found Maria's house cluttered but clean. Several young children, oblivious to the pain
and agony on Maria's face, pushed trucks and other toys around
the small living room. Maria was holding a baby Darby knew
was six months old. Consuela had proudly showed her stacks of
pictures of her newest grandchild.

"Manny, take the children outside." Then she turned to
Darby. "Would you like a drink? Some water, maybe?"

"Nothing, thank you." Darby sat next to the woman on the
sofa and found herself smiling down at the baby, who easily
smiled back. "She's prettier than her pictures," she said.

"After three boys, my mother was glad to finally have a
granddaughter."

"Maria, I am so sorry," Darby began. "I know exactly how
you feel."

She nodded. "The police explained it to me. And they suspect him in the murder of your parents? And he has your
baby?"

"Yes. And I have no idea where he has taken her."

"I'm sorry, but I have no idea either."

"What about the last time you spoke to your mother?"
Darby pressed.

Maria hung her head. "I thought her phone died," she admitted. "My mother had a habit of forgetting to charge the
phone so I didn't really think anything of it when her call
ended abruptly."

"What was she telling you?" Jack asked.

"She was whispering and, like I said, I thought it was just
poor reception or something. It was something about a man."

"What man?"

"Glen. Glen Burnie."

"What about him?" Darby asked.

Maria shrugged. "I think she was going to meet him."

"Did she say she was with Sean?" Jack asked.

"No. I heard voices in the background but it was too hard to make out what they were saying." Maria shifted the baby so she was up on her shoulder. She met Darby's gaze. "I hope they find your baby safe and then I hope they kill your husband. I know I'm supposed to forgive but I don't have forgiveness in my heart, only vengeance."

"I know the feeling," Darby said. "Thank you for talking to me today." Darby reached for her purse. "Your mother was like a family member for me. I'd very much like to cover the costs of her funeral." Darby wrote a check. "Again, I'm very sorry for your loss."

"This is too generous," Maria said.

"No, your mother was too generous. And she died trying to protect my daughter. This is the least I can do. And if you ever need anything, please feel free to call me."

As soon as they got back in the car, Jack called Declan and asked him to try to find a man named Glen Burnie, and to look in Charleston, since that was where Sean's trail seemed to have gone cold.

"I'm feeling hopeful," Darby said. Then she turned and read trepidation on Jack's face. "What?"

"Nothing."

Darby reached out and touched his upper arm. "Tell me."

"Would Sean give the baby away?"

The hope she was feeling drained from her body. "I don't think so. What are you thinking?"

"I don't like the idea that he was taking Consuela to see a man."

"What are you saying."

"I'm not *saying* anything. I'm just thinking about possibilities."

Darby felt nauseous. "You're thinking he might be giving her to someone? As in human trafficking?"

"Forget it. It doesn't make sense anyway."

"How can you say that?"

"Because he and Roxanne went to a baby store to buy supplies."

She let out the breath she didn't know she'd been holding. "You scared me," she said.

Jack reached out and placed his hand on her knee. Darby placed her hand over his and gave it a squeeze. "As long as he has Mia he can torture me," she reminded him. "I think that's all he wants at this point."

"How well do you know Roxanne?"

"Not well," Darby admitted.

"I think it's time we gave her a good look. Maybe Glen Burnie is her uncle or something."

"Her address is at the restaurant."

"The crime scene people are finished there now. Let's swing by there and see what we can find out."

They arrived at Tilefish Grille and Darby unlocked the door but the alarm just beeped. The police couldn't set it after clearing the crime scene. Darby didn't much care. As far as she was concerned, the place could burn to the ground. Preferably with Sean inside.

Jack led the way to the office, which gave Darby an unobstructed view of his impressive body. His broad shoulders tapered to a trim waist and he was wearing khakis with his polo shirt, so he looked very much as if he could fit in with the horsey set. Just watching him navigate through the restaurant was enough to urge her pulse higher.

Get a grip, she thought as she tried to vanquish images of their lovemaking from her brain. Easier said than done. However, standing in the small space where Consuela had lost her life was a sobering experience.

They each took a file cabinet and in no time Darby said, "Got it!" then she waved a folder in the air.

She opened it on Sean's desk and flipped through until she came to the application. Darby scanned the document. No mention of a Glen Burnie. "Now what?" she asked.

"She lists three references. Let's go chat them up to see if any of them know anything about her whereabouts. If we find Roxanne, we find Sean and Mia."

"Let's hope. Unless she's done something to piss him off and he's killed her, too."

CHAPTER SIXTEEN

Roxanne's first reference was a girl named Ali Hoines. They found her at home in a small apartment in Hobe Sound.

"Yes?" she asked.

Jack handed her his card. She took it and surprise registered in her hazel eyes. She was an attractive girl, all of nineteen, and a former co-worker of Roxanne's.

"May we come in and ask you a few questions about Roxanne?" Jack asked.

"Sure, but the police have already been here," she said. They entered the apartment, which could've used a good dusting, and Ali offered the two of them the sofa. She sat on the floor across from them, the space between separated by a flimsy coffee table. She was wearing an off-the-shoulder T-shirt and shorts that left very little to the imagination. Her brown hair was in a messy pile on top of her head, secured by a few twists.

"I'll tell you what I told them. Roxanne came by three days

ago. She owed me some money so she signed over her car title as payment."

"Was she alone?" Darby asked.

"No," Ali answered. "There was an older guy with her but he stayed downstairs in a black Mercedes. I only caught a glimpse of him when I walked Roxanne down to the parking lot."

Darby thought for a moment, then asked, "Did she seem nervous?"

"Very," Ali said. "And she was in a huge hurry. Her car is worth about ten grand and she only owes me three hundred bucks."

"So why would she do that?" Jack asked.

Ali sighed. "Roxie and I had a falling out about the money. We haven't spoken in months. The last thing I told her was that she could have access to the storage as soon as she paid me my money."

"What did she have in storage?" Darby asked.

"Just a couple of boxes. I helped her carry them in and they weren't sealed, just the cardboard edges tucked closed. I could see paperwork in the boxes but I don't actually see what the papers were about but the boxes were marked 'Important Papers.'"

"Did the police impound the car?"

She shook her head. "No. They went down and opened the doors and gave a quick once over but they seemed more interested in asking me where she would go if she was in trouble."

"What did you tell them?" Darby asked.

She shrugged. "Roxie had a lot of friends. Until about six months ago when she started seeing her mystery man, she partied with us all the time."

"Mystery man?"

Ali smirked. "She wouldn't tell anyone anything about him. So he must have been married or something. All I know is that once he came into her life it was as if she was on call twenty-four-seven."

"I know the feeling," Darby grumbled under her breath.

"Anyway," Ali continued. "I picked up on a few things that made me really uncomfortable."

"Like what?" Jack asked.

"Like I ran into her in City Place and her lip was puffy. I asked her flat out who punched her and she just tossed me some shade. Tried to tell me she had tripped on her tile floor."

Darby cringed. Perhaps Roxanne had fallen for Sean's BS just as she had. "You didn't believe her?"

"No," Ali answered. "And I don't think she signed over her car just to pay a small debt."

"Why do you think she did it?"

"I think she was just finding a place to ditch the car. Like maybe she'd been in an accident. But there's no damage to the vehicle."

"Mind if we take a look?" Jack asked.

"Go ahead," she said, standing and going into the small kitchen and returning with a set of keys. "It's the beige Camry parked behind the building."

Jack splayed his hand at the small of her back as they walked across the parking lot to the Camry. The midday sun was high and there was heat coming off the cement. Along with her nervous anticipation, the little thrill of having Jack touch her made Darby begin to perspire.

He used the key fob to open the car, then he walked around to the driver's side while she took the passenger side.

The car wasn't the cleanest she'd ever seen. There were a number of receipts balled and cast aside on the floor. Darby opened each one, not sure what she was looking for. She got down on her knees and moved the seat as far back as it would go. Then, using the flashlight feature on her smart phone, she scanned under the seat for possible clues.

Her flashlight glinted off an item tucked between the carpet and the seat track. Darby had to do any number of contortions to reach the item. Finally, after stretching her arm to its limit, she retrieved a small gold ring.

"This belongs to Consuela," she said.

"Are you sure?" Jack asked.

"Positive. I saw it on her hand a zillion times."

"So we have Consuela's body at the restaurant and your housekeeper's ring in Roxanne's car. Put it back where you found it and I'll call the detectives about it later."

"You think she was involved in the murder?" Darby asked. "I don't know, Jack. Sean can be charming but I can't believe he'd be able to talk someone into helping him commit murder."

Jack shrugged. "Then maybe he used the car without her knowledge. Would Consuela get in a car with Sean?"

"Without question," Darby told him.

"It could be that he strangled her in the car and just dumped her body in his office. That would explain why the office was basically undisturbed except for her body."

"I'm worried for Roxanne," Darby said, then she watched the surprise register on Jack's face. "She is young and vulnerable. Sean is obviously using her and if she's already been seen with bruises, my guess is the controlling behavior has been going on for some time. If I had to register a guess, I'd say Roxanne probably has some variation of Stockholm syndrome."

"You're justifying the behavior of a woman who most likely helped your husband steal your child?"

Darby raked her fingers through her hair. "I'm just saying that Sean is a master manipulator. Hell, I'm on the ugly side of thirty and he was able to do it to me."

"How exactly did that work?" Jack asked when they had finished their search of the car.

"He makes you feel like you're the most special person on the planet. It's really quite flattering. Then he starts to twist everything around. Like complaining about me spending time with my parents. He never said not to do it, he just made me feel guilty for taking time away from our relationship. Somehow, I started to cut ties with people and thought it was my own idea. It's hard to explain." Tears welled in her eyes and each breath was a gulp of air. "Especially after the physical abuse started. It was nothing major in the beginning and he had this way of apologizing and making me feel like it was *my* fault he had to hit me. Then it got worse and worse and then I finally decided to get out and it cost my parents their lives. I'll never forgive myself for that." Darby wiped away her tears but that wasn't enough to wipe away the guilt she would probably carry with her always.

* * *

Jack took her by the upper arm and gently positioned her against the side of the apartment building's breezeway. It was a zillion degrees cooler in the shade but Jack wasn't feeling cool. In fact, he felt the exact opposite. He was aware of her on so many levels. The way her blond hair sparkled in the sunshine. The way her eyes switched from green to gray depending on her emotions. He admired her strength, the way she stayed focused on Mia but managed to keep it together no matter what. And her body—well, that went without saying. Images of her had haunted his brief dreams the night before. All he seemed to think of when she was close was the way she had responded to him. The sexy little noises she'd made and the gentle slopes and curves he could spend hours exploring.

Jack held her in place with his body and braced his weight on his palms, which were flattened against the stucco on either side of her head. "Your parents died because a maniac killed them. You had no way of knowing Sean had wired your home and phones for sound and audio."

"But if I hadn't made that call…"

Hooking his thumb and forefinger beneath her chin, he forced her to look at him. He was going to tell her none of it was her fault but instead he dipped his head and gave her a tentative kiss. Slow at first, barely touching her pliant lips. He knew the timing was off just as he knew he should stop. But when she responded by reaching up and urging him closer, all his good intentions flew out the window.

He deepened the kiss and she pressed against him. His response was quick and noticeable as his erection pressed against her abdomen. He loved the taste of her, the way she used her tongue to make tiny little movements against his lips. He loved the feel of her hands as she bracketed his waist, then slowly and deliberately allowed her fingers to explore at will.

Jack's head was spinning with conflicting thoughts. He wanted her more than he wanted his next breath but this wasn't the right way to go about it. Her emotions were raw and exposed. Her daughter was in peril and it was his job to help her, not seduce her.

Reluctantly, he broke off the kiss and took a step back so his body could return to normal. He heard her breathing, quick and shallow.

"Sorry about that," he said. "I just got caught up in the moment."

She tilted her head slightly and held his gaze. "I'm not sorry."

"Well, you should be. Finding Mia has to be my priority and I'm having a hard time with that because you're such a tempting distraction."

She gave him a sexy half-smile and he could almost hear her brain working. "Distracting?" she asked as she grabbed his belt buckle and pulled him against her. "I don't think anyone has ever called me distracting."

"Then you don't know the right people," he promised.

"I know it feels wonderful when you kiss me. And the sex was incredible."

"You're making my self-sacrifice very difficult to maintain."

"Thank you."

"For what?" Jack asked.

"For making me feel like a woman again."

Was that what this was for her? Some sort of affirmation?

That would make sense. She had met and married Sean quickly and now here they were, barely two months after their first meeting, sneaking passionate kisses in a breezeway. Jack pulled away. Normally he could read a situation pretty well but Darby was a puzzle. He couldn't figure out if, like him, her curiosity was evolving into something more, or if he was just part of her healing.

"Let's see if Ali will give us access to the storage unit where Roxanne stored her stuff," Jack suggested.

They went back up to the second floor apartment and knocked on the door. In their absence, Ali had changed into scrubs and applied makeup.

"Here are the keys to the car," Jack said. He told her about the ring and told her not to drive the car until the cops came back and did a more thorough search. "We'd like to go see if there's anything the storage unit."

Ali went to the kitchen and brought another key." It's at the self-storage on Federal Highway at Salerno. I've got to be at work in less than thirty minutes."

"We can drop the key off to you at work," Darby suggested.

"That's fine. I work at the Manor's Nursing Home. Know where that is?"

Darby nodded and Ali handed over the key.

"Thank you," Darby said earnestly.

"Roxanne is in deep shit, isn't she?" Ali asked.

Darby nodded. "I think so. If I can find her, I think I'll find my daughter."

"I know who you are from the TV," Ali admitted. "So the baby isn't dead?"

"No. Sean took her and Roxanne has been having an affair with my husband for months."

"He's her boss, right?" Ali asked.

"Yes."

"I thought so," Ali said. "I started noticing changes in her about a month after she took that job."

"Is there anyone else you can think of who Roxanne would confide in?"

"She's pretty close to her family. She calls her mom every Sunday at ten-thirty."

"Where does her family live?" Jack asked.

"Charleston."

They were leaving the apartment together when Jack asked, "Did Roxanne ever mention a relative named Glen Burnie? An uncle, maybe? Or a cousin?"

Ali wasn't familiar with the name. "But you might want to talk to her friend Meghan. Meghan Jones and Roxanne moved here together from Charleston. They've been friends since elementary school."

Ali gave them an address. "Good luck."

"Thanks," Darby said.

Darby and Jack got in the car and were just backing out of the parking lot when the throwaway phone rang. She scrambled to find it in her purse and answered on the second ring. "Sean?"

"You sound frantic, my darling."

She cringed at the term of endearment. "Please, Sean. Name your price or whatever else you want and give me back my baby."

"She's my baby, too," Sean said.

"C'mon. We both know you don't want to be saddled with an infant. I promise I'll be fair, Sean. We can even discuss visitation." Her heart was pounding and the only thing keeping her tethered to her own sanity was the feel of Jack's hand on her shoulder.

"That's a joke and you know it. You gave me no choice but to take care of the Consuela problem. I should have known she'd be more loyal to you than to me. All I really needed was for her to take care of Mia until you and I could work out a settlement. Now that time has passed."

"We can still work one out," Darby insisted.

"Right. I'm now looking at mandatory life in prison without the possibility of parole. I won't come back to Florida. So you can forget about ever seeing your daughter again."

"Sean, don't so this. I can give you enough money to move to another country. One with no extradition treaty with the U.S. Just give me back my baby."

There was a brief pause, then Sean, sounding more relaxed said, "Now you're thinking, Darby. But I'll need a lot of cash to start over again."

"Okay. Name the price and I'll do a wire transfer *after* you return Mia."

"I'm not stupid, Darby. The minute you get the baby, you'll renege on the deal."

"Then what is your suggestion?"

"I'll be in touch."

The line went dead.

CHAPTER SEVENTEEN

Their first stop was the storage facility. Jack called the detectives about the ring in the car while Darby opened the padlock on the unit. Cool air whooshed out of the door as soon as she pushed it up and open. Thankfully the unit was air conditioned.

It was a small unit, maybe eight-by-eight and it was packed with boxes, lawn equipment and more boxes. As soon as Darby found the switch on the wall, she bathed the area in light. After scanning the crowded space, she spotted the "Important Documents" boxes.

"There they are," she said as she moved other boxes out of her way. "Someone's been here," she said, finding the boxes open and copies of tax returns in the name of Roxanne Kolkina set off to the side.

Jack joined her and said, "I just spoke to the cops and they've been here. Oh, and they weren't too thrilled to hear we found Consuela's ring in Roxanne's car."

"Doesn't exactly inspire confidence in local law enforcement," Darby said as she began sifting through paperwork.

Jack grabbed the second box and did the same. As they worked side by side, he asked, "I know this is tacky, but exactly how much money do you have?"

She smiled over at him. "Cash, property, investments…between four and five million."

He whistled. "And how much of that are you willing to give Sean?"

"Everything. I want Mia back. By the way, you don't happen to know what countries don't have extradition treaties with the U.S., do you?"

"I can check," Jack said. He took out his phone and asked Siri for the list.

Darby hadn't heard of most of the countries, but the ones she recognized she had a hard time picturing Sean fitting into. With one exception: Sean would probably love Morocco. She found an empty folder marked "passport" and her heart sank. "What if she needed her passport because they're already planning on leaving the country?" Darby's chest constricted with fear.

"He's not going to leave with just the twenty-two grand he got off your credit card cash advance," he reasoned. "If that was enough he would have left the country long before now."

"I didn't hear the baby cry this time," Darby said. Each syllable she'd spoken betrayed her sadness. "What if…"

Jack wrapped her in his arms. "Don't even think it," he reassured her.

"The next time he calls I'm going to have to have some sort of proof of life."

"Make him take a picture of the baby with a current newspaper. You don't want him cutting off her ear or anything crazy."

She rested her head against his chest and felt the even rhythm of his breathing. It had a calming effect on her frazzled nerves. She loved the way he smelled and loved the way she fit so comfortably in his arms. In fact, there was a lot to love about this man. Her world with Sean seemed like a lifetime ago now. Yes, she still felt the shame of not reaching out for help, and the responsibility for the deaths of her parents and her housekeeper. But in Jack's arms she felt safe and special.

Still, there was doubt in the back of her mind. She had fallen for Sean in a matter of hours and look at how that had turned out. She wasn't sure if she would ever be able to trust her choices again. Had Sean taken that from her as well? Not being able to trust her gut was maddening, especially when it came to Jack. He'd shown her nothing but care and concern and yet she still had a nagging feeling in the back of her mind. She felt like he was too good to be true. Then again, she would have said the same thing about Sean. At least in the beginning.

"I'm not seeing anything else here," Jack said as he placed a quick kiss on her forehead.

"Me either. Let's go see Meghan. Maybe she can shed some light on Roxanne."

Jack relocked the unit, then said, "I think Roxanne is going to be the key. If we can find her, we'll find Mia."

"Unless she does something to piss Sean off in the meantime."

They dropped the storage unit key off to Ali, then went on to Meghan's place. It was a small duplex in Jensen Beach with a beat-up Honda parked in the sandy driveway.

Walking up the overgrown walkway, Darby was still warring privately with herself. How could she be so attracted to Jack when she was in the middle of the biggest life crisis known to mankind? They had just reached the door when Jack's cellphone rang.

He mouthed "the cops" to her before he had a brief conversation, then hung up. "They want you—well, us—to come to the station in an hour."

"Why?" Darby asked.

"They've called in the FBI. There's an agent on his way to coordinate with the local cops."

"Is that good?" Darby asked.

"Really good," Jack assured her, then he pressed the doorbell.

A cute brunette with a pixie haircut and big green eyes opened the door. Her smile was bright and genuine. "May I help you?" she asked.

Jack handed over his card. "Can we talk to you about Roxanne Kolkna?"

Meghan shrugged. "C'mon in."

Her apartment was adorable. All shabby chic and creative touches that seemed to mirror the occupant. Darby, at five-four, towered over the tiny young woman.

They sat in chairs across from her sofa separated by a round table, a simple piece of glass over a battered frame filled with sand and shells. On top of the table an ocean breeze candle flickered and scented the air.

"You're the lady with the baby, right?" Meghan asked. "This morning's newspaper said all charges against you were being dropped and that your baby is missing."

"I think my daughter is with Roxanne," Darby said. "Do you have any idea where she might be?"

"I can't see Roxanne stealing a baby," Meghan said, then she pressed her fingers together in a prayerlike position. The tips of her middle fingers touched just below her bottom lip. "Unless it has to do with the guy."

"Who is 'the guy'?" Jack asked.

"Don't know his name," Meghan insisted. "Roxie was really hush-hush about him but she was nutty in love."

"Have you heard from her in the last few days?"

Meghan shook her head. "But I'm sure she's talked to her mother. They're very close."

"Have you ever heard the name Glen Burnie?" Jack asked.

Again Meghan shook her head. "Is that the name of the guy she was all gaga about?"

"That would be Sean," Darby answered.

Meghan's face didn't register recognition upon hearing the name. Darby and Jack left, completely convinced that Meghan didn't know anything helpful.

"I think it's time to talk to her family," Darby said. "I want to go to Charleston. There has to be a reason why he put that copy of the Charleston newspaper in with the divorce papers."

"I agree, but first we have to meet with the FBI."

Darby and Jack returned to the Martin County Sheriff's office. Unlike her first visit, this time she wasn't in handcuffs, which was good since there was a swarm of reporters around the entrance, shouting questions at her. Well, not exactly questions—more like accusations. Had she sold her baby? Was she in cahoots with her husband? Was the baby still alive?

Jack sheltered her with one arm around her shoulders as they pushed through the gauntlet. Once inside, Darby let out a breath but it did little to tamp down the tension in her body.

Detective Lange came out into the reception area and asked them to follow him. "This way, Mrs. Grisom, Jack."

" 'Jack'?" she whispered.

"We've played basketball together a few times."

"I hope you let him win," she said as she entered a conference room. It was a long, narrow space with a massive wood table in the center and enough chairs to accommodate twenty people.

Standing on the opposite side of the table were two people. The woman was tall, almost gangly. She seemed uncomfortable in her blue blazer and blue button-down shirt. Her matching slacks brushed the tops of her lace-up flats. Her thin blond hair was pulled back, though a few wispy hairs fell loose around her long face. She reached out to offer Darby a handshake, and Darby noticed the woman's hand was huge. There wasn't much of anything particularly feminine about Assistant Special Agent-in-Charge Bennett. Which was fine. Darby wanted someone who could find her baby, not a buddy for a mani-pedi break.

The gentleman with her, another Assistant Special Agent-in-Charge, was named Franklin. Darby guessed he was somewhere in his forties, worked out religiously, and had a no-nonsense attitude.

They ran through the basics of the case. As Darby told it, she felt really stupid for thinking her plan would ever have worked. "I really thought Mia would be safe with Lyssa and I would be safe in jail. The whole idea of pretending to have postpartum depression and the issue of mental competence wasn't my finest moment. And unfortunately Sean must have realized I would never hurt Mia."

"Do you think Sean knew about your plan ahead of time?"

Darby nodded. "Maybe not all of it, but since he was taping everything in the house he must have been suspicious."

"And Lyssa Chandler has made no effort to contact you?" Agent Bennett asked.

"None," Darby said. "During his first call I heard a baby cry, so I think Sean got to Lyssa quickly."

"Any idea how?" Franklin asked.

"He had one of my employees open the safe at my office. Lyssa's file was inside. Even though I told Lyssa to go where no one would think to look for her, I'm thinking she went someplace familiar."

"Do you recall what was in the file?"

"Just records for her cat, Mr. Wiggles."

"Your records?" he asked.

Darby nodded. "And the records from her prior vet's office."

"Do you recall where that was?"

"No," Darby admitted. "I don't know where to start, so I'm going to go to Charleston. Roxanne's mother lives there and the car Sean rented was found abandoned there, so that seems like the best place for me to start looking."

The agents and the detective exchanged glances. Then Bennett said, "The best course of action is for you to stay put and wait for Sean's next call."

"You mean you think I should do nothing while he's got my baby?" she scoffed. "No way."

"Look, Mrs. Grisom," Bennett began in a reasonable tone. "I've handled many custodial kidnappings. Sean is most likely to turn violent if you confront him. It's better if you remain at home, where we'll have systems in place to try and track Sean's location."

"I don't think you understand," Darby argued. "Sean doesn't want the baby; he just wants to hurt me for trying to get away, and he wants my money." It was frustratingly obvious that they didn't appreciate the depth of Sean's perversion.

"You do understand that the FBI can't help you with that aspect of the case. If there is a ransom demand, you'll have to come up with the money yourself."

"Not a problem," Darby insisted. "But I'm still going to Charleston."

"We'll send an agent to interview Roxanne's mother."

Darby shook her head. "Still going."

Bennett tented her fingertips on the tabletop. "Mrs. Grisom, we can't keep you and your daughter safe if you go off conducting your own investigation."

"I'm not asking you to keep me safe," Darby replied. "And you can't keep Mia safe because you don't have a clue where to find her. Hell, if Jack and I hadn't gone in after the Martin County Crime Scene techs, we'd never have found Consuela's ring in Roxanne's car. So don't tell me what to do."

"We're here to help you," Bennett stated firmly.

"Then flag the passports," Darby suggested. "Roxanne's was missing from her important papers and Sean has his and Mia's. Now that he's a murder suspect he'll want to get out of the country as soon as possible."

Bennett nodded. "I can do that. But please reconsider going to Charleston. If Sean is as desperate as you think he is, he'll contact you sooner rather than later."

Darby looked to Jack. "Maybe let them talk to the Kolkinas first. If you aren't satisfied, we can fly there in just under two hours," he said.

Reluctantly, Darby said, "Okay. Then she turned to the Deputy and asked, "May I have my things back? My passport, my computers, and my weapons?"

"I can arrange for you to get your things if you can wait a few minutes."

It wasn't a few minutes; it was more like an hour, but Darby finally left the Sheriff's office with all the things they had confiscated after her erroneous confession. Again she was peppered with questions and again Jack protected her from the strobe of flash bulbs and the bright glare of video cameras.

It was nearly dark by the time they got back to the house. They found Declan in the kitchen and an FBI agent in the living room. Darby didn't bother to remember his name; she just listened as he explained how he was going to tap the phone conversation if Sean called.

"If?" she challenged.

"*When*," he corrected.

Darby handed him the throwaway phone and went back into the kitchen to where Declan and Jack were seated at the table. They had their heads together and they were looking at the Declan's laptop screen.

"Find something?" she asked.

"Maybe," Declan said.

Darby walked around so she could see the screen. It was a complete copy of the Charleston newspaper Sean had slipped to her in jail. "What are we looking at?" she asked.

"The personals for that day." Declan tilted the laptop so she could get a better view. "Anything seem familiar?"

She read item after item. Most were tame but there were a few kinky ads. In the second column, about halfway down, she read:

Darby—I miss you, Mr. Wiggles

Her heart sank to her toes. "He knew practically from the beginning," she muttered.

They called the agent over and showed him the paper. He then made a phone call and in about ten minutes he found out the ad had been placed by S. Grisom the morning after her arrest.

"Any idea how he was able to track down your friend so quickly?" the agent asked.

"The cell phone and the vet records. Lyssa must have tried to make contact or Sean figured out where she'd gone from the paperwork. Damn it!"

"Two agents went to the Kolkina house," the agent reported. "The mother said her daughter was there two days ago with a strange man."

"Roxanne told her mother that they were on their way to pick up the boyfriend's baby. That the mother was no longer in the picture."

"And the mother believed that?"

"It was the agent's impression that the mother was actually excited for her daughter after spending time with the man. She called him charming."

"He can be that," Darby mumbled.

"All the mother knew was that her daughter stayed the night—the man didn't, but he showed up early the next afternoon and the two of them took off to pick up the little girl."

"Please tell me she told her mother where she was going?" Darby asked.

"No. Just that she'd be in touch when they were settled."

"What about other people in the house?" Darby asked.

"There is a fifteen-year-old sister, Rachel. But she told the agent she was out most of the time Roxanne was at home."

"If they were going to pick up the baby, why did they abandon the car?" Jack asked.

"Probably because he'd rented it under his own name. Easy to trace with rentals, they all have GPS units."

"So where did they go after they left the Kolkinas?"

"I'm afraid we don't know that yet."

CHAPTER EIGHTEEN

Darby excused herself and went into the bedroom. She needed to cry and she preferred to do so in private. Not knowing where her precious daughter was was shattering her heart into thousands of sharp pieces. If only she hadn't started this whole thing. She'd been a fool for thinking she could outmaneuver someone as evil as Sean. Glancing at her end table, she looked at the framed photograph of Mia, the one from the hospital, taken just a few hours after her birth. Darby's tears flowed in a steady stream. Mia looked so peaceful and precious and just thinking about her being in Sean's custody made Darby feel physically ill. "What have I done?" she cried into her pillow.

There was a light tap on her door. "Darby?"

She wiped her tears with the backs of her hands, then went and opened the door for Jack. "I'm afraid I'm not very good company right now."

He pulled her into his embrace. "I don't expect you to be," he said as he placed tiny kisses on the top of her head. "I just wish I could do something to find that son of a bitch."

"We're down to one lead," Darby said. "Finding Glen Burnie."

"I asked the agent to run the name. He's doing that now."

Darby reached up and flattened her palms against his chest. She vacillated between pulling him to her and pushing him away. Intellectually she knew the smart move was to keep some distance between them. It was no secret that people sometimes became unnaturally close during times of crisis, so she didn't know if this was that, or something real. She knew her desire was real; her body's strong and immediate response was impossible to deny. But what was she doing? Where could this go? She couldn't answer any of those questions until she had Mia back in her arms.

She took a step backward. Jack watched her every move. "I'm sorry," she finally said to break the tension. "I'm confused, Jack."

"About?"

"This. Us."

He held his hands up in mock surrender. "No one is asking you for anything here. No pressure, okay?"

"Why does you being so understanding make me feel even worse?" she asked.

He shrugged. "We called out for pizza. Come eat something."

"I'm not really hungry."

"You haven't eaten anything all day. You have to stay healthy, Darby."

"Pizza is really healthy," she replied sarcastically.

"Want me to go out and find you a salad or something?"

"I'd rather eat pizza," she told him. She was very careful as she walked past him not to make contact with his body. The last thing she needed was more confusion clouding her brain.

She joined the men at the table and ate a slice of pizza without really tasting it. Once they were finished, she cleared the dishes and took the pizza box out to the garage. When she returned, she found Declan looking at a long list of Glen Burnies. There had to be a thousand of them.

"How do you narrow that list?" she asked.

"What list?" the agent asked.

"One of Roxanne's friends said she mentioned a man named Glen Burnie. He's probably a distant relative of hers, but there are too many of them to check."

The agent sat up excitedly. "Maybe you're looking in the wrong place."

"What?" Darby asked.

"I worked out of FBI headquarters at Quantico for a while."

"Isn't that in Virginia?" Darby asked.

"Yes," the agent replied. "But there are three airports that service northern Virginia. One of them is BWI. In Glen Burnie, Maryland."

"It's a place?" Darby asked, feeling excitement surge through her.

"Could be," he answered. "Let me make a couple of calls."

She stood behind Jack and hugged him tightly. "Maybe he went to Maryland."

"Does Sean have any ties to Maryland?"

Darby shrugged. "I don't know. He told me he was from

California but that probably wasn't true. Remember he beat up one woman in Texas and he's a person of interest for a missing woman in Michigan. He left all that out, so I can only assume he lied to me about everything."

"Okay," the agent returned to the kitchen, his blue eyes steely. "I just heard back from the Baltimore office. Lyssa Chandler was killed in a hit-and-run on Monday."

"Oh God," Darby said as more guilt washed over her. "What about the baby?"

"According to the police, the father showed up with her birth certificate and passport so they turned her over to him."

"Was it Sean?"

"Description matches."

"What about Roxanne?" Darby asked.

"No one saw her. He was alone when he picked up the baby. He said Lyssa was his sitter and after they examined the footprints on the birth certificate against the baby's, everything checked out."

"Talk about balls," Declan said. "The guy walks into a police station and claims his kid when he's wanted for murder and kidnapping here in Florida. How does that happen?"

"Apparently no one ran him, just the baby."

"How long ago was this?"

"Two days. Probably right before he made his first call to you."

"So now what?" Darby asked. "Is he still in Maryland?"

"We're checking now."

It took almost three hours for the FBI to determine that Sean hadn't boarded an airplane or used any other form of mass transportation. But they hit pay dirt when they shifted their focus to Roxanne. She'd rented a car near the airport and the GPS showed them travelling southbound on I-95. The tracker placed them a few miles over the Virginia border when it began to just beep in place. A short while later when local police arrived at the rest area, they found the GPS chip in the men's room.

"He's got to be headed back this way," Darby said. "He can't get very far without my money."

"There's an APB out on the vehicle but there's a lot of ground between here and Virginia, especially if he stays off the interstate."

"Again: balls," Declan said. "This guy must think he's smarter than the whole world."

"If I—" Darby was cut off by the sound of the throwaway ringing. She raced into the living room and answered it on the second ring. "Sean?"

"Who else were you expecting?"

Darby heard the muffled sound of a crying baby and drew comfort from it. It confirmed Mia was alive. "Tell me what you want," she said.

"Two million in cash."

"When and where?" she asked.

"I'll call you back with details."

"Sean, don't do this. I need some sort of proof that my daughter is still alive and unhurt."

"You have my word."

"Sorry, but that doesn't cut it. Send me a picture of her with a newspaper showing the date so I know she's okay."

"You're testing my patience, Darby."

"You're the one who needs the money." Afraid of alienating him she added, "Which I am happy to give you. I just need a little good faith from you."

"I'll see what I can do." He hung up.

Darby glanced at the clock. The bank opened in three hours. Hopefully some state trooper would spot them first but if not, she wanted the cash on hand.

* * *

"Are you sure this is a good idea?" Jack asked.

"No. But I don't have a choice. I want my daughter back."

"Okay," he said as he turned into her community. "But we need to have a foolproof system for you to deliver the money. I'm not letting you get within ten yards of that bastard."

"I just want my baby back," Darby said.

"Can you really shoot?" Jack asked.

"Yes."

"Well, that's a good thing. Any other hidden talents?"

"That's about it."

"Declan and I will back you up."

"What about the FBI?"

"That will be your call. I'd just be careful that they don't send so many agents that they scare Sean off."

"No, I don't want that." Her cellphone buzzed and she took it out of her purse. Someone had sent her a picture. "Wait!" she said, grabbing hold of Jack's arm. "Look at this!"

It was a clear picture of Mia lying across a newspaper. Darby pulled the image with her fingers, zooming in on the name and date. "Jacksonville paper dated this morning."

"Christ. How did he make such good time?"

"That doesn't make any sense. You can't cover all that mileage in that amount of time."

"He's not flying," Jack said. "The FBI has him on the Wants and Warrants list. He'd never make it past security."

"Unless he *is* flying," Darby said.

"Privately?"

"Yes. We do it all the time when we go to the Bahamas."

"Do you think that's where he went?"

"Maybe. It's very private. I have a small house on one of the northern islands. The only way there is by boat or plane. And only rarely do they send anyone out to check passports."

"That would be a great place to hide out," Jack agreed.

"And a great place to exchange the money and the baby," Darby added. "There's no real police force to speak of."

"That's bad," Jack said. "I'm not going to let you go there on your own."

"Then I hope you can swim."

* * *

Ten minutes later, Sean called. As she'd expected, he wanted her to bring the money to Marsh Harbour. Even if he hadn't asked for that location, she could hear telltale steel drums in the distance.

"Do you have the money?" he asked.

"Yes."

"Tonight at seven," Sean said. "Come alone."

"Okay," she replied and hung up the phone.

"This is a big mistake," the agent said.

"My mistake to make," Darby said. "You don't have jurisdiction and it will take you days to get cooperation from the Bahamian government."

"You could be walking into an ambush."

Darby went to the living room and opened the evidence box that held her nine-millimeter. "I'm not going alone."

"What?"

"Jack, you and Declan charter a boat over to Marsh Harbour. Rent a Jeep there from Carmine; he knows me. Then wait for me by the airstrip. Go now so Sean won't get suspicious of a boat coming into the harbor."

"Mrs. Grisom—" the agent cautioned.

"It's Hayes. I don't ever want to be called Grisom again," she snapped.

"This is a terrible idea," he insisted.

"Well, it's the only one I have right now. If you come up with a different one, I'm all ears," she said as she filled another magazine with ammunition.

Declan and Jack left Darby alone with the agent and her frazzled nerves. She might have put up a decent front, but she was scared to death. The idea of confronting Sean was scary but her fears were tamped down just knowing she was hours away from getting her baby back.

The FBI agents came and went, each one of them trying a different tactic to get her to rethink her meeting Sean. But all their talk fell on deaf ears. Darby was so anxious that she showed up at the Martin County Executive Airport nearly an hour before her reserved flight.

She had dressed carefully for this. She had on slacks and a loose fitting off-the-shoulder flowy top. It wasn't for fashion. It was so Sean wouldn't notice the nine-millimeter she had tucked into the back of her waistband. She had a small duffle bag with the cash in it tucked by her feet. She wore flats just in case she had to make a run for it. In a bag she planned to leave on the plane, she had packed for Mia. A blanket, clothes, a bottle, diapers, and a small stuffed toy from her crib. She also stopped on the way to the airport and purchased a replacement Pergo car seat so Mia would be safe on the ride home.

She had just the gentle buzzing of the engine for company for the twenty-five-minute flight to Marsh Harbour. The sun was just starting to set as she deplaned. The pilot helped her with the heavy bag of money, then promised he'd wait for her until she returned.

The airport was really just a landing strip and a couple of hangars. There was a token immigration booth but per usual, it was vacant. She walked through an overgrown path to the sandy road and found Jack and Declan waiting for her in the place they'd decided upon before she'd flown over.

"Okay," she said. "Here's the plan. My house is about a mile up this road. Go out to the beach and come up by the dunes. I'll go to the door and hopefully Sean will make the exchange right then."

"I doubt that," Jack said.

"Which is why I want you two to go around to the back of the house and take the stairs up to the second floor balcony.

Sean always leaves the French doors open. No shooting with the baby in the house. Okay?"

Declan nodded reluctantly.

Jack reached out and grabbed her around the waist and pulled her to him. "Be careful," he whispered against her mouth. Then he gave her a quick kiss.

Her adrenaline was already pumping and the kiss just pushed it up a notch. She got behind the driver's seat of the rented Jeep, but waited until Jack and Declan had made their way down to the beach before she drove toward the house.

It was a lovely two-story made out of local wood by local craftsmen. Its construction had been a year-long process and a thirtieth birthday gift to herself. Never could she have imagined that she was going to end up using the house as a location to bargain with a killer.

CHAPTER NINETEEN

Darby willed her hands to stop shaking as she pulled into the horseshoe-shaped drive in front of the house. She wasn't the same woman Sean had taunted only days earlier. Dragging the heavy bag of cash with her, Darby went up to the front door and reached for the knob.

At the same time, the door opened. There in front of her was a badly beaten Roxanne. One eye was swollen; her lip was cut and there were purplish bruises around her neck. Darby felt a pang of pity for the young woman. She had been there too many times herself to not feel something for Roxanne.

Darby looked past her to see Sean holding Mia. The baby was fussing as he tucked her under one arm like a football. She began to cry in earnest.

"Come get the baby."

Darby took a step, but he said, "No. Roxanne."

Dutifully, Roxanne went over and took the baby. She held her properly and tried to sooth her.

"I brought the money," Darby said. "You get what you want, I get what I want."

"When did I ever give a shit what you wanted?" Sean said as he took a couple of menacing steps forward.

Darby tossed the bag forward and it skidded across the polished wooden floor. Without taking her eyes off Sean she said, "Roxanne, give me my baby." She was surprised that she wasn't shaking like a leaf. A mere two weeks ago, she would never have had the nerve to speak with such authority.

Roxanne was frozen in fear. Darby remembered that feeling. "Roxanne?" she tried again. "He wants the money, not the baby."

"Stay put," Sean commanded. Roxanne recoiled into the corner of the room. "Pick this up and hand it to me," he told Darby.

She did as he asked and before she could take a step back his hand shot up and caught her across the face. She fell back onto her bottom and yelled, "Sean!"

The minute she did that, Declan and Jack came flying down from the second floor. Declan tackled Sean and Jack went to her side.

"Stop!" Sean yelled. He had somehow managed to take one of Declan's guns and he had it pointed at Declan's temple.

"Hang on," Jack said as he raised his hands. "No need for anyone to get hurt."

Sean ignored him and glared at Darby. "I told you to come alone."

"And you wonder why I didn't?" she asked as she wiped the blood from her mouth.

"This is going to cost you," Sean warned. "Big time." He

glanced over at Roxanne. "Put the baby on the floor," he said.

"Sean," she practically pleaded. "Don't hurt her."

He kept moving the gun between Declan's head and where Mia was lying on the floor, wriggling as she cried out. Darby couldn't take it anymore. In a flash, she pulled the gun out of her waistband and fired.

Sean screamed.

Declan pounced.

Jack grabbed the baby and ran her out of the house.

"Oh shut up," Darby said. "It's just a few fingers. You'll live."

* * *

The return trip to Martin County was a tad more crowded. They had hog-tied Sean and put him in the aisle. He was still bitching about his wound.

"You are a good shot," Declan said.

"Actually," she admitted, "I was aiming for the gun. I didn't mean to shoot off the two fingers."

"Still," Jack said with a smile. "Remind me not to make you mad."

Darby couldn't be mad at anyone. She had Mia in her arms and she was feeding her a bottle. Darby was in heaven.

The baby seemed to have been well cared for, which probably had been Roxanne's job. Darby actually felt a pang of sympathy for the nineteen-year-old. She was no match for Sean's suave manipulation or his viciousness. Hopefully she hadn't been so involved in his plotting that she'd spend the rest of her life in jail, too.

The pilot had radioed ahead and there were deputies waiting for them at the airfield. They opted to take Sean to Martin Memorial Hospital via police car, though they did replace the hog tying with more conventional handcuffs. Roxanne was in the back of a squad car crying.

Darby was thrilled and exhausted at the same time. She knew she had to give a statement to the FBI and the local authorities but she begged off for the night, promising to come in the next morning. She just wanted to hold her daughter.

She woke up the next morning with a very unattractive swollen lip. Mia was still sleeping in her crib, so Darby made some coffee. Her house felt empty somehow. Jack and Declan were gone. There were no more FBI special agents. No one except Darby and her daughter. That should have been enough.

* * *

It took her two weeks but she finally worked up her nerve to take Mia and head to Jack's office. Mia was in the backseat. "So," she said to her baby. "Do you have a crazy mommy after all?"

Darby watched his office door for a full five minutes before she got up her courage and got out of the car. She released the infant seat and placed the handle in the crook of her arm. "You're getting heavy." Then she grabbed the diaper bag and started toward Jack's office.

She caught her reflection in the window and again questioned her sanity. Here she was weighted down with baby stuff—hardly the impression she hoped to make. Oh well, this was her life.

She didn't get the chance to touch the handle because Jack opened the door for her. "How can I help?" he asked.

"Take the baby," she answered.

He easily carried Mia inside. As usual it was cluttered, but in an organized way. He placed Mia smack dab in the middle of his desk and turned to greet Darby with a proper smile. "You look great," he said.

She let the diaper bag drop to the floor with a thud. "That's nice of you to say but I know different. Single parenting requires a lot of heavy lifting."

He crossed his arms in front of his broad chest. Darby started to lose her nerve. "I wanted to thank you."

"No thanks necessary," he insisted.

"You haven't sent me a bill."

"Consider it my pro bono case for this year."

"I actually have another case for you."

"A referral?" he asked.

She shook her head. "I want to change Mia's name. I mean…eventually I do…not any time soon."

"You're babbling."

"I am," she agreed. "Okay, I have a proposal for you."

"What?"

"I'm proposing we date for a while."

Jack smiled and stroked his chin. "Well, that's a first. No woman has ever come courting me before."

She smiled at his grin. "So you're going to make this as difficult as possible, I see."

"Oh yes," he agreed with a half-laugh. "What does your proposal entail?"

"Well, you may not know this but I have some trust issues I need to work through. And I'm a single mother. So I'm kind of a package deal."

"What's in it for me?" Jack asked.

"Companionship. Free vet care—don't overlook that perk."

Jack whistled. "As attractive as that sounds, I'm afraid I'm going to have to say no."

Darby felt heat begin to rise to her cheeks. Boy, had she read this wrong. "Sorry to have bothered you." She bent to reach for the diaper bag but Jack stopped her.

He stood her up and pulled her close. "I thought this was a negotiation. What about what I want out of this?"

"Which is?" she asked, steeled for his response.

"The free vet care is doable. I'm not sold on the companionship thing. Just what does that entail?"

"Getting to know each other?"

Jack dipped his head and brushed his lips over hers. "Like this?" he asked against her mouth.

Darby swallowed a groan. "Yes."

Jack moved her hair off her neck and placed a tiny row of kisses along her throat. "Like this?"

"Mm-hummm," she mumbled as her knees weakened.

Then a distinctive cry split the air. Jack reluctantly let her go. "This is the single-parent part, right?" he teased.

"Yep. She's just hungry." Darby reached into the diaper bag and got a bottle.

When she turned around, Jack already had Mia out of her carrier and had one hand extended for the bottle. "How about I feed her, then we can go out and grab lunch?"

"Lunch?"

"Yeah, as in a date."

Darby smiled. "I can't promise she'll stay quiet."

"Darby, you don't have to promise me anything. While we're being companions, I hope you'll reach that conclusion yourself."

"I think I'm already on my way."

"Good."

Please see the next page for a preview of
ABANDONED, Book Two in this thrilling new
series.

PROLOGUE

The President put one hand at the First Lady's elbow, giving it a brief squeeze before rising to join the governor at the dais. Brilliant light bathed the podium, which was flanked by the most prominent men in Louisiana politics.

Governor Rossner and his wife applauded politely, as did the dozen or so others basking in the delight of pulling off such an important political coup. Rossner straightened his tie as he turned in his seat and recrossed his legs. *The seat right damned next to the President of the EN-tire U-Nited friggin' States of America*, he gloated in silence. His barrel chest puffed beneath his suit coat. He wondered what his father would think, him just sitting there with the freakin' most important man in the free world. And that man was about to tell everyone in the crowd that he—Gil Rossner—deserved another term. Stifling his grin, Gil folded his hands in his lap and stared at the president's profile.

He took caution not to catch Madison's eye. His campaign manager-slash-brother-in-law shared his disdain for the party leader and current commander-in-chief. It simply would not do for the two men to erupt in laughter behind the man's back, though he was sorely tempted. Gil enjoyed belittling the liberal Yankee in the White House.

President Kent Rawlings wasn't much by Gil's standards, yet women seemed to lose their good common sense whenever he was around. His guess was the rumors about Rawlings were true. He stifled a laugh by covering his mouth and quietly clearing his throat. Rawlings was too refined. He and his wife were snobby and polished. Definitely made for television. Gil tried to imagine the prissy man in the sack with that shapely, young First Lady of his. He wondered if the president screamed when he—

Pop!

Gil's eyes bulged as incredible pain seared through him. He slumped, slowly, to the side. *Sweet Jesus!* were the only words his brain could conjure. There were two more popping sounds. Gil was now lying prone on the floor. A spray of blood blurred his vision. Then he felt crushed beneath a heavy weight as the president fell on him. Gil heard his own wife scream as he expelled his final breath.

CHAPTER ONE

Conner Kavanaugh wasn't normally given to bouts of chivalry, but then there was something decidedly different about the hot blonde currently trying to fend off the off-duty bartender's interest. Frankie may have been born into money but he was still white trash.

The round stool beneath Conner squealed when he turned back to rest his elbows against the scarred and lacquered bar. He put the long-neck bottle to his lips, taking a long pull and allowing the beer to slide down his throat.

He watched the scene in the mirror behind the bartender. Frankie had one dirty boot on the stool next to hers. His hat was pushed back on his head. To her credit, the blonde wasn't even looking at him. Conner snorted and took another sip of his beer. She was obviously thinking that subtlety would work on a guy like Frankie. But Conner knew better. Frankie didn't comprehend anything less subtle than a two-by-four against his temple.

She didn't exactly fit the type of woman who came trolling at The Grill. First off, her clothes were all wrong. Her Harvard sweatshirt was loose enough to cover all but the faintest outline of her breasts. *And those jeans*, he thought as he took another pull of beer. Though they were faded from wear, the material held a distinct crease—a dry-cleaners crease, he figured with an amused shake of his head. *Well, at least she had spruced up her fanciest duds for her night out.*

When she finally lifted her eyes, he felt the impact as if he'd been slapped. Even in the smoky haze of the bar, they were the greenest he'd ever seen. Clear, emerald green. And shimmering with anger.

Frankie apparently wasn't seeing it that way. Conner watched the large man anchor himself on the stool as he pushed it just inches from his quarry. *Why*, he wondered, *couldn't this broad have picked a safer place to find Mr. Right Now?* With her looks she could have sauntered up to the Dairy Queen and found someone eager to spend the night with her. *Maybe she liked slumming*, he considered as he finished off his drink. He watched as Frankie continued to move in on her. The man had less finesse than a teenager on prom night in the front seat of his father's pick-up. His big palm gripped her wrist, wrestling her hand to his sloppy mouth.

The woman's eyes narrowed, but she didn't seem to put up much of a fight. Conner's chivalrous thoughts were dismissed when he realized he'd been wrong. "Happens," he muttered with a shrug. Some women just liked 'em nasty.

He'd no sooner turned his attention away from them when he heard the familiar sound of a bottle being smashed.

"Damn!" he sighed. He was off duty and he sure as hell wasn't in any mood to break up a drunken bar fight.

Expecting to find a couple of townies squared off by the pool tables, he looked there first. It wasn't the townies. He shifted his gaze in the opposite direction. It wasn't Frankie. No, the hand holding the jagged glass weapon belonged to the Harvard blonde.

"You gonna do something?" the bartender fairly pleaded.

"Think I should?" Conner countered without looking away from the standoff. "It's my night off," he mentioned almost casually.

"C'mon," the bartender groaned. "I can't afford no more fights in here. Councilman Tuppman and his holier-than-thou wife are just itching for a reason to get my liquor license pulled. Anybody gets hurt, I can kiss this place good-bye."

Now *that* would be a loss, Conner thought as he slowly got to his feet. His boots scraped the worn floor as he closed the space between himself and where Frankie stood, apparently ready to pounce on the woman or the weapon she brandished—or both.

Conner slipped his hand onto Frankie's tense shoulder. A small semi-circle of interested folks gathered around the participants.

"You don't want to get into a brawl with a woman, do you, Frankie? It sure would give Tarrant Parish a bad name." Conner kept his eyes on the weapon.

"You gonna let that bitch get the best of you?" someone taunted.

"Yeah, Frankie!" another voice echoed. "Can't be letting no woman kick your ass!"

"Take that bottle away from her, Frankie!" someone else called. "Show her what a real man does when a woman gets outta line!"

Conner knew ol' Frankie would rise to the bait. Frankie was one of those individuals destined to spend his entire life being goaded by others. His past was testimony to that. His father had been leading him around by the nose for years. It didn't seem to matter that Frankie was pushing forty-three.

"You really don't want to do that, Frankie," Conner said calmly. "Doesn't take much of a man to beat up on a little thing like her."

Now Frankie turned and snarled at him with eyes that were narrow and angry—just like the guy's brain. Amazingly, the Harvard Blonde was shooting *him* a pretty hostile look as well. Apparently everyone was having a bad day.

Frankie snarled. "This ain't your concern, Kavanaugh." He puffed out his muscled chest and added, "'Sides, you're in no position to tell me what to do in here."

Conner sighed. "I see it a little differently," he countered. "My mamma was real clear on the rules about boys hitting girls."

"Your mamma was a whore," Frankie spat.

Conner's first response was an audible, deep sigh. "Frankie, I don't think you want to make me mad just now. Do you?"

Conner saw a faint flicker of uncertainty pass in the smaller man's eyes. "You don't scare me, Kavanaugh. Never have, never will."

"I'm not trying to scare you. I'm trying to reason with you. Surely you have something better to do tonight than pick a fight with a girl."

"Girl?" the Harvard Blonde scoffed.

The broken bottle never wavered from her target, not even when she tossed some of that long, thick hair over one shoulder. "I am *not* a girl. I don't know why you feel the need to play Knight in Shining Armor, but I can assure you, I'm perfectly capable of taking care of myself."

Conner grinned. "That must be why you're standing in the middle of a barroom full of sloppy-drunk men with a broken bottle in your hand."

She stiffened with indignation and he wished he had just stayed out of the whole situation. "Suit yourself, sweetheart. Sorry for interrupting your fun."

Her eyes burned like fire as she glared at him.

"Go on, Frankie!" one of the men yelled as Conner began to move backward toward the bar. "Teach her some manners!"

Conner had every intention of leaving her to her own devices; let her learn a small lesson so long as it didn't get truly bad. That lasted only until he saw the smallest flicker of fear on her face. He should have ignored it. She had basically told him as much. He should have let the foolish woman get her due. Lord knew she'd asked for it by coming to a place like this and giving Frankie the time of day. But as he thought about her small body being manhandled by a pig like Frankie, he knew he was going to help her. Even if she didn't want him to.

"I'm sure you're right capable of taking care of yourself," he began as he stepped between her and Frankie. "But I wouldn't be much of a gentleman if I—"

He hadn't finished the sentence when he felt an explosion in the area of his ribs. His breath billowed in his cheeks. He heard the Harvard Blonde's sharp shriek. He was almost sorry that Frankie hadn't decided to sucker-punch him in the mouth. At least then he would have had the satisfaction of bleeding all over the dimwitted woman. As far as he was concerned, this whole situation was her fault.

"That," he warned Frankie between clenched teeth, "wasn't real smart."

With a speed belying his size, Conner caught the other man around the mid-section in a move that sent them spraying atop the pool table. Bracing his forearm across Frankie's throat, Conner turned and glanced at the blonde. He caught a faint whiff of her perfume. Annoyed at the world in general and at her specifically, he asked, "May I borrow your bottle, please?"

Stunned, the woman relinquished it to his free hand. Ignoring her for the moment, Conner stared down at the menacing, red face of his opponent. The room had gone still and silent. He was able to hear every rasp of breath. Conner placed the jagged edge of the bottle to the base of Frankie's throat.

"This ain't your fight, Kavanaugh," Frankie gasped in a whisper.

Conner eased his pressure hold on the man. "I beg to differ." He allowed the glass to pierce Frankie's sweaty skin. "You threw the first punch."

"But I didn't mean no harm."

"Sure." Conner put more weight into his hold. The action caused Frankie's watered-down blue eyes to bulge in their sockets. "I don't take kindly to having my ribs punched."

Frankie's thin lips pulled back to expose two rows of capped teeth. He managed to shrug defeat from beneath Conner's hold and the threat of the jagged glass.

Conner moved close to the man's ear. "When I let you up, you'll head on out the door. Understand?"

Frankie was glaring, but he nodded. Somehow, Conner didn't find his attitude very reassuring. He decided Frankie might definitely need just a bit more persuasion. Bracing one leg firmly on the floor, he brought his knee up and applied attention-getting pressure to Frankie's crotch. "I didn't catch your answer."

The combination of the bottle against his jugular, the band of muscle against his throat, and the distinct threat to his privates apparently made Frankie see the error of his ways.

"I didn't really want that frosty bitch anyways," Frankie puffed, casting his eyes in the direction of the woman. "I like my women a whole hell of a lot softer than her."

"Then there won't be a problem," Conner acknowledged.

Slowly, he eased off the man, but kept the broken bottle raised just in case Frankie got another attack of the stupids. He knew from prior experience that ninety percent of Frankie's decision-making was fifty-percent stupid.

Luckily, this wasn't one of those times. Conner placed himself and the weapon between the Harvard Blonde and Frankie while the latter collected his hat. Shoving through the visibly disappointed group of men, Frankie stomped out of the bar. Expelling a breath, Conner had a sinking suspicion this wasn't quite over. Frankie was short on brains but long on memory.

Absently, he kneaded his ribs, relieved when he felt only mildly uncomfortable. Cracked ribs were a pain in the ass. Speaking of pains in the ass...He turned, wanting an explanation from Miss Harvard Blonde.

What she apparently lacked in common sense, she definitely had in looks. He felt the beginnings of a smile. Her hair was beautiful, spilling well below her shoulders in a simple, no-frills style. Judging from the way she had smashed the beer bottle to challenge a man twice her size, Conner assumed her hair was simply an extension of her personality—blunt.

"Come here often?" he remarked casually.

She regarded him with something amazingly akin to defiance. He could see it in the subtle thrust of her chin and the small fists balled at her sides.

"You didn't need to come to my rescue," she responded tightly.

Her accent was Southern, but not Louisiana Southern.

"I could have controlled the situation."

"It didn't look like that from where I was sitting," he told her. Hell, he didn't expect her to fall into his arms and kiss him with gratitude, but it annoyed him that she couldn't so much as say thanks. She owed him that. She could at least show him the courtesy of civility.

"You could have hurt him."

Was that censure he heard in her tone? "Excuse me?"

Her hands moved to her hips. "The broken bottle would have allowed me to make a quick, gracious exit. There was no need for you to hold it against his throat and incite a fight."

His blood pressure went up a notch or two. "I *prevented* a fight, sweetheart."

"Not from where I was sitting," she returned in a near-perfect imitation of his drawl.

"This is crazy!"

"No," she countered. "*You're* crazy."

She breezed past him as if he was nothing more than a minor annoyance. A gnat she might swat, had she been so inclined to donate some of her precious time.

The few men who still lingered parted as if she was royalty. Of course, given the regal way she swayed her tight little derrière, it didn't surprise him. It just made him madder than hell.

"Wait a minute!"

Her step faltered at his thunderous command but she still pushed the door open and walked out into the night. He should just leave this alone. Chalk it up to a good deed for which he would eventually be rewarded. But he didn't feel much like waiting for eventually. She owed him, and he believed in collecting on his debts.

Depositing the broken bottle on the bar as he strode by, Conner stormed after her. Like it or not, the woman was going to get his short lesson on manners.

Cool, fresh air welcomed him as he stepped from The Grill. It took him less than a second to find her. It was easy. He simply followed the chirping sound made as she disarmed her Lexus in the dark parking lot.

She really is slumming, he grumbled inwardly as he jogged over to her car. He got there just in time to see her settle in behind the wheel and blocked the closing of her car door with his body.

When she angled her head up at him, Conner felt his annoyance double at the exasperation he noted in the tiny lines at the corners of her full lips.

"Stop being a jerk," she warned, impatient.

"A jerk?" he parroted.

"Okay," she amended, batting her long lashes at him. "Stop being a complete asshole."

Her condescension didn't bother him so much as her voice. This woman had a cultured cadence, the kind of speech pattern learned only in the finest schools. It was the kind of speech that didn't usually include the names and expletives she had so easily tossed at him.

"If I'm such an asshole, how come you're looking to get laid in a dive like this?"

She blinked once. "And who told you I was looking to get *laid*, as you so coarsely put it?"

"Why else would a woman like *you* come to a place like *this*?"

"For a beer?" she suggested.

"Were they all out at the country club?"

"I've got news for you," she said as she reached for the door handle. "I don't belong to any country clubs, but I do enjoy a beer now and again."

"I would suggest you enjoy it someplace other than here."

"Oh, I get it!" she said in a breathy, sarcastic rush. "This is one of those quaint 'men only' places."

"You could say that."

She gave him an exaggerated dumb-blonde sigh. "Gee, I guess I should have checked the corners of the building for urine. Isn't that how most lower animal species mark their territory?"

Conner chuckled. She was quick. "Would you have liked it better if I would have let ol' Frankie have you?"

"Frankie would not have *had* me."

"There's not a whole lot of you, sweetheart. That bottle trick would have protected you for a while, but not forever. Frankie and his friends would have seen to that."

"Perhaps," she said. "But I still believe I could have handled it myself."

Placing his palms on the polished roof of the fancy car, Conner leaned down. The red interior of the car smelled new. She smelled fresh, like the air after a shower.

"I'm willing to concede that you might have been able to pull it off, if you're willing to concede that it was damned neighborly of me to intervene on your behalf."

Her lashes fluttered against her cheeks. The action caused his body to respond with alarming speed. Her skin was pale, flawless, and slightly flushed from the cool evening air. She was a tiny thing but the word "vulnerable" didn't even enter his mind.

She hesitated, then said, "Okay. Thank you for being neighborly, Mr.—"

"Conner Kavanaugh. Conner to my friends."

"Mr. Kavanaugh," she said. A small smile curved the corners of her mouth.

"And you are?"

"About to leave," she answered, gently tugging on the door.

Ignoring the feel of metal against the backs of his calves, Conner remained planted in the spot. "I'd like to know your name. Telling me would be the neighborly thing for you to do."

"I guess I'm just not as neighborly as you are." Some of the annoyance had returned to her eyes.

"I don't know," he drawled. "You impress me as a lady with potential." Conner gave her his best grin. The one that had talked his fair share of women out of their panties.

She looked as volatile as a fast approaching tornado. "Potential?"

He nodded. "Knew it the minute I set eyes on you."

The lips he'd been admiring pulled into a tight smile.

"I get it. You're under the impression that since you defended my honor—so to speak—I'm now fair game?"

"I'm game if you are," he teased, hoping to get her to lighten up.

"I hate to disappoint you," she said in a tone that told him she didn't mind disappointing him at all.

"I wasn't interested in spoils," he insisted.

"And I'm not interested, *period*."

"Sure you are," he told her without conceit. "Or your eyes wouldn't be flickering between my face and my—"

"My eyes have not flickered."

Her voice was stiff and haughty. Still he sensed just a trace of wariness behind her brave words. The lady wasn't as immune as she was letting on. That knowledge filled him with a hefty dose of male pride.

"Suit yourself. But I'd be right flattered if they did." Conner moved and she closed the door. She surprised him when she lowered the window.

"You're either desperate or a bigger jerk than I originally thought."

"Careful, sweetheart," he said as his fingers reached out to brush the soft underside of her chin. Her skin was silky soft and he wondered what the rest of her body felt like. He also wondered why she hadn't so much as flinched at the contact. Perhaps this lady liked games. Specifically the "convince me" game. "You don't want to hurt my feelings, do you?"

"I really don't give a flaming hoot about your feelings, Kavanaugh."

His fingers traced the delicate outline of her throat until he encountered the edge of her collar. His eyes followed his hands, inspiring all sorts of fantasies.

Then he heard an unmistakable *click*.

His gaze moved toward the sound. His fingers stilled as he found himself looking down the barrel of a small-caliber gun.

"Take your hand off me," she said calmly.

The fingers gripping the gun were as steady as her gaze. Conner wondered how he had managed to get himself into such a mess. *So much for chivalry*, he thought as he slowly pulled his hand back. He knew the answer; he'd been thinking with the wrong part of his anatomy. *Stupid.*

"Do you always use a gun as persuasion?" He was careful to keep his tone conversational. Apparently she didn't like that. He could tell by the flash of surprise in her eyes. She must have thought her little Annie Oakley moment would have had a more intimidating effect. Of course, he still wasn't sure she wouldn't shoot, but he'd gnaw off his own tongue before admitting that to her.

"If you'll recall, Kavanaugh, I asked you nicely first."

"I guess I wasn't listening right," he said, stepping away from the car.

He heard her start the engine. She propped the gun on the window frame. Her eyes never left him. Not for an instant.

"Perhaps in the future you'll remember that *no* actually means *no.*"

About the Author

After selling her first work of romantic suspense in 1993, Rhonda Pollero has penned more than thirty novels, won numerous awards and nominations, and landed on multiple bestseller lists, including *USA Today*, Bookscan, and Ingram's Top 50 list. She lives in South Florida with her family.

CPSIA information can be obtained
at www.ICGtesting.com
Printed in the USA
FFOW03n1305240917
40227FF